Midnight's Fate

The Cynn Cruors Bloodline
Book 4

By
Isobelle Cate

18 July 2015

Dear Caroline,

All the best!

Love,

Isabelle Cate

Isobelle Cate

Zac McBain is on a mission to a place that doesn't exist - a place that disappeared thousands of years ago. The source of the Specus Argentum--the only silver that can harm the Cruors, is sought by not only Zac and the Ancients, but Dac Valerian as well.

Hidden deep in the rainforests of Honduras, the present day town of La Nahuaterique, Faith Hannah is on a mission, both humanitarian and personal. Her medical mission is prompted by her wish to escape the problems that assail her in London. She never expected to be kidnapped and discover a whole supernatural world around her own--and she certainly didn't expect to feel such a sudden, intense need and longing for one of them.

As soon as Zac sees Faith deep in the woods, he's lost to her. In the middle of a hard fought battle for the Specus Argentum, the passion fate has decreed between Zac and Faith begins to consume them.

But the impending war between the Cynn Cruor and Scatha Cruor comes to a head. Secrets are unearthed, loyalties are doubted... and love must struggle to prevail.

Isobelle Cate

This is a work of fiction. Names, characters, places and incidents are either the product of the author's imagination or used fictitiously, and any resemblance to actual persons, living or dead, business establishments, events or locales is entirely coincidental.
All rights reserved.
Copyright 2014 © Isobelle Cate

ISBN-13: 978-1505808926
ISBN-10: 1505808928

Published by Beau Coup Publishing
http://beaucoupllcpublishing.com

Cover by JRA Stevens
For Beau Coup Publishing
© Bareta | Dreamstime.com - Muscular Guy Photo
© Jiss | Dreamstime.com - Cenote Dzitnup Near Valladolid, Mexico Photo

ALL RIGHTS RESERVED. This book contains material protected under International and Federal Copyright Laws and Treaties. Any unauthorized reprint or use of this material is prohibited. No part of this book may be reproduced or transmitted in any form or by any means, electronic or mechanical, including photocopying, recording, or by any information storage and retrieval system without express written permission from the author / publisher.

Isobelle Cate

Prologue

A village close to the Loch Innis Mo Cholmaig, Stirling, Scotland 1399

Zac watched the plume of black smoke dispassionately, unable to bring up any remorse or heartbreak. He had just returned from the burning village, unable to save even the only person he would rather not have anything to do with.

The Abbot of Inchmahome Priory had informed him that a village just off the Port of the Loch had been razed to the ground by bandits. Zac couldn't understand why he was being asked to see to any survivors. He was neither a monk nor a postulant. He had been left at the Port of Loch Innis before he was brought to the Priory in the island. He was just Zachary McBain. It was the name given to him by an old monk who had taken responsibility for him. The monk had arrived from the Green Isle, together with his fellow Irish who sought to convert the heathen.

"I still cannae understand why I have to go," Zac mumbled beside his friend, Colm, as they obediently prepared for the boat ride that would take them out of the island.

"When you reach the village, you will ken. Brother Aodh will accompany you to give extreme unction to the dead."

Zac whirled around at the Abbot's voice, his cheeks reddening with embarrassment. "Yes, my lord."

True enough, when he arrived, all objections to what Zac thought was a useless journey disappeared.

It was the village where he was born. It was where

a man had sired him and a woman had given birth to him. Nothing more. For if his parents loved him he wouldn't have been left at the port with only a homespun and tattered plaid to clothe his squalling form instead of the warmth of a mother's embrace.

"Zac, *abhos*! This *boireannach* is alive." Colm called him away from his thoughts to come over. Zac turned just in time to see Colm carry a woman out of a nearly burned out hovel to gently place her against a sturdy tree trunk. Slippery cold settled on his lower spine because for some unknown reason, he knew who she was. He walked slowly towards her, his sandals flapping softly against the ground damp from the misty rain and blood. Brother Aodh, already nearing his dotage turned to look at them but continued to tend to those who had perished, making the sign of the cross over their bodies.

Zac stood over the woman as she winced in pain. Her blonde hair matted her face, limp with dirt and dried blood. Her clothes were torn, exposing her right breast that bore deep scratches. Her jaw bloomed with a bluish-purple bruise. She allowed Colm to take her hand away from her stomach so that he could attempt to stem the red tide of life ebbing from her.

"She isna going to make it," Zac said, his voice devoid of emotion.

Colm whirled around from his kneeling position, disbelief on his face. "We have to at least try. She is still alive, isna she? Come and heal her."

Zac refused to move.

"Zachary!" Colm said his name as though it was a swear word.

"Leave us," the woman croaked, her dry lips cracking and causing welts to appear on her mouth. When Colm hesitated, the side of her mouth lifted as she tried to smile. "*E do thoil e.*"

Colm nodded but glared at Zac before he left. He hurried to Brother Aodh, who gratefully took his arm as he moved from body to body. The woman looked long and hard at Zac, who still remained standing. She had difficulty breathing as though there was something heavy on her chest. Then she averted her gaze, looking at a point behind Zac's form.

"I cannae expect you to forgive me," she said.

Zac wanted to taunt her, to ask her if she knew him, but he kept silent, waiting for her to speak.

"You couldna stay with us." She faced him once again, her face a picture of the discomfort she was feeling. Her breathing became shallow by the minute. "You couldna stay with me."

Zac knelt down slowly, his gaze assessing her. Couldn't stay with her? He had vowed never to ask, never to wonder. Now he had this overwhelming need to find out why. Whether it would do him any good he didn't know, but he'd always had a thirst for knowledge of any kind. He was a thinker, the monks called him a philosopher. How could he tell them that knowledge was the only thing he believed in? It wouldn't hurt him. It wouldn't abandon him. His favourite place in the Abbey was the Scriptorium where he voraciously devoured the written word. He cursed inwardly. He rarely did. But this was one occasion that merited it.

He moved his hand toward her and she stiffened.

"I'm only going to look at your wound," he said.

"Why?"

Zac shrugged. "It's what I do." Early on, he had felt no remorse at seeing that she was about to die. Was he beginning to feel a little sympathy for this woman in front of him? The niggling heaviness that settled square on his chest was something he wasn't familiar with.

Reluctantly, she removed her hand, exposing the gaping wound in the side of her belly. Zac could see from its shape that the wound had been inflicted by a cutlass. *Caterans,* he thought grimly. Bandits and discredited clan warriors that roamed the lands. Not as many as it used to be, but they still existed. The wound was also very deep. While some of the blood had begun to clot, half of the wound still trickled. Zac opened his satchel to take out strips of sterilized cloth and placed it over the wound. Soon, the cloth bloomed red.

"*Tapadh leibh*," she said, thanking him.

"Was I that unlovable that you had to leave me by the dock?" he asked instead, not acknowledging her gratitude, inclining his head to one side. "What made me so different from the rest of my brothers and sisters, Elspeth?" There, he had called her by her name because he couldn't call her by any other.

Elspeth drew a ragged sigh. She wanted to laugh but coughed instead, her reddish spittle trickling down the side of her mouth. "Because you were not born of Kenneth. He is not your father."

The revelation pushed Zac to lose his balance, his eyes widening in shock.

"Thank you again for making me laugh before I die," Elspeth cackled, her face a mixture of pain and mirth. "You look daft falling to the ground on your backside. Not so almighty after all." Then she added in a softer tone, "More human."

Zac didn't care at how comical he looked. His mouth suddenly felt very parched, he could have choked on the air he was breathing. More human? What did she mean by that? Had he taken on the very airs he detested seeing, no sensing, from the nobles who came to visit the Abbey? With a holier than thou attitude? And as though Elspeth could read his thoughts, she answered his unspoken questions.

"No, you were not born a bastard either." Elspeth wheezed. "I left your father. He wasna human."

Zac reeled at the words that came tumbling down his mother's lips. In the long years he stayed with the monks, he had harboured a despairing resentment towards the people he knew were his parents. He had pleaded with the abbot to help him get word out of the island, to ask if not beg to see his family. But each request the abbot sent was refused, and Zac was at a loss, unable to understand why. Was he so unwanted that even the woman who bore him wouldn't want to see him? The abbot refused to allow him to visit them either, telling Zac that it was for the best. Zac couldn't comprehend what "for the best" exactly was until he resigned himself to the fact that his parents didn't want him. With Elspeth's revelation, he didn't know what to think. He, Zachary McBain, whom the monks believed was the most gifted healer with a brilliant philosophical mind, who thought things out logically and rationally, couldn't get his head around his origins.

"You are not one of us, Zac."

"My father wasna human because he beat you, didn't he? And because I'm a *mac na galla.*"

"You are not a bastard." Elspeth shouted, if the breathy voice could be called that. "Take it as I say. Your father wasna human." She grimaced. "I don't have much time, Zac. You know that. I cannae ask you to forgive me. All I can ask of you is to hear me."

Moments later, Elspeth was dead.

Zac cleaned her body to prepare it for burial before he helped Colm carry the dead and pile them up by the side of the road. They started to dig a mass grave and once done, Zac moved away to start digging another. Colm didn't stop him. Zac could feel his friend's gaze on him as he continued to dig. He knew that his friend would eventually ask him why but now wasn't the time. The bodies were beginning to reek and if they wanted the elderly monk to ferry the dead to the afterlife and not vomit at the stench, then they needed to work fast.

It took longer for Brother Aodh to get to where they were and they had to wait for him to catch his breath before he could administer the final rites. Zac and Colm placed the dead bodies over each other before covering them with earth. Then they moved to Elspeth's grave. Thunder boomed and one bolt of lightning zigzagged across the Scottish sky. The wind churned, flapping their coarse habits against their legs and their cowls against their necks. Brother Aodh continued with his prayers unmindful of the coming storm. Zac held on to the monk, but his thoughts were elsewhere. For one brief moment, his conversation with Elspeth overshadowed everything. He would take his time. After all, didn't she say that he was immortal?

By the time they returned to the Priory they were drenched. Colm and Brother Aodh shivered in their sodden clothing while Zac felt nary a chill. After making sure that the other brothers had helped Brother Aodh, Zac went to his cell. He stripped off his habit and used it to dry his hair. He dressed in the only set of clothes he owned before gathering his belongings in a bundle and making his way to the Abbot's office. An hour later he merged, closing the Abbot's door one final time.

Colm was outside the Priory when Zac made his way to the Priory's gates. Colm's snood was over his head in an attempt to protect his head from the drizzle. Zac paused as his friend approached him, noting his change of clothes from his white leine to this dark trews and leather shoes.

"You couldna wait until the morrow. Why?" Colm asked. "If the cauld does not take you, the caterans will."

"I don't belong here." Zac gave him a brief smile. He cinched his satchel against his body and tightened the plain green woollen plaid around the upper half of his body. The rain pelted the gates softly while here and there, the sound of water dripping to the ground joined the sound of the rain hitting the lake.

Colm looked around before he spoke. "I ken you were different. But immortal?"

Zac froze.

Colm's mouth quirked, disbelief and awe marring his face in equal measure when he faced Zac. "I dinnae ken whether those were the ramblings of a lass about to come face to face with our Maker or if 'tis the truth." He paused and placed his hand on Zac's shoulder. "Your secret is safe with me, my friend. You have nothing to fear."

Zac sighed, sadness weighing down on him. Colm was the closest friend he had and now he had to leave. He was a man of few words, and he didn't know how to express himself other than through the lines of the tomes he had been fortunate to read, that he knew almost by heart.

"When one of those that come together is incompatible with certainty, then certainty cannot be achieved."

Colm broke into laughter. "Where did you read that? I dinnae ken a word you said."

Zac chuckled. "John Duns Scotus."

"Whoever he was, I'm sure he was right," Colm remarked wryly. "You should cease to talk in a language only few people understand, Zac."

"I shall do my best." Zac grinned before his smile slowly disappeared when he saw the same sadness he felt reflected on his friend's face.

Colm held out his hand. "Fare thee well, Zachary. If you ever pass this way again in your long life, come and visit and tell me of what you've seen."

Zac grasped his friend's hand firmly before squeezing Colm's shoulder, then he made his way out in the pouring rain, allowing the night to embrace him.

Chapter One

The Caribbean, off the coast of Honduras, Present Day

Waves from the water's reflection covered the walls of the indoor pool. Several women splashed water at each other, their shrill laughter echoing and bouncing against the walls. One of the women swam towards the shallow part of the pool before surfacing to walk on the steps. Water glossed over her naked body, the droplets hanging precariously on her nipples and glistening against her trimmed mound cradled by her lean thighs. A puddle formed by the side of the lounge chair when she stopped to get her towel to dry herself. Wrapping the towel around her waist she left the pool.

The cold air from the air conditioner slammed against Kamaria's skin, making her shiver for a moment before her blood warmed. She made her way through the narrow hallway of the lower deck. When she turned a corner, she met a group of men who were initially surprised at her semi-naked appearance before their lips curled in appreciation, sweeping her with eyes that glittered with lust. Kamaria's mouth lifted in the barest of smiles. The men parted to let her through, but one of them raised his hand to flick her nipple. The rest of the men howled and hooted. Kamaria's mouth lifted further to smile, coyly looking at the man from beneath her lashes. As soon as she turned another corner, she heard the man's scream before the sound became guttural. The next moment, she heard the sound of snapping jaws. Some Scatha never learned, Kamaria sighed inwardly. She would need to find a replacement for the warrior killed by her own kind.

Kamaria exited the lower deck of the yacht, walking through the salon before going out to the sun deck. She inhaled deeply, closing her eyes as she allowed the peacefulness of the night wrap her in its embrace. Overhead, the moon looked like a half-eaten wafer of white, its reflection rippling over the whispering waters of the Aegean Sea. At that instant, she felt the quickening. After all these centuries she still couldn't get used to the moment when her blood became thicker and ran furiously through veins so narrow that any mortal would have had an embolism. If Kamaria didn't transform her veins wouldn't be able to contain the thicker life giving force speeding through her body and she could die. A silver bullet stopped someone like her in their tracks because the silver shrunk the blood vessels, causing her kind to implode.

That was really how werewolves died and the reason why they had to transform on the night of the full moon.

One of her kind found a way to counter the need to shift into animal form. Her niece, Alaghom Na-om, daughter of her cousin, the Lycan shaman. Her niece refused to tell Kamaria how she did it. Kamaria could only imagine how it felt to have the ability to control the quickening. She could walk through the villages and mingle with the humans, watch their every move. When the night of the full moon came she could feign that she had no place to stay and she could live with a human family until the call of the hunt lured her victims to their death. If she chose, Kamaria could make a potential victim become part of her kind.

But Alaghom disappeared, taken by the sorcerer her niece believed herself to be in love with. They took their secret of controlling the quickening with them. Kamaria had been furious. She confronted her cousin and demanded to know where his daughter was, but he was as baffled as she was. She decided to spy on her cousin, following him into the woods where he bid his daughter and her chosen mate a final farewell. The shaman waited until he couldn't see his daughter anymore before he turned to walk back to the village.

"Have you come to kill me, Kamaria?" he asked, his footsteps never faltering as he walked back to the village.

"Where did they go?" she demanded, walking away from the huge tree where she had been hiding.

"Why didn't you come out when I was talking to them?" the shaman asked instead.

Kamaria laughed. "I'm up against two werewolves and an alchemist. You think so less of me."

The shaman looked at her sadly. "No, Kamaria. You think so less of yourself. If you are here to kill me, do it. I won't tell you where they've gone."

Kamaria's eyes flared. She would grant her cousin his wish. Who was she to deny the last request of a condemned man? In one swipe, she slashed her cousin's human form, slicing him vertically. Her fury knew no bounds. She ravaged him with her claws, her anger fuelled by his refusal to scream his agony as he was ripped to shreds. Guttural moans emitted from his mouth the same time blood bubbled from it. Kamaria dug her claws into her cousin's chest cavity and tore out his still beating heart, the source of all life. The greatest gift anyone can give a god or goddess. They were, after all, Mayan.

Kamaria smiled as the shaman's blood trickled down her arms. Her long tongue swiped at the liquid and she sucked her breath sharply. Her cousin's blood was as potent as anything she had ever tasted. He was steeped in magick, steeped in the old ways that time had covered in mist and whatever he had done while alive was infused in his blood. Kamaria could feel power surge through her, the tendrils of forbidden knowledge curling around her veins. Insidious. Delicious. Painful. Part of the shaman's blood seemed to come alive inside her veins, encircling her own heart and squeezing it so tightly that Kamaria thought she, too, would die. Then the tightness immediately disappeared as quickly as it came. She looked at the heart in her hand. It had stopped beating. Kamaria's mouth curled sideways.

"Thank you for your sacrifice, cousin." She licked the few droplets of blood from her lips. "You daughter's heart will be the next one I take."

****

"Enjoying the view? Or are you planning on shifting before the moon peaks?"

Kamaria briefly looked over her shoulder before resuming her contemplation of the moon.

"I have learned to accept my lot," she stated. "You, on the other hand, Dac, cannot be thankful for what you have."

The Scatha leader chuckled before zooming beside her in less than a second.

"Liar," he murmured softly into her ear, sending shivers down her spine.

Kamaria whirled to clamp a furry hand over Dac's throat. Dac gurgled his surprise before his eyes glittered.

"Do it, Kamaria. I'm a sucker for pain. You should try it sometime."

Kamaria repressed a shudder before she moved away, her arm quickening to a normal limb.

"No thank you. I wouldn't want my arm to be soaked in your tainted blood." She leaned against the deck's railing, experiencing a sliver of triumph when she saw the furious tick on Dac's jaw.

"My blood isn't tainted."

Kamaria tutted. "Anyone housing a smattering of vampire blood is always tainted."

A growl rumbled from the recesses of Dac's throat before he lunged at her. With one swipe, Kamaria flung Dac across the railing and into the water. His scream of fury alerted the yacht's captain.

"See to it that someone fishes him out of the water and takes him to his cabin." Kamaria ordered. "His vampire blood might just bring him to the bottom of the sea."

Kamaria wouldn't have minded seeing Dac dead, but she needed him. Until she found her niece, the Scatha Cruor leader would be useful. He had the brawn which she lacked. She looked at the flailing Cruor from her vantage point on the deck, her ears closed to the curses he hurled. She gave an imperceptive shrug, disappearing from sight.

Chapter Two

The jostle of the truck hitting a pothole on the road jerked Faith awake. Sharp pain cut across her neck and her shoulders, the ropes digging into the skin of her wrists. The young man to her left beside her gave her a cursory glance before looking at the dirt road their vehicle was traveling on. Slightly disoriented, Faith eventually noticed her surroundings. Trees surrounded them from all sides. Faith heard the splash of water from the potholes, the water spitting to hit the trunks so close to the moving truck. She had to duck and bend forward every time they neared a low hanging branch so as not to get whipped. Every bone in her body screamed in protest at the jarring ride, her tailbone bringing shafts of pain up her lower back when she was thrown against the steel seat underneath her.

Then it was over. The truck came to an abrupt stop that threw her against another of her captors on her right. He held her steady before giving her a toothless grin. Faith felt his hand underneath her breast slowly kneading her flesh. She jumped away, glaring at him when he guffawed. When her captor stood to move towards her, she automatically cowered, but he didn't continue where he left off. He made his way out of the truck before slinging his rifle over his shoulder.

"*Vamos,*" her young captor said. She understood a little of Spanish, she had to what with her grandmother often talking to her in the Iberian tongue. Her knowledge was enough for her to know that she was being asked to go with them. Getting up from her seat, she walked to the edge of the truck and jumped the short distance to the ground. She clamped her mouth shut to stifle her groan. Faith dared not stretch in front of the men, especially her older captor, who was leering at her cleavage. Her younger captor poked her back with the end of his rifle and she gratefully walked away.

"*¿Dónde estoy?*" Faith asked, surprising her captor. "*Hablo español, pero un poco.*"

"It doesn't matter where you are," her young captor said in fluent English.

So much for trying to speak in a different language. "What are you going to do to me? Why are we in the forest? Why did you bloody kidnap me?"

Her captor looked at her with annoyance. "You ask too many questions."

"Why shouldn't I? I want to know what you're going to do to me before I get killed."

Suddenly his face was only a few inches away from hers.

"If you don't shut up, you *will* get shot," he snapped. "Now move!"

Faith gasped as a wave of his angry aura slammed against her. *No, not now*, she scolded herself. This wasn't the time to see inside him. She needed her wits about her. She needed to shield herself, to keep her mind focused on finding a way to get out. At the moment she didn't know how. She hoped the medical mission in La Nahuaterique would soon notice she had disappeared and send a search party.

The mission had been nothing out of the ordinary. Sometimes she joined them, other times she didn't, preferring to monitor the several medical missions she sponsored from the Mission house in London. *Caridad de la Salud*. It was a simple phrase meaning health charity. It was an organization she named after her deceased grandmother who had made it possible. But the debacle that culminated in her grand-aunt being imprisoned and the treachery of the man she thought she could spend the rest of her life with came all to a head. She just had to leave the British Isles and plunk herself into a different place where everywhere she looked didn't remind her of betrayal. So when she read about La Nahuaterique in the news she decided to organize a medical mission there. If a place wasn't recognized as a part of the countries who shared a common border, the people there wouldn't be getting the support they needed. They'd be in limbo. They'd be in a place that didn't exist.

The path they were walking on became narrower until they had to traverse single file. Faith stumbled and nearly slipped on the muddy way, her hiking boots making sucking noises on the ground. As the trees closed in, her heart started beating fast. She swallowed but there wasn't enough saliva to go down her parched throat. Her chest felt heavy and she was close to hyperventilating. Closed spaces made her panic. Immediately, she forced herself to think of something else. The colour of the trees, yes that was it. She concentrated on the flora, her interest honing on the orchids that grew on some of the trunks and the ferns that brushed against her legs as she walked. Pain, yes, the discomfort of having her arms tied behind her back.

Concentrate on everything else other than the small space around you. She continued with her disjointed thoughts, anything to prevent her from hyperventilating.

Faith felt sweaty, sticky, and smelled. She was hungry and thirsty and hoped that before she died, she could at least be fed. Why was she thinking of dying? Because she didn't want to entertain the idea of being raped. Suddenly, the path widened and as they entered a glade Faith heaved a sigh of relief.

Several huts lined the periphery of the clearing. Men with rifles slung over their shoulders and machetes strapped to their waists came and went from one dwelling to the other. To her far right, she saw people inside what appeared to look like a mess hall. Her stomach growled in response. Her young captor looked at her, a hint of a grin on his lips, but Faith glared at him.

"Come," he said, grasping her upper arm to half pull her towards the squat house in front of them.

A man sat behind a desk, writing, the window behind him offering the only source of light. He wasn't much older than Faith's captor. When he glanced up and nodded, her young captor took out a small serrated knife strapped against his thigh and stood behind her. Faith almost whimpered, her fear nearly overtaking her. She felt her arms being lifted behind her back that she had to bend her elbows.

Then her wrists were free.

Blood rushed through her arms, flooding them with sensation. Faith massaged her wrists and shoulders, rounding them to get the feeling back. She wanted to speak, but her gut told her to keep quiet. Lord knew how many times her mouth got her into trouble.

The man finally stood up. He ran his hand through his hair to move it away from his face that was still covered in shadow until he moved towards her. He was one of the most handsome kidnappers she had ever seen. His beard only softened the harsh planes of his face and his dark eyes, hooded at the moment, were fringed with lashes she herself envied. Why did a good looking man like him turn to a life of crime?

Why, must evil men always look ugly?

Faith slightly scowled at her taunting mind. Yes, bad men didn't need to be ugly to do ugly things.

The man's eyes raked her from head to foot and back up again. Faith controlled the urge to squirm. He may be handsome, but he made her skin crawl.

"What are you going to do to me?" she asked, her use of Spanish halting, unsure.

He didn't reply. Instead, he brushed against her as he walked out of the hut. The nozzle of her younger captor's rifle nudged her to follow, and when she didn't he nudged her harder, causing her to wince.

This is it. Heart in her throat she bade her legs to move, terror causing her to walk as though in stilts. Faith felt herself going numb as she followed meekly, but as soon as she got out of the hut she veered to the left in an attempt to flee. Her young captor's fingers immediately dug painfully into her upper arm that she screamed. The leader turned around slowly, watching her struggle. His face remained inscrutable.

"You do not stop struggling and *El Jefe* will give you to the rest of the men. You know what that means," her captor hissed in her ear.

Faith couldn't think. The laughter around her particularly from the man who had touched her breast was enough for her to nearly crumple where she stood. El Jefe swung back to see what was keeping them. His face contorted with annoyance and everyone stopped laughing. He retraced his steps and grabbed Faith by her other arm. Her two captors dragged her towards a hut far away from the centre of the clearing. Her life flashed before her eyes.

What an ignominious way to die.

They entered the hut and pushed her that she stumbled on the packed earth. Faith stiffened her resolve, stood up, and turned towards them. Her younger captor's weapon was trained at her while El Jefe had no weapon.

"Turn around," her captor ordered.

"No." Her voice shook, but she stood her ground.

He raised one brow before looking at El Jefe. Wait, was that a smile pulling at El Jefe's face? In one instant, anger burst inside her like a flame.

"If you're going to kill me, kill me now. I'm not going to turn so you can shoot me in the back." Fury became a ball inside her gut and this time, she didn't care. To hell with it if they saw something out of the ordinary. She was always careful, not allowing her anger get the better of her, but this was an all-or-nothing situation. She was going to die anyway. Until they snuffed her life completely, the intense heat she could generate would continue and could burn whoever was near her. She gritted her teeth.

Her young captor approached her to turn her around.

"*¡Putana!*" he swore, immediately releasing her. His eyes rounded like saucers as he looked at his reddened hand then at her. He lowered his weapon. "Turn around and see why you are here."

"I'm not falling for that." She lifted her chin.

"You are in our clinic!" he snapped. "Did you think we'd kill a doctor?" He swore again before leaving the hut.

His admission shocked Faith that when El Jefe guffawed enjoying her discomfort, she couldn't find a fitting retort. As El Jefe exited the hut, a cough broke behind her. She pivoted slowly, still disbelieving what she was told. She wouldn't be surprised if there was a gun trained at her head and the moment she had her back to the door they would pull the trigger, her brain matter scattering all over the packed earth. But what her young captor said was true.

Eight beds covered in mosquito netting flanked the makeshift hospital walls. Four of the beds were occupied. At the farthest end of the hut was a dispensary filled to the brim with medical supplies, a table, and a chair.

Faith choked at the dryness of her throat. She could feel the blood drain from her head and her face, inching its way to her feet, as though the earth was siphoning the life out of her. She just about made it to the first unoccupied bed before she fell on it and passed out.

****

Zac fell back from the Ancient Eald's group. The Ancients' personal guards flanked them on all sides. Except for Zac and the Ancients, all of them were covered up from head to foot. Although they were shielded from the sun's rays by the canopy of trees above them, the orb was still too high in the sky for the Cynn Cruor to be able to comfortably walk without having to cover their skin. It was just as well that they all wore their amorphic armour, flexible suits that could stop the hack of a blade or a silver bullet, bouncing of the material. Except that the suit was not good enough for the special kind of silver that had been used in the bullet Graeme had taken during the siege of Dac Valerian's stronghold on the Isle of Man. While Zac had the seal of the Manchester Faesten on the left arm of his suit consisting of the wolf, griffin, and crane, the Ancients and their retinue had the seal of the wolf, griffin, and the two headed eagle.

Anything wrong? The Ancient Eald telepathed.

His retinue and the Deoré halted.

Someone who isn't one of us is close by, Sire. Keep walking. I will find out who it is.

The Eald nodded.

Zac heard the Deoré growl softly before the Eald held her hand and she quieted. Iain, one of the Ancient's personal guards, walked back to Zac.

"Hey, McBain, do you have anything to take the leeches off me?"

Zac chuckled, playing along. No leech stuck to any Cynn Cruor's skin. The Kinaré was too strong for even the parasite. As soon as they latched on, they immediately fell to the ground.

Dead.

"You smoke. Use your lighter to burn them." Zac sized up Iain covered in the suit before shaking his head.

Iain snorted, his huge shoulders bouncing. "Don't like fire."

Zac shook his head. "There are some wipes in my backpack. Don't finish them all, okay? The ship is too far to trek back to and I've only brought enough for a couple of days." He handed Iain the pack with all of the vials and chemical supplies needed to analyze the silver that nearly killed Graeme.

Thanks, mate. Zac telepathed.

Iain nodded before slinging the pack over his shoulder as he trudged back to the Ancients. Zac knelt, pretending to tie his bootstraps but his senses were attuned to his surroundings, the vampire DNA that was part of the Kinaré making his sense of hearing as sharp as the katana, wakazashi, and tanto swords he favoured. He heard the slithering of the snake several meters away from him before it made its way up the trunk of tree, waiting for its unsuspecting meal. He heard the footfalls of his fellow Cynn Cruors and the Ancients as they moved away from him, the sound of branches and leaves they moved out of the way as they trudged through the forest, making a whipping sound as they flicked back. Zac inhaled, his sense of smell enhanced by the werewolf DNA in the gene that all Cynn Cruors carried. Rain. He could smell rain that would arrive in three days' time. Zac's ears perked.

There. He could hear it as clear as though the sound was just beside him.

He called forth the Cynn Cruor's ability to alter an ordinary human's sight and mind so that he wouldn't be seen by either human or Scatha. His ability to cloak was nothing compared to Luke's gift of moving between planes. Zac had seen that during the siege of Dac Valerian's fortress in the Isle of Man. No one knew that Luke had already been a part of the Cynn Cruor's assault group for a long while, attaching himself to Colin Butler's unit.

He dug deep, sending a gradual blast of sense alteration to everyone around him. The blast siphoned a lot of his strength than was needed. Nevertheless, a Cynn Cruor's oath was to protect the Ancients. If the people coming towards him were unfriendly, their next destination would be a shallow grave in the middle of nowhere.

Except for the Manchester Cynn Cruors, no one knew that the Ancients had joined Zac to look for the silver. Not even the Faestens in Central America knew that their progenitor was in the vicinity. Until Zac found an antidote to the nearly fatal effects of the silver which nearly cost Graeme Temple his life, the Ancients agreed it was best that only a few knew what they were up to.

And what they were up against.

Several hundred metres away and perpendicular to his location, he saw a group of men with guns and machetes holstered on their waists and assault weapons slung over their shoulders. Two men carried a crate between them.

Must be a cache of assault weapons. Zac mused.

He looked back at the direction of where the Ancients had gone. They were too far to send a telepathic message to warn them. Zac was torn between following the men and returning to the Ancients. His gradual loss of strength made the decision for him. Iain was a tracker and another excellent Cynn Cruor recon. Zac would ask him to find the men's location. His eyes narrowed as he watched the last man in the group disappear through the thicket before he let his guard down.

His fellow immortal was waiting for him, his arm extended with the backpack.

"Thanks."

"How did it go?" the Ancient Eald asked from underneath one of the trees, his arm resting on his bent knee. He looked ageless and no one would have thought he was more than two thousand years old. Beyond him, the Deoré was busy taking out food and laying it on a huge banana leaf that was cut from a nearby tree.

"I saw a group of men walking with a lot of ammo, Sire. They headed to the opposite direction."

"Probably an anti-government group," the Deoré spoke, looking over her shoulder. Her long black hair was braided and reached her waist. It swung when she turned her head to face Zac.

"Or a kidnapping syndicate," the Eald said.

"That's possible." She shrugged, walking towards the Eald. She looked around, inhaling the thick air.

The Eald stood up and held his mate's hands. "How do you feel?"

Zac could feel the love and tenderness the Eald had for the Deoré. He turned away. It was a private moment, but he could hear what they said.

"I really don't know," the Deoré said softly. "It's been so long."

"Yes it has." The Eald bent his head and the Deoré raised her mouth to meet his.

Iain and Zac looked at each other, grinning before walking to the food laden leaf. There was no point talking about how the Ancients loved each other since it was plain for everyone to see. Besides, they were powerful enough to read Iain's and Zac's thoughts.

After the brief stop they continued toward their destination. Only the Ancients knew where this was and the Cynn Cruor warriors had no choice but to follow suit. Zac and Iain surveyed the forest, eyes peeled and ears honed in on every sound. Two other Cynn Cruor warriors stayed on the sides of the Ancients, their weapons each at the ready.

All of a sudden the Ancients stopped. Zac saw the shock then fury that bathed both Ancients' eyes. Zac's eyes widened when he saw the Deoré transform. Gone was the Cleopatra like beauty and in its place was a figure with its mouth open in a silent scream. Simultaneously, its skin stretched and tore, slashing her amorphic armour into shreds. Bloodied sinew was exposed to the elements for the minutest of seconds before skin that looked like shiny leather covered the gaping wounds. No fur grew from her body. Neither did her hands and feet morph into paws. They just elongated, lengthened, and webbed together. Zac's jaw tightened as he bit back his grimace at hearing bones crack and break as the Deoré's back elongated, curved, and hunched. The Deoré whimpered between exhausted puffs of pain and stood straight. Her face transformed. Hollow cheeks and mouth with razor sharp teeth replaced her human beauty. Her nose remained the same. Ears pierced through her hair and stayed back on her head. She lifted her head and opened her eyes. Her eyes were now the colour of molten gold and diamond.

Zac inhaled sharply as he faced the Deoré's terrifying beauty of who she really was.

A werewolf.

Chapter Three

"Alaghom," the Eald said, standing in front of his beloved. His voice firm, commanding, but gentle. "She will not hurt you. She cannot hurt you anymore."

"She will," the Deoré whimpered, her voice slightly guttural. "Through you."

"I will not allow her to do so."

Zac was in the middle of pondering who they were talking about when the hair on the back of his neck rose. He watched in stupefaction when the Ancient Eald transformed as well. His eyes glowed blood orange so unlike what Zac was used to seeing when battle and blood lust consumed a Cynn Cruor warrior, for the Ancient's pupils were a fathomless black. His short cropped hair lengthened, falling to just below his shoulders. His lean frame bulked to thrice his size that Zac thought the armour that covered his body would tear apart, but it adjusted to cover the Eald's new frame. His fingers and toes lengthened and curved, almost looking like claws, but they didn't change the way the Scatha Cruor's hands and feet did.

"Sire." Iain's voice cracked like thunder in the still air.

"Dac is here," the Eald growled, fury thrumming through his body. In the blink of an eye, he raised his arms towards the sky. The rest of the Cynn Cruor drew back at the sight of a glowing ball of fire in the centre of the Ancient Eald's chest. Fissures of electricity crackled between his fingers before fire pulsed through them. He looked up, the muscles of his neck cording and straining as he tried to keep his anger at bay. Suddenly, he chanted in a language Zac had never heard nor come across in his immortal life. He felt the strength of the words and the power it called forth. The sky gradually darkened. The leaves rustled in the branches of the trees as well as underfoot while the trees began to violently sway.

The Ancient Eald and the Deoré looked at them. Trepidation laced Zac's spine and he swallowed hard when two pairs of unholy eyes looked at him, Iain, and the rest of the Ancients' personal guards.

"It's time to stop Dac Valerian once and for all."

****

Faith placed the kidney pan on the table before wiping the sweat off her brow. Three days. She had been in the camp for three days tending to the four members of Los Tiradores. The heat was debilitating to say the least. Cloying, sticky, stifling, it didn't allow for sweat to evaporate. There was no breeze at all and it made her work much harder. Thankfully, the groans of pain had stopped for the moment. Three of her patients kept on asking for morphine to relieve their pain but as time passed, Faith realized this was only an excuse to satisfy their addiction. When one of the patients shouted at her threatening to kill her, she ran out of the makeshift hospital and straight into the viper's pit. All who saw her run to El Jefe's hut followed her, their weapons drawn, their shouts piercing the humid air. One even trained at gun at her head. Faith whipped around. The fright that paralyzed her body at seeing the nozzle of the rifle in the middle of her head gave way to indescribable fury.

Damn!

She felt that energy curl into a ball in the pit of her stomach. Her chest rose and fell with difficulty, the air entering her lungs slowly. Her mind wanted to lash out, but there was still a part of her mind that still clung to one rational thought.

I can't kill anymore.

The man's eyes widened and he faltered, his weapon slipping a notch before he raised it back up. Faith knew he could see the fire that burned in the middle of her pupils, which looked like licks of flame. No one else would see the change. Only the person who was the target of her rage would.

"I'm going to speak to El Jefe and you are not going to stop me." Her voice dripped ice as she spoke in fluent Spanish. She had no idea how she was able to do so. She just didn't give a shit.

Faith turned away and started towards the hut, the rest of the men's weapons still trained on her. If she was going to die, then she would die. There was no point delaying the inevitable.

Besides, it would put her out of her misery.

The hut's cool interiors did nothing to dampen the heat roiling inside her body. She gritted her teeth, her jaw hardening with the strain. The sooner she finished her business with El Jefe, the better. She would make her way back to the makeshift hospital, put her hands to the ground and let the extra heat generated from her body bleed into the packed earth. Only then could she be comfortable in her own skin.

Or she could be shot after she spoke to the renegade leader. Either way, she had to find an outlet.

"You wanted to see me, señorita," El Jefe drawled, his back to her as he faced the window. The foliage beyond was a deep green.

And still.

"Your men are using up the medical supplies."

"I didn't realize you could speak Spanish fluently."

He turned to her, his face shadowed by the gloom.

Faith scowled. "I didn't come here to discuss languages. I came here to warn you."

Even from the shadows, Faith's sharp eyes saw El Jefe's brow arch.

"Warn me?" His voice turned glacial. "You are in no position to warn me."

"By the time your men go through your drugs there won't be enough painkillers to go around if any one of you are wounded. You will have men dying all around you."

El Jefe laughed softly. "You forget, señorita, being killed is part of our lives. My men knew that the moment they joined my group."

"When there is no one left to recruit, you will be no more," Faith murmured beneath her breath.

Pain suddenly exploded from a blow to her head, causing a cry to wrench out of her. The stars she saw in front of her eyes were bright, adding to the discomfort. Something trickled down the back of her neck, making its wayward trail down to her soiled shirt. Faith jerked, wanting to escape what cascaded down the side of her throat. She placed her hand on the offending pain and it came away with blood. She closed her eyes. Her hand was slapped to the side that she lost her balance and sprawled on the ground.

"*Jefe, por favor, Jefe.*" It was her young captor's voice pleading. "For my brother's sake, let her live. We can kill her after."

"She has no manners!"

"*Pero,* señor, we have no doctor," her captor reasoned. "It's true what she says. Jaime, Oscar, and Rodrigo are already healed but they pretend to be ill so they can stay in bed and get doses of morphine."

Words of anger flew over Faith's head. She didn't

care. The only thing she thought of was the pain that decided to spend the rest of its time in her skull. Suddenly, she was hauled to her feet.

"Don't say a fucking word," her captor hissed in her ear.

"Make sure she learns her place, Xavier, or else she won't be the only one having to face the gun's barrel. And it won't be you."

Faith felt her captor stiffen beside her.

"*Arreglado, Jefe.*"

Faith half ran and half stumbled as her captor pulled her out of the hut. She lost a bit of her spatial awareness and her head began to loll from side to side in time with her captor pulling her forward. As soon as they entered the small hospital, she was hurled onto one of the bunk beds. A mirthless smile cracked upon her mouth.

"I'll kill you if you even as much as touch me," she said, then flinched at the breath she felt on her face.

"Be glad that I'm desperate to keep my brother alive and that I have enough influence with El Jefe." Xavier gritted against her ear. "Or else you would have been sport right on El Jefe's floor, where each one of us would enter your holes several times before a bullet scattered your brains on the forest floor."

Faith sucked in a harsh breath at the crudity of her captor's words. The apprehension she felt overran the nearly blinding pain in her head. She bit back a whimper when she felt something cold against her cheek.

"It's only a bottle of alcohol," her captor said flatly. He wrenched her hand from the bed and placed a swath of gauge in it. "Clean yourself."

"Wait!" Faith grabbed his arm, his muscles

stiffening under her fingers. "I need help." She swallowed. "Please."

Her eyes were slowly turning into slits as the pain wound its way through her veins, throbbing and splintering into minuscule pockets of agony.

"I can't see the wound," she continued. "I need your help to guide my hand to the wound." She inhaled sharply and smelled her own coppery scent in the air. "Please...." If she had to end her every sentence in "please" she would do so. She just wanted to ease the pressure in her skull. "You have a name?"

"El Jefe said it earlier."

"Does El Jefe speak for you as well?"

"¡Putana!"

"I have been called worse since I got here."

"I am going to kill you."

"What happens to your brother if you do? I thought you wanted me alive to treat your brother." Faith looked at him through hooded eyes. His hair was shorn close to his head. He was lean, though Faith knew he was muscled after having held on to him earlier. He wasn't too tall and it was easy to see that his growth spurt had been stymied by the lack of proper food.

"Xavier."

She hid her smile, bowing her head. "*Gracias,* Xavier. Will you please help me now?"

He grunted.

"Okay." She licked her dry lips, wincing at the shot of pain traversing her neurons. "There is a bottle of *agua oxinada* in the cabinet. That is what I will use instead of the alcohol." Her gaze tracked him as he did her bidding. She closed her eyes momentarily, hoping that her wound wasn't as bad as it felt. It didn't matter, though. The heat generated by her body would heal it.

Whatever internal injury she may have received would be stitched internally. She just needed to stop the blood flow.

Xavier returned and unscrewed the cap before pouring the solution on the gauze that Faith held.

"Now, guide my hand exactly to where the wound is. I have an idea where it is, but it may not be the exact spot."

She hissed and couldn't stop the groan that was forced out of her when she felt the sting and smelled the solution hitting the lesion.

"Señorita! Your wound is bubbling!"

"It's all right, Xavier." Faith's voice was weak with exertion but said with assurance. "The bubbles you see means that there's dirt being removed."

She asked Xavier for more gauze and once her wound was cleaned, they bandaged it. By the time they were done, Faith was close to collapsing and Xavier close to passing out. He sat down beside her on the bed. She turned to him slowly, gauging how her head felt with the movement. Relieved that the pain she felt didn't increase, she chuckled.

"For someone used to killing people and seeing blood..." she began.

"I am not used to it?" Xavier finished for her. "I shoot people, señorita. I don't help them heal. I let them bleed to death."

She should have been appalled at his callousness. But seeing the way they lived and having glimpsed the dog eat dog culture prevalent among the poor, it didn't come as a surprise anymore. After all, hadn't she been through something similar?

"Rest," Xavier said. "You are not good to my brother if you are too ill to treat him."

Just then four of El Jefe's men came into the hut.

Xavier stood up, his body covering Faith from view. They approached Jaime, Oscar, and Rodrigo, asking them to get up and join them. The three men pretended to walk slowly, painfully out of the hut. Faith looked up at Xavier, his face ashen. He looked down at her, his Adam's apple moving as he swallowed. Her head leaned to the sound of the voices some distance from their hut, raised in a heated argument. Blood, whatever was left in her head, drained from her face. Her three patients were begging for their lives. Then she stifled her scream, her hand covering her mouth when she heard shots fired, disrupting the stillness of the day. Wild-eyed, she looked at Xavier's dead ones.

"Consider yourself lucky, señorita," Xavier said before he sauntered to the bunk of his sleeping brother.

Chapter Four

Dac was a vision of calm. The fury was all inside, eating him, consuming him. The last time he felt this way was when he was castigated by Caesar having been caught taking a woman in the Senate's august halls. Caesar knew of his proclivity towards women but didn't know the pleasure he felt in making them scream in pain, no matter how they begged for Dac to stop. He snorted at the memory. His raping women was no different from how Rome raped and conquered the lands beyond its borders.

Kamaria had bested him, putting him at a disadvantage, making him depend on her despite having some of the Scatha on board the yacht. Dac would allow Kamaria this one short victory.

For now.

He walked across the spacious cabin to the sliding doors that led to his private deck. Kamaria's yacht skimmed the dark waters smoothly and fast. He couldn't care less how long they had been travelling as long as it took to get them to their destination. Dac hardly felt the waves underneath. Neither did he admire the opulent interiors of the cabin, from the king sized bed on the raised dais to the rich wood panelling and exposed beams softly lit by recessed lights, or the private bar stocked with the finest alcohol from all over the world. No, Dac Valerian was more engrossed with visiting a time when yachts were mere triremes taking Roman soldiers to distant lands to plant the Roman eagle, staking the area and its people as belonging to the empire. He was more interested in the information he unearthed from the research done by supposedly brilliant human minds blinded by the amount of money they received for their efforts. He would ply them, with all the riches at his disposal, cajoling them to live the life and spend unwittingly in the establishments he owned. It was a vicious cycle. Humans he employed later spent more than what they could afford, shackling themselves to become indebted to him.

Greed was a beautiful thing.

They had crossed the Caribbean Sea the night before, inching their way through the Panama Canal before dropping anchor off the coast of El Salvador. Kamaria had several werewolves and transfuges at her disposal, much to Dac's chagrin. Being fished out of the water after Kamaria swiped him off the deck was something he would never forget because as soon as he hit the water, he had started to sink. After more than a millennium of sowing fear in the hearts of the Scatha and humans, the tables had been turned.

He was introduced to fear during those seconds he lost buoyancy, and he didn't like it one bit.

Had he still been a Cynn Cruor, Dac knew it wouldn't have been too difficult to tread water since the Kinaré's vampire DNA only absorbed the best qualities of the blood. Since breaking away and forming the Scatha Cruor, the vampire and werewolf blood had started to mutate. Like a dormant virus, the Kinaré inside him and his Scatha immortals made room for the evil that was part of each individual blood. It caused the coldness, the cruelty of the vampire and the rabid bloodlust of the werewolf to dominate and eventually kill off whatever goodness it had. It also made the Scatha's blood thicker and heavier, enough for Dac or any other Scatha to sink to the bottom of the sea. Dac had stayed in his cabin for the duration of the journey, pacing across his luxurious prison, plotting, planning, and contemplating his next move.

He never felt as vulnerable as he did now.

The fact that he had to depend on a werewolf stung like a festering wound cauterized and doused with alcohol again and again. He hated the fact that he couldn't even command his own men, for while on Kamaria's ship her word was law. And he loathed to admit that he needed her to reach their destination.

La Nahuaterique.

Dac sat down on the plush cream armchair. For one rare moment, he allowed weariness to creep into his bones. Allowed the weight of his decisions to flood him. Gave in to that seed of doubt that made him think his end was near. If only the Ancient Cynn had listened to him all those millennia ago. If only the Cynn Cruor leader allowed the Cruors to be recognized for their assistance in the progress of mankind. If only the Council of Ieldran saw that the Cruors could rule the human race.

"No!" He stood and turned on his chair in anger. He swiped the chair off the floor, sending it flaying across the cabin to smash against the mirror suspended over the fireplace that shattered in huge pieces before breaking further as it hit the mantle on its way down to the floor. Dac's fury knew no bounds and he welcomed his transformation. His hands curved with nails so sharp it could cut through a thick block of wood. And the pain, the excruciatingly glorious pain of his flesh stretching to accommodate his bigger bulk. The agony of feeling his teeth pushing hard against his gums, narrowing to incisors that filled his mouth as his jaw broke and reformed. Dac closed his eyes, his breath coming in rapid bursts, his stomach tensing, his body straining against the torturous change.

And it was heaven.

The last time he allowed himself to transform was when one of his own dared to challenge him for the right to be called the leader of the Scatha Cruor. It didn't matter that the Scatha Cruor was drunk and was thinking out of turn. That was enough for Dac. He rarely showed the monstrosity of what he could become. He was powerful even without the change. But when fury consumed him, overrode his reasoning with fear, he allowed the transmutation to take him. Dac opened his eyes, his pupils dilating to a dark neon green with fathomless dark flecks, resigned for now. Until he could secure what he needed, he was at Kamaria's mercy.

Suddenly he growled, his enhanced senses picking up footfalls along the corridor outside. He envisioned the gentle sway of hips, the eternal length of legs ending in feet fettered into five inch black patent leather stilettos, the flat fertile belly, the gentle caress of inner thighs brushing against each other guarding that orifice no red blooded heterosexual human or Scatha could resist. Three holes to be precise. And the gentle bounce of natural breasts topped with dark nipples he could sink his fangs into.

By the time the door to his cabin opened, the reflection of his fury was replaced by his human form.

And a raging hard on that tented his slacks.

The side of his mouth lifted when he saw his visitor. "You touch me by coming here to tell me we have arrived."

Kamaria raised her brow. "We've dropped anchor. Are you up to travelling over water?"

Dac chuckled to hide the slight trepidation he felt. "I applaud you for catching me unawares." He pinned

Kamaria with all the hatred in his gaze. "That will never happen again." His lip curled. "Ahh, Kamaria, I see fear in your eyes. It suits you."

Kamaria immediately banked the emotion before sauntering to the telephone located on the bedside table. She punched one number and waited only for a split second.

"Raise anchor, Captain," she snapped as soon as the phone was answered. "We return to Europe."

"Wait!"

"How long before we set sail?" Kamaria continued as though Dac hadn't spoken.

"Kamaria." Dac gritted his teeth.

Kamaria looked at him, her gaze the golden hue of the werewolf. In the background, Dac heard the Captain answer her. His entire body began to shake with humiliation before he spoke.

"Please."

The word jolted Kamaria speechless that she wasn't able to respond to her captain's query.

"Kamaria?" the captain called.

Startled, she replied, "Yes?

"Where exactly in Europe do we head to?"

She paused, her eyes hooded. "I changed my mind. Prepare to go ashore."

"Understood."

Dac wanted to say more but decided against it. The humiliation of his request made his stomach roil.

Kamaria returned the receiver to its cradle.

"La Nahuaterique is important to you," she began. "Why?"

"Silver."

She sucked in her breath. "You bastard."

"I'll take that as a compliment." Dac sat down on the sofa, relishing the anger that made the werewolf's body hum. It teased him, stroking his lust, inviting his cock to take notice. "However, I won't be able to use it. If it hasn't been smelted and refined, I don't have a viable weapon to use."

"Where is the mine?" Kamaria remained wary.

Dac became pensive, looking at a point beyond her. "I can't exactly say. The human I paid didn't give me time to tell me before I killed him. He wanted to keep some of the silver for himself." He snorted. "I paid him to process the ore, not get a cut from it."

"Then how do you know it's there?"

"He left several diaries of his observations which he concealed from the Scatha. All of his writings about this special silver and the coordinates of the mine's location pointed to this area."

Kamaria moved to the sliding doors. "Did this human know the name of the place?"

"The entry in his diary only said it was a place that didn't exist."

****

Kamaria reeled from Dac's information. Impossible! All this time, the one that could have catapulted her to incredible power and sow fear among the packs had been right under her nose. She cursed herself for being so foolish. Her overriding aim had been to find Alaghom Na-Om and the sorcerer who found a way to stop the quickening from happening on the night of the full moon. Her kind could shift and return to their human forms at any time, but shifting was impossible when the white orb dominated the dark sky. It was the only time they couldn't control their bodies' transformation. She had been so incensed with her cousin who refused to divulge any arcane knowledge so she had to grope her way through the darkness of her existence. Yet there was one thing she always knew. Her village had never been found and didn't exist in any cartographer's masterpiece because by the time the Spain's conquistadors arrived in Cuzcatlan and Copan, present day El Salvador and Honduras, the forest had overrun her village. There would be no trace of a culture or a people having lived there for anyone to discover.

She had made sure of that.

She looked at Dac over her shoulder. A wave of disgust scrunched her features at the sight of the tenting bulge between his legs.

"You're not putting that abhorrent maggot of a cock inside me," she stated through gritted teeth.

Dac's chortle slithered down her spine. She couldn't stay inside the room any longer. A low vibration at the back of her throat was the only warning Dac got before she pounced on him, her mouth against his throat, her hands gripping his shoulders with inhuman strength, the stiletto heel of her shoe grazing his hard shaft and forcing it down.

"One more sound out of you, I will deflate your dick and rip your neck apart."

Dac hissed.

Kamaria's mouth slowly curved. She enjoyed the feel of the Scatha's hardness under her heel. It was so...symbolic. She laughed softly at his discomfort.

"My dear Dac. I thought you liked pain?" Kamaria thought she would be sick of his stench. She zeroed in on the scent of the were blood inside the Scatha leader, that part of the Kinaré gene she could stomach. It was the only way she could stay put to bring her message home.

"You will die by my hand soon, Kamaria."

Kamaria's laughter floated when she catapulted herself away from him before landing without a sound in a crouched position by the door. She stood up with feline grace.

"I wouldn't have expected anything less." She turned on her heel and left.

Chapter Five

Faith couldn't dispel the foreboding that coated the back of her nape like a cold towel. Not even the pain in her skull that dulled to a throb could shake it off. She knew by the sudden change in the weather and the quick darkening of the sky that something was about to happen. Thunderstorms didn't immediately blanket the sky in less than five minutes if it was Mother Nature behind it, despite the fact that man had so altered the world that the weather had become more unpredictable. The only consolation was that the sun wasn't beating down on them, humidity was at a standstill, and there was a stirring of a cool breeze. This wasn't Gaia's making. She knew it all too well as she had also dabbled with the elements when she was younger.

This was being done by someone with the gift of controlling the elements.

Xavier busied himself by stripping the cots of his dead companions, occasionally checking on his sleeping brother. He spared Faith a glance when she sat up before standing unsteadily.

"Do you think that's wise?" He continued to strip the beds.

Faith didn't bother to tell him that she had already healed. Her gift had healed her too.

"Something's not right."

"It hasn't been for a long time."

"Xavier, listen!"

"I don't hear anything."

"Exactly!" she whispered. "Everything is so...still."

Xavier inhaled deeply, doing as Faith said. A crease formed on his forehead as he walked to one of the open windows. Faith followed, standing beside him.

"Clouds that are nearly black and pregnant with rain don't happen immediately," she said. "Someone is manipulating the weather."

"You believe in that?" He snorted, shaking his head before going back to the beds. He slung his rifle diagonally across his body snugly.

"Don't you have curanderos? Or shamans in your past who were powerful enough to do so?" she countered.

"When you live in the streets where every day is a battle to even just exist, a past obscured by time and a future shielded by the unknown don't matter. What counts is the present, to prevail over everything and anything thrown at you."

Faith was about to speak when they heard one of the men shout.

"¡Alto!"

The crackle of guns zeroing on a target reached their ears. Xavier strode to the door of the hut as Faith trailed behind. A man and a woman accompanied by several men had just entered the hideout's periphery. The unholy feeling that seemed to have been glued on Faith's nape strengthened. She looked at the woman. She was breathtaking. Her hair fell to her waist like a dark silken curtain. Faith wished she had a whistle bait figure like what the woman had—flared hips giving way to shapely legs, a narrow waist, and ample breasts. The woman looked like a movie star.

A cold movie star.

The woman's eyes surveyed her surroundings, not missing anything.

"Hide!" Faith mouthed. What she saw in the woman's eyes nearly paralized her. She had glowing gold eyes that spoke of cruelty.

Xavier didn't argue, his own gaze filled with apprehension. He looked at his brother, uninterrupted in his sleep. Faith placed a finger over her lips and continued to watch from behind the gap on the wall.

El Jefe stepped out from his hut, a double serrated knife in his hand. The men who came with the couple growled low.

Growl? Faith frowned. The sound that came from them sounded more animal than human.

Her attention shifted to the man. If there was an epitome of evil, this man fitted the bill. His bald head gleamed even in the dim light of the sky. His easy smile reminded her of a crocodile's grin. His eyes were hooded and in the stifling heat, he was wearing a leather jacket. How the hell could he not be sweltering underneath it? She belatedly realized that some of the men behind them also wore leather jackets. Was this some kind of biker gang that lost its way in the forests of La Paz? Almost all of them had looks women would die for. Faith wasn't immune to their fitness model builds, handsome features and eyes that made women melt and do their every bidding. But the sneers they had, which seemed permanently plastered on their mouths, told a different story. Each of them focused on one kidnapper, causing El Jefe's men to fidget where they stood and unlocked the safety of their weapons.

"We have lost our way," the man explained in Spanish without waiting for El Jefe to speak.

"I doubt very much that you have come here for some sightseeing, or even trekking the forest." El Jefe looked at all of them. His stance was relaxed but guarded. "Be careful what you say next, señor. My men are just itching to pull the triggers. Who are you?"

"Señor," the visitor cajoled. "*Mi nombre no es importante.* We're not here to fight. We're only looking for a mountain."

"There are many mountains around us," El Jefe quipped, his mouth quirking as he looked around. "Take your pick."

Watching from the makeshift hospital, Faith swallowed against the lump that suddenly clogged her throat. Her eyes had strayed from what was happening when she noticed that this wasn't the only group who had arrived. Her eyes picked up a movement to the right up in the trees and just a few feet away behind the biker gang, but the ball of apprehension grew when she saw that the unseen group had two figures that could have come from graphic novels or Comic Con. A werewolf without the elongated snout and someone that looked like...a vampire? Didn't vampires only come out at night? He exuded something out of the ordinary, something beyond human. Then Faith clicked at a truth.

This was the sorcerer responsible for the dark skies.

What's going on?

There was someone else, someone she barely saw, but felt. Amidst the rising tension of the moment, his presence was like a salve in the chaos she knew was about to happen. Protective, caring, sensual. Faith was bewildered. How could she feel that when death was about to strike any moment? Yet she knew this man she couldn't see was looking at her. How else could her body be thrumming, her skin becoming sensitive in the most sensual of ways? The feeling was no different from the sensation she got when someone looked at her from across the room. She just knew. It was as though his breath was on her skin, teasing her, making her hunger more of what he offered, making her want to beg? Who was this unseen being who called out to her?

The visitor's harsh voice cut through her thoughts, also severing the connection she had with her sensual stranger.

"We're not here to play games either," the man said. "But we will not be averse to play if that's what you want. Why don't we play hunters and prey? We are the hunters, you and your men are the prey?"

Several clicks of hammers being cocked back and the unlatching of safety locks sounded in the still air.

"Get out of my sight and my men won't kill you," El Jefe growled.

"Gladly." The stranger grinned. Faith couldn't stop the shocked gasp that came out of her mouth. Disbelief made her eyes round. It couldn't be. This wasn't possible. The stranger's teeth changed to fangs!

Hell, there were so many people who had their teeth altered. He could be one of those, couldn't he? Faith's mind honed in on the only possibility.

There was a Comic Convention in the middle of nowhere.

Yeah right. The rain forest is making you loca.

"Either that or I'm seeing real paranormal beings that are not supposed to exist," she whispered to herself.

The stranger pivoted on his heel before returning to face El Jefe.

Shock and confusion painted El Jefe's face before the knife in his hand fell to the ground. The next thing that slid and kissed the earth was El Jefe's head, bouncing before rolling away from the body that spewed forth a fountain of blood. Pandemonium broke as El Jefe's men started shooting.

Faith clamped her hand over her mouth to stop her scream from being heard. Horrific disbelief assailed her at the sight of the men in leather changing into the most hideous creatures of claws and razor sharp teeth, reminding her of the deep sea angler fish. And the stench. Faith jerked away from the wall. Their stench of unwashed bodies and garbage drifted all the way to where she was. Those without leather jackets jumped into the air and landed as werewolves over their targeted prey. Her blood turned to ice.

They had to leave. They couldn't stay and be flayed alive.

Just then, the other group she noticed in the background launched themselves at the intruders. Screeches akin to nails on a blackboard and indignant howls rent the air. Except for the sorcerer and the werewolf with them, this group of men carried swords.

Faith had enough.

"Xavier!" she shouted over screams, the clashing of metal, and the rapid fire of guns. Faith looked at her captor, his face ashen at what he saw. He didn't hear her as he stood frozen.

"Xavier, it's me!"

Xavier's eyes were wild, frantic with fear. Faith felt her panic resurface. She swallowed hard, closed her eyes to momentarily concentrate on taking one deep breath. "We have to go. We can't stay."

Piercing screams split the air. It galvanized them both to sprint to the farthest end of the hut. Xavier bent down to get something from underneath his brother's cot. He took out his firearm and placed it at the foot of the bed, slung the duffle bag over his body before criscrossing the firearm back over the bag's strap.

"Felipe," Xavier coaxed his brother gently.

"*Vamos. Tenemos que ir.*" He continued speaking to Felipe despite his brother's protests.

"Let me help you with the bag." Faith said but stopped dead when Xavier pointed the gun at her.

"I have no need for you anymore," he said, fear still mirrored in his eyes.

"What do you mean?" she asked in bewilderment. "You saved me earlier because you needed me to heal your brother."

"I've changed my mind."

"Xavier, that's the panic talking. How far do you think you will get carrying your brother and that bag of medicine?"

"If I go now, we will get far. You are free to go wherever you want."

"Free to go?" Faith's voice rose, hysteria bubbling to the surface. Anger came in a close second, and she could feel the fire inside her curling into a ball. Soon it would reflect in her eyes, and she might not be able to hold back. She hands balled into fists to quell it as much as she could. "Where the hell will I go? You kidnapped me! I don't know squat about this place!"

"*Tus ojos!* Your eyes!" Xavier sucked in his breath, his eyes widening in alarm.

"Make your eyes bigger and they're going to bulge out of your skull."

"*Pero tus ojos!*" He waved his firearm in front of her face. "There's fire in them!"

"Then shoot me. Either you take me with you or you end my misery. I'm not going to be fodder for the horrors fighting each other at the moment! I'm no one. Just another body you've put down to pave your way to hell. Do it. You will do me a great service."

She closed her eyes, waiting for the shot's report. For the bullet travelling from the chamber into her head. What would it feel like? Would it be hot like the fire that constantly burned her from inside out? Or would she only hear the discharge before she entered nothingness? She waited.

"No, señorita."

Faith's eyes snapped open. From the frightened young man she saw before she closed her eyes, Xavier had suddenly changed to the resolute hardened man standing in front of her now.

"I will not have your death on my conscience. You helped my brother. You don't deserve to become a part of the path leading to my damnation." He gave Faith the duffel bag. "Come. We've already wasted too much time."

Chapter Six

Zac welcomed the blood orange colour of fury in his eyes, the kill call that raked every sinew of his body. He called forth the vision of all his brethren, his friends who were now part of the pantheon of the Cynn Cruors' fallen. He thought of his mother's rejection and his father who didn't know he had a son. Someday this war had to stop.

It just had to.

The Ancients' enhanced senses had followed Valerian's scent to a clearing with ramshackle huts. One hut looked sturdier than the rest and was separated from the group of squat bungalows. Zac inhaled sharply. Drugs, but it didn't smell like the men were manufacturing the substance. The smell of antiseptic and alcohol tickled his nostrils.

A clinic.

There was another scent.

A woman.

Zac would have known a woman's scent anywhere, but hers was different. He could scent her fear yet there was courage mingled with it. What was she doing here? Bloody hell, had the woman been kidnapped? His fury increased. He vowed he would take the woman away and bring her back to her family after this face-off was over.

He turned his attention to the scene unfolding in the clearing. Dac Valerian was alive. He had survived the siege in the Isle of Man. Herod wasn't with him. Instead, a woman with the same beautifully flowing hair as the Deoré was with him. Her beauty wasn't as ageless as the Ancient's beloved, but she definitely had the allure to turn men into lapdogs at her feet. And her eyes, were a deep golden colour bordering on brown, the shape of her visage no different from the Deoré's. Zac's eyes darted from the Deoré to the woman with Dac Valerian, the truth dawning on him

Yes, McBain, they are related. The Ancient Eald spared him a glance. *Let's concentrate on the task at hand, shall we?*

Aye, sire. Zac flushed.

No offense taken, Zac.

The decapitation of the man who appeared to be the leader of the group became the signal for the Cynn Cruor to engage the Scatha.

"Now!"

The Cynn Cruor launched themselves at the Scatha and the other men who had transformed into werewolves. Dac and the rest of the Scatha whipped around in surprise before they were tackled to the ground and the fighting began in earnest.

"I'm going to relish slashing you for the weres to feast on, Cynn Cruor," one Scatha snarled at Zac as soon as he righted himself, his saliva flowing from his maw.

Zac held his wakizashi straight at the Scatha before swinging his sword to slice diagonally across the body. The Scatha fell to the ground, dark blood pooling around him, the skin where Zac made the slice sizzling and adding to the stench.

"You were saying?" Zac looked down at him, a brow arched.

"Fuck you."

"You're not my type," Zac said before hacking the head off the Scatha's shoulders.

He didn't wait for the dust to settle before killing off several more. Werewolves...bloody hell. He really had his work cut out for him, but he grinned. The Manchester Cynn Cruors would have loved to join the fray. And what Zac wouldn't do now to have them by his side because as the ash settled, he could see that the Scatha and werewolves outnumbered the Cynn Cruor almost nine to one. One of the Ancients' bodyguards was pounced on by three Scathas and decapitated, making the Scatha shout in victory. Zac roared, flying towards them, turning his body to one side, holding his sword in two hands. But before he could reach them, a huge furry body slammed into him sideways that caused him to almost lose his grip on his weapon. Momentarily disoriented, two huge paws kept him to the ground while its muzzle dripped saliva on his amorphic armour. Zac hissed in pain when the claws pierced the armour to clamp on his shoulders. Blood rushed out of the wounds, bathing Zac's shoulders. In the distance, he saw more Scatha approach, loping towards him without a care in the world while all around them, the Cynn Cruor were getting decimated. He knew he only had a few precious moments before they arrived. He zeroed in on the pain the claws made.

Then he erased it.

"Today you die, Cynn Cruor."

"You first." Zac sneered before the werewolf collapsed, his body neatly sliced at the waist. Its distended flesh sizzled from the sword's silver grooved blade. Zac kicked the body away and wrenched the claws from his shoulders.

Get up, McBain! You've been through worse! he snapped at himself. Point was, he had used most of his energy on cloaking earlier. He knelt on one knee, his breathing slightly laboured. He held his sword aloft, twisting his torso in preparation. When the Scatha screeched in for the kill he swung the blade. The

Scatha fell howling in agony, its legs mere stumps flung away from its body. Zac brought his blade down on the Scatha's neck, enveloping him in vile ash. The two other Scatha warriors bellowed seeing their comrade disintegrate. Zac stood almost doggedly. All around him the Ancients and the Cynn Cruor battled it out. Not wasting a moment longer, he surged through the Cynn Cruors' nemesis as his sensei had taught him to do. Without turning around he swung his blade and closed his eyes before the billowing dust covered him.

"Bloody hell, I'm going to need a bath," he grumbled.

He moved on to the next Scatha, maiming them before taking their heads. He ran towards Iain who kept his silver grooved modernized securis or Frankish axe circling while he twirled almost like a dervish, hacking at every Scatha and werewolf that approached him. But no matter how many he, Zac, and the rest of the Cynn Cruor killed, the Scatha and werewolves kept pouring in.

Suddenly, a werewolf flew over Zac and landed on Iain's back. Iain roared in pain before it was cut short when the were snapped his neck, removing it from his body, turning Iain to a pile of ash.

"Iain!" Zac bellowed his anguish at the loss of another Cynn Cruor. In one swing he severed the were's head before he felt the weight of another mangy mutt at his back. Zac closed his eyes as he struggled. All around him, his brethren were joining the Pantheon. There weren't any Cynn Cruor left to guard the Ancients. They couldn't be held hostage by Dac. He refused to see this as the end of the Cynn Cruors' progenitor. He had to keep them safe, but no matter how hard he struggled to get the werewolf off his back, he was just too weak.

Then, Zac heard the whistle of several arrows being fired and the indignant screeches and howls of the enemy. The were on his back yelped as it was knocked away. Swiftly turning around, he was stunned at who he saw.

"Long time, McBain."

Zac took the proffered hand and he was pulled up to his feet. "A very long time. A few centuries. I'd ask what you're doing here, but I doubt you'd tell me."

The man gave him a tight smile and a slight nod. "You don't have time either. You need to get the Ancients away. The Scatha and werewolves have a yacht load of reinforcements."

Zac wanted to find out how his friend got the intel, but they had to fall back. He looked at the Ancients. Both were in pitched fights. The woman he saw earlier had morphed into a werewolf, trying to take a swipe at the Deoré. The Deoré's body suit was ripped in several places, but as soon as she was wounded, she instantly healed, much to the chagrin of her opponent.

"I'll have what should be mine," the female werewolf growled.

"I'll willingly give it to you, Kamaria," the Deoré snapped. "Your death." She hurled herself at Kamaria and they both tumbled to the ground.

A shot rang out. The silence that followed, deafening. Zac watched the scene unfold in slow motion in front of him.

Dac had his arm extended, a smoking gun pointed at the Ancient Eald, who fell to the ground.

The Deoré screamed, forgetting Kamaria as she sprinted to her beloved. Seeing the Eald's wounded shoulder she raised her head and gave a howl of anguish and fury before training her gaze at Dac. She was about to launch at the Scatha leader when he pointed the gun at her, stopping her cold in her tracks.

"One more move and this silver enters your body." Dac leered at her. "I wasn't ready the last time, bitch. This time I am."

Zac spotted Iain's securis. In less than a second, he hurled it, the axe making a wobbling sound before severing Dac's hand. The Scatha leader bellowed in pain, holding his stump that oozed green blood. He turned to Zac.

"You! You Manchester Cynn Cruors are a bloody thorn on my side!"

"We aim to please," Zac snapped.

The Ancient Eald slowly stood up much to Dac's shock. The blood from his wound made rivulets down his armour.

"That's impossible! You should be writhing in pain!"

"I made you Dacronius!" the Eald thundered, calling Dac by his Roman name. "Do you think your progenitor weak?"

The Eald then raised both his arms up to the sky without a wince, spoke an ancient tongue and the heavens poured immediately in torrents. The wind lashed against the trees, breaking up the canopy above them. With a swiftness that belied the pain it must have caused him, the Ancient Eald's hands curved before a ball of fire erupted between them. Immediately, he threw the ball at Dac. The force was so strong that Dac went through several tree trunks before falling to the ground.

"Kamaria, kill him!" Dac's shout reverberated through the din of the rain.

"I will empty my crossbow in you, she-wolf, if you do," Zac's friend shouted as he pointed his Cho-ko-nu at her. "Your choice. Die now. Or later."

Kamaria growled in frustration. She went down on all fours, walking with measured steps towards the remaining Scatha Cruors and werewolves. They waited for Dac to zoom back to them. One Scatha made a move toward the Ancient Eald but before he took his second step he was obliterated, his neck pierced by two silver bolts.

"This isn't over." Dac said, his chest heaving, water dripping from his bald head to his tattered leather jacket.

"Agreed," the Eald said. "It will only be over when your ashes are no more. Even the ground won't accept your offering."

Dac, Kamaria, and the rest of their contingent inched their way out of the clearing. The Ancients, Zac, and his friend only relaxed when they couldn't sense Dac anymore. Suddenly the Eald knelt on the ground with a thud, but he looked at Zac's friend with gratitude.

"Zac told me about you once, but I have never had the pleasure of your acquaintance. These were not the circumstances I would have envisioned for our meeting. Thank you, Armourer."

The Armourer nodded curtly in acknowledgment, his ponytail plastered against his back, his chiselled features occasionally lit up by the lightning.

"Dac will be back," he said, his voice loud against the pelting rain.

"We have to get you out, my liege." Zac informed the Ancients.

"In a moment," the Eald winced and inhaled sharply.

"Sire, the silver."

"I think I have enough magick in my body to stave it off for a little while, McBain." His progenitor's smile was sad. "Many Cynn Cruors died today. The rain has allowed their ashes to soak the ground. This is now hallowed ground. The least I can do is to send them properly to the Pantheon."

Zac nodded curtly. While the Eald's actions were laudable, he was more worried about the effects of the silver he knew was already trickling through the Eald's veins.

"Alaghom, I need you."

"I'm here." The Deoré had changed back to her human form, her braid plastered against her tattered suit. She held her mate around the waist. The Eald closed his eyes and placed his hands, palms down. He started to chant, the sound growing in increments until his voice was as loud as the downpour. Zac watched as bits and pieces of earth soaked with the Cynn Cruors ashes separated from the ground.

And there were a lot.

Almost everywhere he looked huge masses of dirt hovered at shoulder level like unspent meteors before bursting into flame that not even the deluge could extinguish. The steam generated by the mixture of fire and water swirled around all of them and they bowed their heads in prayer. Slowly the vapour disappeared, rising above the clearing to make its way to all Cynn Cruors' final resting place.

Zac walked to where Iain's axe was and knelt to say a short prayer for his fallen brethren, his grief sharp and keen. The ache in his heart flowing through him as liquid anguish, the water that fell over him symbolic of the tears he couldn't shed. He spied Dac's firearm and took it. The Scatha leader's limb had already disintegrated once it had been severed from its source. If there were still bullets left in the chamber, he would be able to study them.

The Armourer shouted again to be heard. "My lord, do you think you can make it stop raining so we can hear each other?"

The Ancient Eald waved his hand and in no time, the deluge lessened to gentle rain.

"Thank you," the Amourer said before walking to Zac. "I'll take the rear. Stay by the Ancients' side. Then you know I have to leave."

Zac stood, nodding. "Understood."

Chapter Seven

Faith winced with every flash of lightning and nearly yelped with the sharp crack of thunder. Dammit! She should be used to this! Her eyes bore holes at Xavier. He continued to trudge on, his brother slung over his back. It wasn't exactly the best way to carry him what with the wound in Felipe's side. Faith turned to look over her shoulder to see if someone followed them, but the curtain of green shielded them from what they left behind.

Suddenly, Xavier turned around to face her.

"Give me the bag."

"What do you need?" she asked as she handed it to him.

"I don't need anything. This is where I leave you."

"What?" She puffed, flabbergasted. "In the middle of nowhere?"

Xavier shook his head. He pointed to his right. "See this path? Follow it all the way and it will take you to the nearest village. I have used this path several times." He walked to a nearby trunk and carefully laid Felipe on the wet ground. He opened the bag to pull out a bottle of water before handing it to her. "I cannot let you join us anymore."

She looked at the path, which was only slightly discernible. "Xavier—"

"You will leave!" He held his rifle in one hand and the bottle of water still extended to her in the other.

"How do I know you're telling the truth? Don't think I'm stupid." Faith's anger was getting the better of her.

"I didn't say you were, but this is where we part. I'm sorry I kidnapped you."

Faith bit back a growl of frustration. "No. I won't do it."

Xavier cocked his weapon.

Faith raised an eyebrow. "Either way, I'm dead."

"You're intelligent, a doctor. You can speak Spanish. The village you will hit needs a doctor too. The government doesn't exactly care about what happens to us."

"I don't speak Spanish fluently."

Xavier arched an eyebrow.

"That was a fluke," she snapped. How the hell could she explain the things she did when she couldn't even understand it herself?

Felipe woke when thunder resounded in the sky.

"Xavier…"

"*Esta bien, Felipe.*"

"*Tengo frio…*" Felipe started to shudder and in no time was shaking uncontrollably. "*Tengo dolor.*"

Xavier placed his weapon and the bottle of water on the ground and scrounged through the bag's contents. "What should I give him? Where is the morphine?" He took out the vacuum packed syringe. He found a vial of morphine. His hands trembled when he took out the syringe.

"Xavier!"

The wails and cries of his brother ringing in his ears, Xavier couldn't stop his hands from shaking to plunge the needle into the vial. Panicked, he held them out to Faith.

"You do it," he said. "Give Felipe the morphine."

Faith remained standing.

Every nerve in her body screamed the Hippocratic oath.

Every neuron in her brain focused on her survival.

"Give him the morphine!"

"If you are going to be alone with him, you will need to learn to steel yourself against his cries if you want to administer medicine," Faith said, her voice steady, calm, unemotional. It didn't matter that she felt horrified by what she was doing.

"Señorita, *por favor!*"

"Why, Xavier? You were going to leave me to fend for myself and yet when you need me, you expect me to help?"

"Xavier…" Felipe's voice squeezed Faith's heart, his supplication killing her. She didn't know anything about the forest. She couldn't risk getting lost in the jungle when the malevolent creatures she saw could still be around. If she wanted to return to the world alive, she had no choice.

Self-preservation was such a bitch.

The wind whipped in gusts, tossing Felipe's frail body from side to side, the movement causing him to groan in pain.

Xavier's harsh countenance cracked as his eyes welled. "Felipe is my only family. I cannot lose him. Please. I cannot lose him." He turned to look at his brother, saying his last sentence over and over again.

Bile rose to her throat. This was not who she was. How could she deny her captor his family when she knew how painful it was to be alone?

Oh, what the hell. Faith walked towards the brothers. Taking the syringe and vial, she efficiently extracted the required dosage before depressing the syringe to push the bubbles out.

"Hold Felipe down," she instructed, inserting the needle into his arm. Felipe's wails slowly stopped, the strain easing from his face. "You have to find shelter.

Felipe needs to get away from the cold." She threw the syringe away.

Xavier turned to her, his jaw tensing to stop himself from crying. He nodded.

"Can you spare your knife?" Faith asked while taking the bottle of water and standing. "How far will the village be?"

"No."

"I should have known better!" she breathed. *Shit!* She felt her anger begin to consume her. It didn't matter. She was outside, she had the ground at her feet, she'd be able to let it bleed. "Here I was thinking there was good in everyone. Some compassion, some humanity, some—"

"You're coming with us. It's not very far. When Felipe is comfortable, I will take you to the village myself and make sure you get home."

Xavier's statement stopped Faith from her diatribe. She searched his face, his eyes. There was no guile.

Just resignation, fatigue, and gratitude.

****

Save for the wind that had cooled the humidity around them, Zac was only too glad that his suit kept his body temperature comfortable. It was a good thing the Armourer was with them, to help carry the provisions they had left at a designated point before engaging the Scatha Cruor and the werewolves. There were still some more provisions they had to leave behind. Zac would come back for the rest later once he knew where their destination was. After the Scatha left and she had changed back to her human form, the Deoré took the dagger hidden in her boot, slashed her wrist and made the Ancient Eald drink from her. The Armourer turned away, reddening at the sounds the Deoré emitted, becoming more orgasmic the deeper the Eald drank. Even amidst all the carnage, Zac couldn't help the grin pulling at his mouth. It was normal for Cynn Cruor warriors and their mates battling it out against the Scatha to find secluded places to heal each other through sex once the battle was over. There was no time to find a secluded place. The Ancients were no different. Zac was used to it.

The Armourer wasn't.

Taking pity on his friend, Zac pulled him to the side.

"Let's look at that hut," he said, pointing to the makeshift hospital. "I noticed the scent of antiseptic coming from it."

The Armourer readily agreed. "If there are any more medicines that may help the Eald…" he sighed, chuckling ruefully. "The meds won't help, will they?"

Zac shook his head, sobering. "We're dealing with a special kind of silver which nearly killed Graeme Temple."

"Graeme?" the Armourer asked, surprised. "The Phantom Templar? I didn't know you knew him."

"Nor I, you." Zac grinned. "We both belong to the Manchester Faesten of the Cynn Cruor. It's why we're here. The Ancients went to Manchester and helped me heal Graeme, they realized that the silver bullet from Dac's weapon was the same silver they encountered a long time ago. When the Ancient Eald first met the Deoré." He paused. "How do you know Graeme?"

"A long story." the Armourer adjusted the weight of his crossbow against his shoulder. "I've met so many immortals in my travels. We meet, then lose touch. The only thing they have of me as part of their memories are the weapons I craft for them. Just like your swords."

"This is something I hold in high regard." Zac looked at his weapon before deftly sheathing the more than razor sharp silver grooved blade in its scabbard. "It has served me well."

"And it should considering we had to fight side by side at the time of the Tokugawa."

"Those were bloody days. Literally." Zac chuckled as he looked around. "Let's take what we can. I doubt that any of the men who lived here will need them in the afterlife."

As soon as they entered the hut, Zac inhaled sharply. The female's smell still permeated the air. Her unique scent. He closed his eyes. Any ordinary mortal wouldn't have noticed the scent, but with the Cynn Cruor's enhanced abilities, it would stay long after it became a memory. She smelled of jasmine, of rose, or cocoa? He opened his eyes to see the Armourer looking at him quizzically.

"A woman was here," Zac replied to his unspoken question.

"I didn't see any woman apart from the Deoré and the she-wolf."

Zac inhaled again. "She was hiding. I sensed her with one of the men."

"You sensed her?"

"Partly. They must have escaped when we joined the fray, but I didn't see her leave the hut. They must have left through the window." He pointed at the low window facing the jungle.

"You would have noticed her disappearance even while you fought?"

Zac gave his friend a dark look.

The Armourer raised his hands in mock surrender.

"No need to be testy, Zachary. If I didn't know any better, that look you're giving me is saying 'she's mine. Trespass, and I'll gut you'." He shook his head as he filled a bag he found with medicines.

Zac stopped before raking his fingers through his short blond hair. "How the hell can that be when I've not seen her?"

"And yet you say she was here."

"Her scent is still here."

"Ahh…her scent."

"Bloody hell, mate. Since when did you become a pain?" Zac muttered.

"Since I realized my life stretched endlessly before me without any end in sight."

Zac sighed. "I'm sorry." He placed his hand on his friend's shoulder. "Maybe if you stayed in one place it wouldn't be too bad."

The Armourer grunted. "Not my lot."

"I said the same thing, my friend. Now that I've become part of the Manchester Faesten, the sadness does ease."

"Of course it does. After you have your share of feeding from women, but for how long will you be satisfied even without a mate?" The Armourer shot him a skeptical glance as he continued to put medicines into the bag.

"Women in my bed are enough for me even without a mate." Zac's chuckle was hollow. The talk of women made him think of the woman who had been in the hut. Who was she? The scent of fear permeated the air, but it wasn't just hers. It also belonged to the male with her. Zac made a sound at the back of his throat.

Mine.

Where the fuck did that come from?

"Zac." It was the Deoré's voice. Though softly

spoken, he heard her. "We need to stem the Eald's blood."

"We better go," he motioned to the Armourer.

The forest was a huge place. If the woman had run away, she wouldn't get far. Once they reached their destination and he made a call to the Faesten, Zac vowed to find her and take her back to her home.

Why did he suddenly wish her home was with him?

Chapter Eight

Faith was about to collapse. The longer they travelled, the heavier the duffel bag became. It didn't help that the rain had picked up and she had to constantly remove her wet hair away from her face and spit the water that entered her open mouth to breathe. Eventually, the downpour abated to a gentle rain, though it still didn't make things easier. Xavier struggled both with his firearm and his brother's weight, but he didn't complain. It was this one attribute that made Faith continue trekking behind her captor without a word. Finally, Xavier stopped and slowly sat on his hunches to lay his brother on the wet ground, his face straining with the effort, his sweat trickling down the same path as the rain water down his face. Faith set the bag down and groaned as she stretched her aching limbs, feeling the blood rush through her numbed limbs, causing her to feel pins and needles. It didn't matter because she was alive. She lifted her face to the falling wetness, sighing at its coolness.

Xavier moved a few metres away from them to remove several thick branches to expose a cave opening. He returned to carry his brother, again not waiting for Faith to follow. The cavern's darkness nearly swallowed them had it not been for Xavier striking a match to light the torch held by a sconce on the wall. They made their way deeper into the cave and several minutes later Xavier stopped.

"Take that torch." He pointed with his chin at the torch lying on a flat surface of the rock wall. Faith took the torch and lit it from Xavier's. "Start lighting the rest."

"The rest?" Faith asked in confusion.

Xavier pointed to something behind her. "Those torches. You go right. I'll go left."

Faith slowly turned on her heel. Thick wooden torches were positioned almost five feet apart along the cave wall. She went to the first torch and lit the rest, sparing a glance back at Xavier who did the same, still carrying his brother. Something prickled the back of Faith's eyes and she had to blink several times. Xavier's devotion to Felipe was enviable, something she'd never had a chance to experience considering that she had been an only child and her relatives preferred not to have anything to do with her until she came into wealth. She turned back to what she was doing and once all of the torches were lit she turned around and gasped.

Facing her was a city within a cave that made her think she was watching a clip straight out of National Geographic. Pathways carved out from rock led to several levels filled with dwellings carved into the cave's walls. Windows cut from the rock face appeared like eyes, lifeless and unseeing, yet held the secrets of those who had lived. The flames from the torches played peek-a-boo with the dwellings, casting them into the shadows one minute, lighting them up the next. Faith looked up at the stalactites high above the cavern, sharpened by time into both blunt and jagged teeth. In the centre of the cave was a pool of still blue water like a flat slab of Murano glass.

"Come." Xavier beckoned. "We need to get Felipe to one of the dwellings."

"How did you find this place?" Faith breathed, quickly following Xavier up the shallow flight of steps. "Can you still carry your brother's weight?"

"Yes, I can," he said, taking several steps at a

time. "After I was recruited by El Jefe I became bored one night. The men were asleep and it was my turn to guard the camp. When I was walking around the periphery I saw the path we took and became curious."

"That was foolhardy of you," Faith muttered. "You could have been punished or killed."

"Not really. No one knew this. El Jefe was my uncle. Before my mother died she made him promise to look after me and Felipe." He gave a sound that was in the middle of a snort and a puff. "Being part of El Jefe's group wasn't exactly how I expected us to be taken care of."

Faith stopped mid-stride. No wonder Xavier had been able to stay her near rape and execution.

Xavier continued talking as they reached the next level. "I found this cave totally by accident. All the torches you see were already here. I just made sure they were ready to light." Faith smelled the faint scent of kerosene in the cloth attached to the torches.

He stopped at one of the dwellings and entered. Faith followed suit into what was an anteroom, the scent of kerosene hung lightly in the air mixed with the cool smell of rock and disuse. There were several rooms towards the back of the cave. A cot was flushed against the left wall while a table and chair was by the opposite wall. An unfinished chair lay on its side on the floor with several tools beside it. Faith placed the bag down and rushed to Xavier's side. She took his torch and hers to put it on the wall containers provided before helping lay Felipe on the cot. Felipe groaned, his face a mask of temporary pain before it smoothed, sleep taking over. Heaving an audible sigh of relief, flexing his back, shoulders, and neck, Xavier looked at Faith before walking out of the dwelling.

"Follow me."

This was it. Faith thought. Xavier was finally going to take her to the village. Yet, looking at Felipe and knowing that his wound was deep, it would take longer for him to heal.

"Xavier, wait," she said.

Xavier turned to her. "You wanted to leave, señorita. I'm taking you to the village."

"And leave your brother here?"

He pinched the bridge of his nose. "Señorita, I'm very tired. What else do you want? Had I known you were this difficult I wouldn't have kidnapped you."

Faith bristled. "Felipe isn't out of the woods yet."

"We will manage."

"The way you managed to find the morphine for him?"

"Don't push your luck, señorita," Xavier warned. "I can still kill you and dump your body and no one will be the wiser. You will just be another foreigner lost in the wild."

"I'm not pushing my luck, Xavier." Faith closed her eyes, asking for patience. "I'm a doctor. I have an oath."

"I absolve you from your Hippocratic oath. Now let's go."

"I just want to make sure your brother will be okay. When I see that he's on the road to recovery, you can take me back. Besides, what if he wakes and you're gone? Has he been here?"

Xavier reluctantly shook his head.

"Not seeing anything familiar will freak him out."

He placed the heels of his hands on his temples.

"You also need to rest," Faith said gently. "Believe me, I want to return to civilization as soon as possible. But I can't in all conscience leave someone to die."

I already did that.

Xavier's dark eyes bored into hers. She didn't flinch. He didn't say a word but left her to follow him again. They went into the next dwelling where there were the same basic furnishings except that this time there also was a generator wired to a lamp on the table and several half burned candle stumps on two broken plates. And books. Faith's eyes widened at the find. Gabriel Garcia Marquez and Miguel Cervantes hobnobbed with Aristotle and Plato. Even Bram Stoker's *Dracula* was atop books on Math and English grammar. Several pencils were in a cup and beside it was a paring knife. It was obvious from the lead in the knife's grooves that it was used for the pencils. Xavier looked at her sadly.

"You think that just because I lived a life of crime I am beneath learning."

Faith flushed. "I never said that."

"But you think it," he said, shrugging. "I never wanted my life to be this way. I wanted a better life for Felipe and myself. I still do. Being part of a gang doesn't mean Felipe and I have to be illiterate."

"It's not that. Why do you keep on putting words into my mouth?" Faith scowled.

"I'm not," Xavier said gently. "And I don't blame you. What do they say about first impressions?"

Faith groaned in frustration. "Look, I'm sorry. You can't blame me. You have a gun, you're one of the men who kidnapped me, you're taking me away from your wounded brother and how sure am I that you're really going to take me to the village. For all I know you're going to leave me in the forest—"

"Didn't I agree that you could stay?" Xavier interrupted in exasperation. "*Dios mío* you talk too much! I was taking you here so that you could stay!

This is going to be your room!"

That stopped her tirade. Fear had made her irrational.

"This would have been Felipe's room, but I've used it as a place to read and study. You can stay here in the meantime while he gets his health back. I will watch over him."

Remorse flooded her. "This isn't necessary, Xavier. I can stay with him."

"Do I have to point a gun at you to force you to take this room and rest?"

Faith looked at him, askance, but saw that there was a twinkle in her captor's eyes. She couldn't help the smile that lifted the corners of her mouth.

"You win." She raised her hands in mock surrender. "You tell me if he wakes up in pain, okay? If you don't, I'm going to kick your arse and no amount of gun waving from you is going to stop me."

Xavier laughed, the sound echoing around them. His face lost its harsh lines, youth replacing it.

"*Si,* señorita, I will. Because I'm sure your kick is worse than your bite." With that parting shot, he left chuckling.

For the first time in nearly a week, Faith smiled. It widened when she also realised one thing. She was inside a cave and she wasn't hyperventilating.

Chapter Nine

Zac took the rear with the Armourer just ahead of him. He watched the Ancient Eald meander through the thicket with the Deoré at his side. The longer they trekked, the more the Eald leaned on his beloved. It worried Zac not knowing how the silver was affecting their progenitor's body. Yet he was also in awe that the Ancient could still stand and walk unlike Graeme who almost died. Zac's face hardened at the memory. He'd be damned if he didn't find a cure. He wasn't going to give up and he wasn't going to let the silver get the better of him. He was a healer for Chrissake! He never failed. And he vowed he never would.

But Graeme had almost died. Had it not been for the Ancients, he might have had his first casualty on the operating table. With the Ancient Eald weakening, they needed to get to their destination soon so that could extract as much of the silver he could get from the Eald's bloodstream.

Suddenly, the Cynn Cruor leader fell to his knees and groaned.

Zac made his way to the Ancients, who were a few feet ahead of him.

"Sire, we need to check your wound."

The Eald didn't protest. His face was pinched, his skin ashen. Blood completely soaked the bandage that had been placed over the wound.

Zac's mouth tightened. "We need to get that bullet out, my Lord. Are we still far from the mine?"

The Eald shook his head. "We're here."

"Thank God for that," Zac murmured in relief. He tended to the wound while the Deoré moved away from them still carrying the bottle of soil where the Ancient Eald's blood fell. Since leaving the kidnapper's lair, the Deoré had constantly made sure that no drop of the Ancient Eald's blood was left on the ground. Not only because it would leave a trail but because a single drop of the Ancient's blood was enough to infuse with temporary untold strength. The rain conjured by the Eald had washed away remnants of his blood. No one would be able to retrieve his life essence.

Zac replaced the bandage with a fresh one, putting the soiled bandage inside a container for him to dispose later. He turned to see that the Deoré's eyes had turned to molten gold and diamond again. Zac followed her gaze. The foliage around the cave had been disturbed. Footprints leading to the cave's entrance muddied the ground. Someone else was inside the cave.

"No, this isn't possible!" the Deoré hissed.

Immediately, Zac and the Armourer became alert. Zac examined the footprints. One set was heavier than the other. The indentions looked as though the owner had been carrying something heavy. Or someone. The other set was slimmer, more like a woman's.

The Ancient Eald tried to stand but flopped back down against the Deoré, who growled like a jungle cat.

"It isn't Kamaria, Alaghom," the Eald said. "There's no one here who will harm you or me." He looked at Zac and the Armourer. "We must get inside. If they are still inside, we'll find them."

Once inside the cave, the Eald turned towards the cave's entrance and raised his hand, palm facing outward.

Aperio adque Tueri

Zac's ears perked when he heard the words he

knew so well. It was Latin for open and protect. He hadn't heard those in a very long time.

The foliage outside the cave righted itself, moving slowly to cover the opening.

"That should keep us safe for the moment," the Eald said. He gave a rueful chuckle as he faced the Armourer. "I have to impose on you one last time."

"It's no imposition at all." The Armourer waved his hand absently. "I gave McBain my word. We will get the rest of your things once we get you comfortable."

The provisions Zac and the Armourer carried clinked softly. Zac noticed light coming from the far end of the cave as though they were about to reach the end of the tunnel into golden sunshine. However, the deeper they went, the more he realized that the light was coming from lit torches whose glow bounced against the cave walls. They stopped at the mouth of the new part of the cave and his jaw tightened. He inhaled sharply, the scent of jasmine, rose and cocoa permeating his nostrils.

She's here.

The Ancient Eald raised his hand for them to stop, using telepathy to speak with all of them, including the Armourer. When the warrior heard the Eald in his head, his mouth went slack and he stepped back in shock.

"Don't give our location away by clinking what you're carrying." Zac scowled.

"Easy for you to say," his friend retorted. "You're used to voices in your head."

"Immortals, please." The Deoré's voice was calm yet urgent.

The Armourer sighed, nodding. He scrunched his face in concentration.

Zac rolled his eyes. *It's not that difficult.* He telepathed. *Just think what you want to say.*

The Armourer huffed. *Lead the way, my Lady.*

A smile ghosted on Zac's mouth, knowing his friend would have a lot of questions but was too circumspect to ask. Only the Armourer took a torch while Zac and the Ancients' eyes immediately accustomed to the gloom. As they made their way up the shallow steps, he marvelled at the way the dwellings had been carved out of rock. His eyes scanned the place, trying as much as possible not to miss anything. The higher they went, the less Zac noticed her scent. His mysterious lady.

He curbed the hiss that almost came out from him and immediately shut down the communication line he had with the Ancients just for a split second to gather his thoughts. His eyes narrowed, his brow furrowed to concentrate on where he was. Her scent kept teasing him without giving him a point of reference to her location.

Finally the Deoré led them to a chamber dusted with age. Zac let go of the provisions and took his satchel and the bag of surgical instruments he'd taken from the makeshift hospital to administer to the Cynn Cruor leader. He gave the soaked bandage to the Deoré once more before laying out what he needed.

"I will be back, my love," the Deoré said, brushing the matted hair from the Ancient Eald's forehead. "We need to burn the bandages that have your blood."

"I'll be waiting." The Eald gave her a tired smile before accepting her kiss.

When she and the Armourer left, the Eald looked at Zac. "I am in your hands, Zachary."

Zac snorted. "Is that supposed to make me feel better?"

The Eald chuckled before immediately wincing. "Yes. It isn't every day you are given the chance to let me live or die."

"My Lord, cease that prattle," Zac muttered, taking out the alcohol to clean his hands and the scalpel he would use. "You are made of the strongest stuff of any Cynn Cruor. You have survived that silver inside you without convulsing unlike Graeme. You have magick, and I think that's what's keeping the silver's deadly effects at bay." He spared him a quick glance before positioning the scalpel over the wound. "You will live, Sire. There's no two ways about it."

"And if I don't?"

Zac paused at what he was doing. "Dying isn't an option."

The Eald's skin sizzled, making his blood bubble as Zac extracted the metal from the shoulder before suturing the wound. An hour later, the bullet lay on a wad of cloth just as the Deoré and the Armourer returned. The Deoré knelt beside the Eald and they both placed their hands right over the wound and said the same incantation they used when they pulled Graeme from death. This time, however, the Eald was too weak to go on and his hand fell to his side when he lost consciousness. The Deoré faltered but continued with the chant until it was done.

"He's just resting, my lady," Zac said.

She nodded. "It still doesn't stop me from fearing the worse."

Now as he and the Armourer inspected the remnants of silver outside of the chamber, Zac worried about the potency of the Kinaré gene inside the Eald, but he was sure that with the blood exchange between the Cynn Cruor leader and his beloved, it would counteract the effects of the unique silver. Besides, the

Eald was a sorcerer, something Graeme was not. Zac thought of his fellow Cynn Cruor. If Graeme had a mate at that time, it might have been easier to counteract the silver's effects. Or could it? Knowing what he knew now about the metal, would a mate's blood have been strong enough to heal a Cynn immortal? Zac shook his head. He needed to do more tests on the ore. He had left Graeme with Roarke and Finn. He was glad that Blake had shown up, even for a little while. Zac knew how close Finn and Graeme were to Blake and the youngest Manchester Cynn Cruor's disappearance soon after was hard on all of them. He pressed the bridge of his nose with his thumb and forefinger. He may be the quiet one among the Faesten's inner circle, but he cursed Dac Valerian to the high heavens for bringing mayhem back into their lives.

Now the Ancient Eald had been shot.

"Bloody hell!"

"What's with you?" The Armourer raised an eyebrow.

"All this! Valerian should die once and for all." Zac scowled. "The Ancient has to heal. If he doesn't—"

"He will heal, M_cBain. You have to believe that. And from what I know of your leader, he wouldn't have lasted this long if he wasn't stronger than you think he is." The Armourer stretched out his hand with the bullet nestled in his palm. "We need to get the rest of the gear. Where do you want me to put this?"

"Over here." Zac strode to the dwelling nearby where a flat surface was carved out of the rock to make it look like a table. "I'll grab the rest of the things from the Ancients' quarters and then we can gather the rest of the provisions."

"The Ancient Eald has closed the cave's entrance. We need to find another way out." The Armourer's voice echoed softly around them. They both walked closer to the ledge, surveying the dwellings and walkways around them. "I'm sure the cave's mouth isn't the only egress."

"Agreed. Let's check the other levels." Zac said.

They found another doorway carved from the mountainside that gave them a view of the entire forest. Quickly jumping down and landing softly not too far away from the cave's entrance, they made their way to where they hid the rest of the provisions. In less than an hour, they had everything inside the mountain.

Zac was in the middle of setting up his mini laboratory to analyse the silver when the Armourer entered the room.

"It's time for me to go, McBain."

Zac felt the pull of sadness in his chest. Centuries ago, he had left Colm, the only friend he had then. Now the tables were turned. The Armourer had been one of his closest friends and he was leaving. He clasped his friend's arm before embracing him.

"I would ask where you're off to, but you never answer," he said.

The Armourer's chiselled features softened as he grinned. "You know me too well, my friend, but I'll answer you. I'm off to Dos Pilas in Guatemala to meet with my fellow armourers."

"There's more of you?" Zac's brows raised in surprise. "I thought you were the only one."

The Armourer chuckled. "We've only found out ourselves recently. There are eleven of us. How we became armourers and immortal is a long story."

"Bloody hell." Zac laughed for the first time since the Ancient Eald was shot. "A reunion?"

His friend's smile dipped. "No. It's a meeting to decide what happens to us. We don't think the world needs us any longer."

"Then stay with the Cynn Cruor." Zac suggested. "Your expertise in crafting magnificent weapons will be valuable to us. This war with the Scatha Cruor is far from over."

"You know I don't take sides, McBain."

"I'm not asking you to take sides. I'm giving you a reason to exist."

"Oh, I will exist, have no doubt about that. It's just a matter of knowing where to put down roots."

"I wish you luck with that, my friend." Zac replied. "Should you ever find yourself in need of shelter, or a place to stay, I extend the Manchester Faesten's welcome to you."

"Thank you, Zac."

Zac acknowledged the Armourer's thanks with a nod. Once the Armourer had left, Zac walked towards a clearing unhindered by trees and took out the laptop and BGAN terminal he brought with him to call the Faesten. Much had changed since he used to travel on horseback to bring messages from one Faesten to the other. The Broadband Global Area Network linked him directly to the satellite in the stationary orbit and he'd be able to communicate with Manchester easily. Switching on the laptop, he waited to be connected.

Ancients! He missed his brethren! He could make small talk, telling them of the skirmish with the Scatha Cruor, but there was no time. With the Armourer gone, they were in danger. He waited for the blue screen to disappear. When he saw the familiar surroundings of the Faesten's nerve centre, relief and joy flooded him.

"Zac!" Eirene cried, happiness and relief in her voice.

"Good to see you, mate." Roarke's face broke into a grin. "How are you?"

"Dux!" Zac's mouth widened in a relieved smile when he saw the patient he left behind. "Graeme, I see you're up and about. That's fantastic! Finn, Eirene, Deanna." He paused, his eyes widening in surprise before he laughed. "Colin and Luke? Everyone's there. Don't tell me something happened while I was away."

"And more." Graeme's smile was happy before he pulled a woman to his side. "This is Kate, my mate and beloved."

Finally, Graeme had found his mate. Three of his brethren had found mates. Zac felt a twinge of envy knowing that he could never have one. Despite that he was elated for his brethren.

"Kate." Zac nodded with a grin. "I shall have to tell you stories about your mate when I return."

Graeme rolled his eyes, his shoulders shaking with mirth. He also saw the adoration shining in his fellow Cynn Cruor's gaze when he looked at the woman who would be with him forever. And Kate was beautiful. She, too, had a wide smile filled with love on her face as she looked at her immortal warrior.

"When are you getting back and where's here?" Roarke queried. "You've been gone for several weeks now."

"La Nahuaterique."

"Lana what?" Colin's face scrunched in his attempt to pronounce the name of the place.

"Nahuaterique," Zac enunciated the syllables, allowing himself the luxury of a full blown laugh at how comical Colin looked. Then he sobered. "Dux, I don't have much time. We've found the mine and it's in the middle of nowhere, but I need extraction."

"I have the coordinates." Zac heard Eirene say.

She gave the piece of paper to Graeme.

"Just waiting for Daniel to pick up." Graeme informed Roarke, calling the Cynn mortal working for NASA.

"Babe, can you alert the Faestens in the area on scrambler?" Finn asked his mate.

In the background Zac saw Colin fish his phone from his jacket pocket before speaking in a hushed tone. He watched as Roarke spoke to Luke who readily agreed to man the Faesten while everyone prepared to leave for Central America. A grin pulled at his mouth when he saw Luke grasp Roarke's arm in acknowledgement of his gratitude. Roarke turned back to Zac.

"We'll contact the Faestens close by and have some of the Cynn Cruor there to extract you." Roarke informed Zac.

"Daniel will send us the satellite feed soon," Graeme said.

"All right. I hope it's soon, Roarke." Zac sighed. He was really running on adrenalin now. Sleep and his serum would strengthen him, something which he didn't allow himself until he attended to the Eald. Sex would have increased his strength more. His thoughts immediately strayed to the elusive female whose scent was like catnip to him.

"There's something else." Roarke's eyes narrowed.

Zac knew there was no other way to break the news to the Cynn Cruor except to tell them the truth.

"It's the Ancient Eald. The Beloved's blood is healing him but not as fast as it needs to."

He saw the thunderous frown building on Roarke's face.

"What are you saying?" Roarke asked, his voice

hardening.

"The Ancient Eald has been hurt."

Gasps and swearing filled the room.

Deanna took out her own phone and spoke to the person on the line quickly. Roarke looked at her and nodded. "Deanna is having her plane fuelled. We'll be there as soon as we can."

"How did the Ancient Cynn get hurt without healing?" Finn shook his head in disbelief. "He's always been able to heal himself. The Beloved would have brought down anyone who hurt him."

"Not this time." Zac's face was grim. "He was hit by the same silver as Graeme. Dac is here, Finn. He shot the Ancient Cynn."

Chapter Ten

Calling the Faesten and knowing that his fellow Cynn Cruors would be arriving soon took out a lot of Zac's tension. It would take them roughly a day and a half to get to the Honduras before making their way inland. He heard curses all around while he waited for the news to sink in.

"So that's where he's been all the time," Finn growled.

"He isn't alone, Qualtrough."

"Herod is with him?"

"No," Zac replied. "He has werewolves on his side. He is in league with Kamaria, the Deoré's aunt."

"Fuck!" Graeme swore. "Werewolves? The Deoré is a werewolf?"

"Easy, Temple. I'm furious too, but we won't get anything done if we burst a vein," Roarke said.

"It isn't that, Hamilton." Graeme turned to Roarke. "Zac has no covering fire."

"We're safe at the moment," Zac interjected. The Cynn Cruor faced him. "Dux, you know the Ancients didn't want the Faestens in the area to know they were here."

"No one anticipated Valerian appearing there, McBain. Besides, the game plan changed the moment the Ancient Eald was shot," Roarke said firmly. "You're sitting ducks as it is. Let me handle him when the time comes."

That statement made Zac's eyebrows rise. "Understood."

Roarke's mouth lifted, his eyes amused. "It's still possible the Ancients will chew my hide when we get there."

"I don't doubt that," Zac replied with a wry grin. "I'll be in touch again in a few hours. We're still safe."

"But not for long," Roarke stated. "If Dac is there, I'm very sure it's because of that silver."

"Then this isn't just a matter of extracting the Ancients." Colin approached and stood beside Graeme. "This is a race against time."

****

After Zac ended the call, he returned the laptop and BGAN terminal into the bag. He scanned the surrounding area, watching for any unusual movement that no human would be able to detect. He trained his senses on any sudden movement in the trees or the sound of Scatha footsteps as opposed to a jaguar's tread. He heard the screech of the macaws as they flew and the slithering of the fer-de-lance, a pit viper, as it made its way up a tree. He listened to the wind, able to distinguish between the rustle of the breeze from the whistling of the air as it passed through crevices of tree trunks. Zac inhaled, his lungs filling with the smell of water clogged earth mingled with the freshness brought by the rain. A film of heat swathed the entire rain forest, shimmering for miles all the way to the Caribbean Sea. He waited for the sun's rays to burn his skin, but like any other time, he was immune. Unlike the rest of his Cynn Cruor brethren who had to dodge direct sunlight, he could walk in the sun without fear. He found out early on when he analysed his own blood that he carried a recessive gene which no other Cynn Cruor had. How he happened to have it in his system still remained a mystery. Roarke had been about to help him get an audience with the Ancient Eald so they could find out why he wasn't affected by the sun. The siege of Dac's fortress in the Isle of Man derailed that. Now, even though he was with the Cynn Cruor leader, Zac didn't think it was the time to ask.

With one last look around he entered the cool interiors of the cave. Zac sighed as the cold air hit him. He was tiring and he knew he had to rest. He knew he needed to inject himself with the serum.

He knew he needed sex. It would have been faster to regain his strength if he had a woman.

He thought of the woman whose scent called to him. She could be a potential candidate to help him regain his strength. Just the thought of tasting her, being surrounded by her essence stoked the fire inside him, thickening his blood, anticipating her heated quim as it surrounding his raging hard on. He closed his eyes, groaning. She was so real in his mind that thinking of her seemed to conjure her. Reality splashed.

He didn't need to conjure her. She was near.

Need like nothing he had ever known slammed into him, the ridge between his legs growing, getting harder. Zac was at a point when he was running on empty and that was bad. He needed to get to the serum fast. It would curb his lust, stave off the Kinaré's hunger, its demand to fuck. Who was he kidding? It wasn't the Kinaré that demanded it. It was him. The serum wasn't enough when the source was in his midst, when he could picture himself between her thighs, his mouth inches away from her heated arousal, taking her all in before he took her with his mouth and tongue.

He couldn't help it. He, Zachary McBain, whom his Cynn Cruor brethren admired for his restraint, couldn't withstand it. Couldn't stop the pull of her call.

Couldn't help but give in.

****

Faith looked longingly at the pool below. What she wouldn't do to swim in those waters and remove the grime from her skin. She knew she smelled. She wondered if there was any part of the pool that was secluded enough to bathe. She went to Felipe's dwelling to ask Xavier when she stopped to see him riffling through the duffel bag to take out another syringe and morphine.

"What are you doing?" Curiosity marred her face.

Xavier looked at her with worry. "Felipe, he's very hot."

"His fever isn't going to go down with morphine." Faith shook her head. "Let me check him." She inhaled sharply after feeling Felipe's forehead. This wasn't good. The boy's temperature had jumped from cool to burning in less than an hour. The heat crawled up her arm as though she had dipped it in a cauldron of boiling water. His body was battling an infection, and in his weakened state, it could be fatal.

She checked the bag. "Xavier, there are no antibiotics here." She rifled through the contents.

"I don't know what they are." He raked his fingers through his hair before pulling at them. "*Madre de Dios*, Felipe needs them and I don't have any." He sat on the cot by his brother's feet. "What will we do? Please help him. I can't lose him."

Faith knew exactly what she would do, what she could do. What could heal Felipe was what she was cursed with. What had killed people in the past.

It was Felipe's only chance.

"Xavier…"

He didn't respond.

"Xavier!" Faith snapped.

He stared at her.

"Listen to me. I need you to be calm. I won't be able to heal your brother if I have to take care of you as well."

He came out of his stupor and nodded.

"Good." Faith took out the bottle of alcohol from the bag and doused her hands with it. "Now, I want you to leave the room. Stay outside."

"Why?"

Her eyes flared. "Do you want us to debate this matter now and let your brother's temperature rise rapidly? Or do you want to save the questions for later?"

"Your eyes! They are on fire again."

"Dammit, Xavier! Go! Now!"

Xavier turn-tailed immediately. Faith turned her attention back to Felipe. She closed her eyes, feeling the fire intensify within her, an incendiary ball in the middle of her chest. Her forehead puckered, her skin heated, her pulse increased even as her blood started to move slowly through her veins. She opened her eyes, the heat coming out in waves from her pupils, from her palms, from her fingers. Then she laid her hand over Felipe's wound. Felipe groaned in his sleep and writhed before he woke.

He gave a guttural scream that gave Faith goose bumps.

"Felipe!"

Faith stopped Xavier with her other palm face up toward him. "Stay away!"

Her heartbeat sped up. Faith could feel the wound, her palm siphoning the infection, absorbing the pain. Her chest started to burn, like hot gas trapped in her oesophagus. She brought her other palm down and gripped the earthen floor, her nails digging so hard that the earth crumbled underneath it. As soon as she did, the pain and infection her body took from Felipe rushed through her veins, her blood becoming the conduit before it flushed out through her palm and on to the ground. The area around her palm darkened before it heated up, gradually spreading through the entire floor. Faith dimly heard Xavier gasp, her mouth thinning in concentration when she heard him shuffle back and away from her. Away from Felipe. Away from the curse that had spared his brother's life.

When it was over, she collapsed to the ground.

****

Zac rushed in without thinking, anxiety making his heart speed up.

Mine.

He had no time to process why he thought that. All he wanted to do was to make sure she was all right. He saw what she did, and part of him refused to believe it. But the heat inside the room was akin to an oven, the ground underneath her a baked brown that made a system of fissures rippling away from her like the cracked earth of a dried up lake.

"What happened?" Zac spoke in fluent Spanish, wanting to know what her captor saw.

"Who are you?" Xavier's eyes were wild as he pointed his weapon at Zac.

Bloody hell. He wasn't thinking straight, was he? His reserves were past empty, he was too far away from his bag with the serum, and he was getting a hard on just looking at her body. She lay on her side, one leg slightly higher so that her inner thigh was exposed.

"A friend." Zac began to weave in mind control. "Now tell me what happened."

"She placed her hand over Felipe's wound and her other hand on the ground. The room became very hot and Felipe screamed and she fell and—"

"It's all right. She'll be fine." Zac checked her pulse, her skin hot but soft underneath his fingers, her heartbeat slowing to a normal beat of someone sleeping. He lifted her hand gently from Felipe's wound and his eyes narrowed, unable to believe what he saw. The wound had been cauterized. The only way it could happen was to either apply a heated poker to burn the flesh, removing the infection and sealing it, or to apply intense heat from a different source. There was no doubt that his woman was the source.

His woman.

Ancients! He must really be losing it. He had to leave or he would be no different from the Scatha, ravaging her without her knowledge. The thought of the Scatha doused Zac. No way was he going down that road.

"What's your name?" He turned to the woman's captor.

"Xavier."

Zac closed his eyes, gently infiltrating Xavier's mind. "Your brother will be fine. I have no doubt that what this woman did has healed him completely. What's her name?"

"Señorita," Xavier said, his dark eyes lightly glazed. "I call her Señorita. We were told not to know our captives' names so that it would be easier for us to kill them."

Sound thrummed at the back of Zac's throat at the thought that she could have died.

"I would never kill her, señor!" Xavier said

quickly. "She has saved my brother's life."

"And if she hadn't, would you?"

Xavier shook his head, looking down at his feet. "No. I'm not a killer. I just had to be one. This isn't the life I want for me and my brother. I would have taken her back to the village and helped her return to La Nahuaterique."

Zac nodded. "She can't stay here. Show me where she can lie down, then leave us. Once you do, you will not remember me." He lifted her slowly into his arms and nearly groaned at the softness of her body. His cock jumped when she moaned before snuggling her cheek to his. The side of her breast, the dip of her waist, the curve of her hip, and her thigh burned him through his suit. Zac's body came alive, recognizing that this was not just any woman, but his mate.

His mate.

Cynn Cruor warriors often tasted a woman's blood while they were having sex to know if she was their mate. Zac hadn't tasted her blood nor tasted her essence to see if she was a potential mate. Yet, without tasting her, he could smell it in her sweat, feel it in her body heat.

She belonged to him.

He closed his eyes for just a moment, stalling to catch a whiff of her, the sweet blood that could strengthen him like no other serum he made could. His chest expanded when he inhaled the faintest trace of her musk, her cream that was inside her, that he could coax out of her with his fingers, his lips, his mouth.

His tongue.

That same cream would wrap him, envelope his burgeoning cock while he slid in and out of her beautiful pussy, scraping her clit at the same time. This was the essence he needed. It was the essence he craved.

And he was about to bloody come just thinking about it.

"Here." Xavier's voice broke through his reality.

"Return to your brother, Xavier. Watch over him while I take care of the Señorita."

Xavier didn't even nod. He just left. Zac gently laid her down on the cot, easing his arm out from underneath her shoulder blades and the back of her knees. With the flickering light from the sconce on the wall, Zac looked at her face in repose. Long lashes lay delicately like curtains over her cheekbones. Shadows danced across her oval face, her exotic cheekbones, her nose, her kissable mouth slightly parted with her breathing. Zac closed his eyes, gently entering her mind, searching for her name. Who was she? She didn't look as though she was from the area. Faith Hannah. She wasn't from here. Zac was having a hard time reading her mind. His face scrunched at the effort. Talk about running on the dregs of empty.

"Just a little more," he muttered. There. He found what he was looking for.

She had indeed been kidnapped. Her memories flooded his mind. A medical mission. Sudden wealth.

Betrayal.

His weakened state broke the connection. He needed the serum. Fast.

Zac was about to stand when he froze midway. Faith snuggled more to him and placed her arms around his neck.

"Stay with me," she whispered.

Had she awakened? Her lids remained shut, her eyes moving underneath. She was dreaming. Invading a person's dreams was something the Cynn Cruors could do the same way that they could read people's minds. Zac had broken his connection with Faith to husband his strength. Besides, intruding into someone's dreams wasn't something he cared for. But now that she was dreaming of someone, jealousy hit like a brick thrown against his chest, and he would have given anything to know who he was. He couldn't take advantage of her. He wouldn't take advantage of her even if what he wanted to do was to kiss her senseless, bury his face between her thighs and lick her dry.

He gently pulled her arms away from his neck.
She stopped him. "Kiss me."

Chapter Eleven

Zac sucked in his breath. This tempting morsel was giving herself to him, giving him permission to kiss her.

Faith wasn't in her right frame of mind. She was dreaming, giving her permission to the lucky bastard behind her eyelids, to taste her.

"Please…." Faith's hand trailed down his chest, lower, lower, down to rub her hand up and down his hard shaft. "I need you."

"You don't know what you're saying." Zac stilled her hand from teasing him, but she kept on sliding it up and down his encased shaft. "You need to rest, Faith."

"Take me…please."

Zac's tenuous hold on his willpower snapped. Whether it was because he was already weak and needed sex to heal or his attraction overrode his logic he didn't care. He wanted her.

He desired her.

He took her mouth in a primal kiss, his tongue swiping against her teeth before parting them to tease her tongue. Zac's blood roared and rejoiced. Faith moaned, her body arching toward him, her breasts pressed to his chest in offering. His kiss demanded that she give in and she did, the sounds she made spurring his lust. He held the back of her neck, keeping her head still so he could devour her. Even in her sleep her tongue tangled with his and explored his mouth. She tasted sweet, hot, and Zac could smell her liquid heat.

Slowly he covered her body with his, nudging her legs apart to graze his painfully hard cock against her mound. She lifted her legs, whimpering as she moved her hips to grind against him to position her core against his shaft.

"More," she whispered against his mouth.

Zac thrust against her jeans encased sex.

"Yes!"

Desire became his blood. He had to taste her, needed her like a man starved of water. He grazed his teeth against her jaw before nipping on her earlobe. When she gasped, he sucked the sting, flicking the flesh with his tongue.

"Off…" She gasped.

Zac did as she asked. He rose to kneel in front of her. He took her shirt off, threw it to the side of the cot and leaned forward to graze his mouth against her breasts. Then he took one nipple into his mouth and sucked on it, hard, while his hand played with the other. She cried out, tangling her fingers in his hair. Then he lavished her other breast with the same attention. His tongue loved the feel of the hardened nubs grazing his taste buds, enjoyed the taste of her delicately salty skin, salivated for more of her. The smell of her skin, her sweat was intoxicating, her gentle musk bringing the sweet scent of her blood into his nostrils. His palm went lower, caressing her as he moved to the dip of her waist, the gentle valley of her stomach, and the feminine swell of her hips. Ancients! She was so responsive. He smiled against her hardened peaks when her hips bucked.

Her jeans had to go.

Deftly, Zac undid the button of her waistband, pulled the zipper down and dipped his fingers into her wetness. He inhaled sharply and groaned. The scent of her arousal enveloped him, strengthening his senses, feeding the Kinaré, igniting his passion. His mouth watered when his thumb found her sweet spot, bathing it more with her cream. He circled it before inserting his third finger inside her sex. He made a sound at the back of his throat when her vagina squeezed his digit. His cock was jealous and wanted in, but Zac didn't listen even though his shaft was in pain and wanted to shoot its load. He inserted another finger.

"Oh God, yes!" Faith clung to him as she bucked her hips in tandem with his hand. Her eyes were still closed tight, her breath coming out in short sexy puffs. "Almost there…."

Zac flicked his fingers inside her before taking them out and thrusting them back in. He felt her climax coming, her channel tightening in response to his finger fucking her. But there was something he needed to do. Wanted to do.

He leaned back to remove her jeans, taking her panties off with it before settling between her legs. Her smell nearly drove him to his own climax, feeling his pre-cum trickling from his cock inside his suit. His fingers were coated with her cream, her pussy glistening in invitation. He swiped his tongue against her clit. She shuddered. His body immediately absorbed her essence. His growl of satisfaction at the same time he laved his tongue against her folds from top to bottom approving her moans. He licked between her folds, taking her bundle of nerves gently, sucking it before inserting his tongue inside her hole. Zac gripped her thighs, digging into her flesh while he lapped up her sweetness. He closed his eyes, his lust flaring when she held on to his head while she humped his mouth. He loved the way she held his head, pushing his mouth away from her mound when she had too much but still coming back for more. He gave her what she wanted.

She gave him what he needed.

Then Zac placed his fingers inside her and sucked

her clit at the same time.

She came with a keening cry, flooding Zac's mouth with herself. Pleasure like nothing he ever felt before flowed through him. He felt gratified that he had brought her ecstasy. Her body trembled from her orgasm and he continued licking her dry until she came back from the clouds. Zac made his way up her body, licking the salt from her sweat, flicking her hardened peaks before kissing her deeply, making her taste herself on his tongue.

"Thank you," he whispered.

Then he was gone.

****

Faith opened her eyes, blinking to take the remnants of sleep away. She had the most erotic dream of her life. She had been seduced by a man with dark blond hair, and unusual hunter green eyes, because of the gold flecks that radiated from the pupils like the sun's rays. For some reason she felt that this was the stranger she vaguely saw hiding in the clearing, belonging to the group who fought those who murdered El Jefe, before she escaped with Xavier and Felipe. Faith turned to her side, a contented sigh parting from her lips. She smiled. Who would have thought she would have an erotic dream during her captivity, in the middle of nowhere, inside a cave while she lay naked on the bed.

Her eyes snapped open.

"Holy shit!"

Faith sat up. Her pulse raced so fast she almost passed out. She looked down at her body as though it didn't belong to her. Her nipples still tingled from the tongue that praised it. She felt her juices still coating her plump labia lips, a reminder of the mouth and tongue that brought the best orgasm she'd had in her life. If this had been a dream, why did her mound feel as though she had been thoroughly finger fucked and tongued? She was slightly sore. She could still feel the tongue against her sex, causing her to become moist again.

"Oh my God…" She quickly donned her clothes and strode to Felipe's room, her sensual mood obliterated.

"What the hell did you do to me?" Faith shook Xavier's sleeping form. But Xavier only moaned in protest beside his brother and resumed snoring.

She spun around. What happened to her? Anxiety wormed its way into her gut. Did she dream all of it up? No way would she heal Felipe naked. Did she take off her clothes after taking Felipe's fever away? She couldn't remember.

"Xavier!" She shoved him. Like a bullet, her young captor jumped up and pointed his rifle at her. Her short scream cleared all of Xavier's sleep before he relaxed, putting his weapon down.

"*Putana señorita*! What is the matter with you? I almost shot you!" He glowered.

"Did you rape me?"

"What?"

"You heard what I said."

"*¡Madre de Dios!*" He looked at her as though she had developed two heads. "Where did you get that idea?"

"I was naked when I woke up."

"Didn't you remove your own clothes?" He looked at her in bewilderment.

"Would I ask you if I did?" Faith snapped, agitation making her tremble. She placed her palm against her forehead.

Calm down.

"Why would I do that? After I took you to the other dwelling, I came back here to watch over Felipe, but I fell asleep."

She could see Xavier's puzzlement was genuine, but she couldn't stop the next thing that came out of her mouth. "That's impossible. We're the only two people here." She paced the length of the room.

"*Hijo de puta*, I didn't touch you!"

"Then who did?" She stopped angrily to face him.

"I did."

Chapter Twelve

Even before Faith turned around, she knew it was him. The man whose presence she felt from the trees. Her face flamed at the memory of his heavy petting. She should have been shocked at her body's violation, but was it really? How could she feel violated when he had coaxed her release and made her body come alive?

And she wanted more of what she knew he could give.

She turned and sucked in her breath. It hadn't been the imagination that spurred her erotic dream. It had been real. Her dream lover was standing right in front of her. And what a sexy dream lover he was. The man wore something like a scuba diver's suit that hugged every muscle like second skin. It wasn't exactly the garb for a walk in the jungle, even if it could be termed on the wild side. Yet Faith could see that body was perfection, muscled but not as though he spent hours pumping iron. It was just right. His clean cut hair looked like spun gold amid the flickering light in the room and behind him. She remembered caressing his scalp, holding on to his head while he led her to oblivion. She remembered how his shoulder and arm muscles bunched underneath her hands while he pulled her to him, the length of his torso, those rock hard abs, down to the…Faith hoped he didn't see her blush at the thoughts of rubbing her hand over the hard ridge between his muscular thighs, the heat of his arousal emanating through his suit. She reddened even more when his crooked smile made her realize that he did.

And it made her hot and wet.

Did he know what she was thinking? Her racing

pulse and her stomach twisting into a delicious knot told her that he did.

The sound of the assault weapon's safety lock being removed ricocheted in the room.

"*¿Quién eres?* How did you get here?" Xavier demanded.

"I might ask you the same thing." The stranger leaned against the door frame, his arms over his chest, his stance relaxed but alert.

"Answer the question!"

Faith saw the fear in Xavier's eyes and didn't blame him.

"I'm a friend." He straightened and walked in the room, causing Xavier to level his weapon at his chest. Faith's eyes widened when he continued toward Xavier, the weapon just ten inches away from his chest. "I mean no harm."

"Then why did you touch me?" Faith's face burned at her question before she could stop it.

His mouth lifted to one side, amusement in his eyes. "You asked me."

"Of all the most absurd things to say!" His arrogance riled Faith, and she was hating her body right now for reacting to his velvety voice that had a VIP pass to make her throb down south. His confident stance dominated the room, a man not to be trifled with, dangerous and appealing.

And she wanted back in his arms.

There! She saw his eyes darken and the gold flecks she remembered appeared as though by magick. His nose slightly flared with every breath he took as though he wanted to smell her.

Where the hell did that come from?

"You haven't answered my question." Xavier lifted his chin.

"I have." The stranger's authority was unmistakable, facing Xavier. "I said I was a friend. My name is Zac McBain. Now what are you doing here? You're not supposed to be here. It's too dangerous."

"This is a free cave."

Zac turned to her when she spoke. "This cave was meant to disappear for a reason."

"What do you mean?"

"How did you find it?" He turned back to Xavier, not answering her question. *What an arrogant bastard.* His face hardened. The muscle ticking against his jaw was the only indication of his sudden coldness. *What? He can hear my thoughts now?*

"I stumbled upon it several months ago. I was bored during my watch so I went to explore the forest," Xavier replied.

"At night?" Zac's mouth curled slightly. "You must be very brave."

"What do you think you're doing?" Faith took one step towards him and grabbed his arm. She gave a soft gasp as the bolt of awareness travelled through her arm and down her spine that she let go. He must have felt it, too, because Zac inched away from her, his eyes darkening. Faith blushed as she felt his heated gaze invite her own lust to surface from the pit of her belly. His eyes lowered to her breasts and she felt her nipples harden in invitation. Faith gritted her teeth to stop her chest from arching toward him.

Then as sudden as the spark ignited between them, he shut down.

"What do you think I'm doing?" he asked softly as he caressed her face with his eyes. "I only asked a question."

"Fine." She exhaled, pulling clarity out from where it hid in her mind. "If this cave wasn't supposed to be discovered, why are you here? You haven't exactly told us who you are either."

He looked down and slightly shook his head. Then he spun on his heel and left the room.

"Hey!" She followed him but didn't touch him. Her body's betrayal was enough for the moment. "I'm talking to you."

"And this conversation is over," he shot back as he strode away, lengthening the distance between them.

"Of all the arrogant pricks I have met in his hellhole—" She stifled a scream when he zoomed back to her. Zoomed? Her mind tried to process what had just happened. No human could zoom that fast. Shit, no human could zoom, period!

"Leave. The three of you," he bit out, his face so close to hers that she felt his breath against her cheeks. His visage flickered copper between shadow and light cast by the torches that lit the cavern from below.

"How can I? I don't even know where I am." *How can I when I'm about to melt here right in front of you. When I can't think of anything but holding on to your ass when you thrust into me. When you go I'll be a puddle.*

Zac let out a growl of frustration before moving away. He placed his hands on his narrow hips. Faith's eyes glued to his firm butt.

"Keep thinking of that." His eyes flickered.

Her eyes flew to his. "Thinking of what?"

"Keep thinking of my ass or any part of my body because there's nothing I'd like more than to lick you wet and fuck you senseless."

Faith's breath came out in a whoosh. A wild yearning flushed through her. She swallowed hard past her heart that seemed to take residence in her throat. Her body thrummed in anticipation as her nether lips moistened once more, preparing itself to welcome his shaft. What the hell! How could she just give in to a stranger she just met? It didn't matter that he had touched her before because she had given him permission, or had she? If he could play mind games with Xavier, what would stop him from doing the same to her? Yet, her mind told her otherwise. Her attraction to him was unquestionable, even when she sensed him in the forest. Amidst the deadly situation they were in, she was drawn to him.

But did she want to get hurt again? One of the reasons why she decided to join the medical mission she funded was in order to get away from the humiliation of a broken heart. She hugged herself, wishing she would stop thinking of Zac inside her, but it was so hard. Yes, his hard body was what she wanted. Dammit!

Get a grip, Hannah!

"This isn't the time or the place. Not an offer I'd consider either," she said, smarting at her own words. Was that disappointment briefly marring Zac's features? He probably thought every woman fell immediately for his crude charm.

He chuckled. "Well, you didn't."

"I didn't what?"

"Fall for my charms."

"Okay, that's it! You're freaking me out! You seem to be able to read everything I'm thinking." She stormed away from him. She squealed when he caught her, his grip tight around her arms.

"As soon as Felipe can stand on his own two feet, you have to go. In less than two hours, he will be as good as though he had never been shot."

What Zac said doused whatever thoughts of sex Faith had, replaced by dread. "How—"

His face softened. "I saw you. I saw what you did." Zac looked at her mouth. Faith parted them involuntarily when he grazed her lower lip with his thumb. "I've never seen any human do that before." He bent down and Faith raised her mouth to his, but he didn't kiss her.

"Who are you?" he whispered, his breath sending ripples of desire coursing from her ear, her neck, and down to her core. His face had a hint of stubble that added to the tendrils of carnal awareness coursing through her. "You have a wonderful gift. Why do you hide?"

Faith closed her eyes, sadness battling for dominance against the lust that incessantly plagued her in Zac's presence. She sighed when his lips finally brushed her skin, edging closer to her mouth. She opened her eyes when he leaned back, held by his gaze that made her want to drown in them. Something compelled her to tell him, a total stranger who already intimately knew her body. Perhaps if she did, he would stop hitting on her and let her be.

After all, who would want to get involved with a murderer?

"My name is Faith and I am cursed."

But it didn't stop him. It didn't faze him. In an instant, his mouth was on hers, licking the seam, her teeth, prodding, exploring, before demanding to be let in. And let in she did, putting her arms around his neck as he crushed her to him, his arousal hot, thick, and long against her belly. His mouth moved over hers in a sensual exploration. Their tongues mated, getting as much as they could from this brief moment. Frenzied, almost desperate not to let it end. Desire was palpable in the way Zac held her, slanting his mouth against hers, deepening the kiss. When it was over, they were both breathing hard.

"Leave, Faith Hannah. I won't be able to tell you again."

Chapter Thirteen

"Faith…" Zac said her name over and over again like a prayer to sustain him. He hadn't meant to speak what was on his mind but bloody hell, she was so difficult to resist! All he could think about was to kiss her mouth swollen, to suck her breasts and rub his tongue forward and backward against her engorged bundle of ecstasy and take in as much of her essence until she was dry, to make her writhe underneath him, to thrust his hungry cock inside her and ride them both to where he would see the beauty of her coming apart in his embrace. He whispered her name again, a woman who belonged more in the ethereal plane than in a cave that would soon see war between the Cruors to take control of the silver that would change everything for all of them. Her accent was British with a mixture of something more, as though she conversed with the outside world in English and used another language all together at home. She understood and could speak Spanish too. Multi-lingual.

Zac was impressed by that and more. She was strong yet fragile that he wanted to cover her with himself and protect her for the rest of his life. He could see she had also been hurt and the pain went beyond a broken heart. It was a pain that almost destroyed her. Zac didn't need to read her mind completely no matter how tempted he was because her mind opened willingly to him. Splotches of her life registered in his own mind like a film reel that had disintegrated with age, but he could put them all together. Why did she call her very precious gift of using the fire inside her a curse?

Whose dead body did her mind conjure for him to see?

He, too, had his reservations, though they weren't directed at her. Far from it, he wanted to stay away because he wasn't worthy of her. Wasn't worthy of anyone's love. That's what his mother said before she died and there was no one in the world alive to refute it.

He had to leave her. Not doing so would break the Cynn Cruor code. Technically, Zac didn't break it. Faith had begged him to take her when she was in the throes of her dream. He didn't break it either when he kissed her, her body giving him permission to do so. But until she said yes completely awake, he would stay away. That tryst had been enough to get his strength back. He had been running beyond empty and when he drank from her, he felt like a tank being filled with jet fuel that when he left her the first time, he had been able to return to the Cynn Cruor's part of the cave in less than three seconds.

Zac entered his quarters, a frown creasing his forehead. He needed to concentrate on finding an antidote for the effects of the silver. He looked at the bags carrying all of their provisions that lay beside the bag carrying the laptop and BGAN terminal. He opened the padded case that carried the serums, gazing at the vials stacked securely inside. This had been meant for all of the Cynn Cruors who had been with them in the mission. A serum powerful enough to heal them, returning them back to fighting form after a fight or battle. Except for the Ancients and himself, they were all gone.

Zac closed his eyes, deeply hurting at the loss, anger boiling that the Scatha had killed his fellow Cynn Cruors. He would soon avenge them.

He took one of the serums and jabbed it into his thigh, immediately feeling the elixir conjoining with Faith's essence increasing his strength. He thought of Faith while he disposed of the empty vial and began to set up his lab, a frown ploughing his forehead. He couldn't be the person she wanted. He wasn't capable of being the man any woman wanted. His mother's words still rang in his ears centuries later. If a mother couldn't love the child she bore, what hope was there for another woman to love him for who he was? To know that he was a hybrid would be the final nail on the coffin.

He set up the microscope before taking out the crucible and the propane torch. He used tongs to pick up the silver bullet and drop it into the vessel before firing the torch at it. The ore's fumes could kill him, so Zac held his breath comfortably until the fumes disappeared and only the scent of the Ancient Eald's blood remained. Zac didn't have the time nor the inclination to clean the blood from the silver. What was more important was to find the cure for any Cynn Cruor injured with the more dangerous form of silver to save their kind. He set out heat resistant glass slides and placed a drop of the melted silver into it. While it cooled, he took out the silver specimen the Cruors regularly encountered, something which vampires, werewolves, and humans would be familiar with. One for which he had a cure. He placed both slides side by side under the microscope.

"Bloody hell." Zac sucked in his breath as he watched the silver mutate with the Ancient Eald's blood. Shock didn't even begin to describe what he felt. Blood rushed into his head. He swallowed hard to get a hold of himself. "That's not possible."

But it was, and he had just discovered something

that defied explanation about the silver's effects. If the silver fell into Scatha hands, they wouldn't only hold a great weapon. They would also have something that would make the Scatha invincible in the battlefield.

The human race wouldn't have a prayer of surviving.

That wasn't the only thing he discovered.

He took out another clean slide and pricked his finger, the prick closing in less than a second. He swiped the glass with his blood before adding it to the surface underneath the microscope. Zac felt the blood drain from his face. The truth stared him in the face. He balked and slowly slid to the floor, his eyes looking at the walls as though trying to find the answer there. Zac's heart thundered in his veins. He found out something that affected him and only him. His logical mind tried to impose rationality but he only came up blank. How could this be? Then again, he didn't know the entire story of how the Ancient Eald came to be, did he? For the first time in his life as a Cynn Cruor, he felt cold. Totally, morbidly cold. For centuries, he had searched for his father. As he began to discover the world of the Cynn Cruors, becoming one of the doctors of the race, he had asked to leave for the Council of Ieldran to test the blood of all of the Cynn Cruors. They refused. It was only when The Hamilton and Roarke himself pleaded his case arguing that, knowledge of the different Cynn Cruor blood types would help the species determine familial primogeniture should the parents of Cynn Cruor children die, did the Council reluctantly agree. However, there was a proviso. All his findings had to be reported to the Council and the Ancients.

How could he tell the Council or the Ancients about this?

No. He would keep this part of his findings from them. It was something he would keep secret for the rest of his immortal life.

Because loyalty was more important.

Washing the slide that held his blood with alcohol he returned the sliver of glass into the padded case before leaving his room. As he neared the dwelling where the Ancients stayed, he faltered. With his renewed strength, he hoped he had enough to block his secret from the Eald.

The Deoré had her arms wrapped around herself as she stared at the pool below. Zac had never seen her this way, strained, anxious, even fearful. She looked like a statue in black, her braid undone, her silky hair flowing to her waist.

"How is he?" Zac asked.

"Not very well." Her mouth was pinched. "My blood is healing him but not quickly enough. We have both used magick to extricate the silver's poison the same way we helped you with Graeme. The Eald is too weak and there isn't enough strength in him for his magick to work completely." She moved closer to the ledge. "I never thought this could happen. I didn't expect her to be alive helping Dacronius."

Zac's ears perked at what she said. To call the Cynn Cruor's nemesis by his Roman name was something hardly anyone did. However, he wasn't presumptuous to think that old ways died hard. Roarke still called Deanna "my lady." The Deoré was no different.

"He will always be Gnaeus Valerius Dacronius to me, Zac. A name I will forever associate with the attempted murder of my mate."

Pain exploded in Zac's mind so quickly that he froze. He gritted his teeth, trying to remain standing, but the agony was so debilitating that he succumbed as his knees buckled and he fell to the ground by the side of the Deoré.

"I meant no disrespect, my lady," he bit out. "Forgive me."

"Alaghom! Enough!"

The Deoré whirled at the Ancient Cynn's voice before turning back to Zac in alarm.

"Zac!"

Suddenly, Zac felt the painful grip on his mind disappear and he fell face first on the ground. Firm but soft arms lifted him.

"I'm sorry Zac," she whispered. "By the goddess Ix Chel, forgive me."

Instantly, Zac was allowed to both the Ancients' thoughts and the first time Dac Valerian tried to kill the Cynn Cruor leader. He saw how the former Roman general tricked the Ancients' personal guards before attempting to assassinate the Eald. If the Deoré hadn't attacked Valerian, it could have been the end of the Cynn Cruor's progenitor. He felt the Deoré's anguish for her mate and remorse for what she did to him. He felt her fear growing like a tidal wave at the thought of losing the Ancient Eald. The hurt she felt ripped through his heart and mind.

Never had he seen such a strong and beautiful woman brought down so low at the thought of losing the only reason she loved and lived in the world.

Zac stood. "I know you didn't mean any harm, my lady. Life without love is no life at all."

The Deoré's eyes crinkled at the sides. She squeezed his shoulders.

"The sage," she said. "I believe I will learn a lot from you, Zachary McBain." The Deoré released him and walked towards the Ancient Eald. Zac saw love's glow in his leader's eyes despite the pain caused by the silver in his blood stream.

Immortal love like what the Ancients had was a gift every Cynn Cruor warrior and mortal longed for. The Cruors' Wars had cut short so many love stories that were meant to last for eternity. Zac had witnessed multitudes of his kindred fall, turning to ash. The mate left behind wilted in front of everyone. Death could last for mere minutes, to hours, days and even weeks. The suffering of the mate left behind cut deep into every Cynn Cruor. Seeing the life force slowly seeping out of a mate wasn't a pretty sight. The mate became gaunt, unable to eat, drink, or sleep until they were skin and bone, until they breathed their last and slowly disintegrated into ash themselves. That was why Roarke's situation when he thought that Deanna had died during the siege of Hamel Dun Creag was very unusual for he didn't exhibit the symptoms of languishing which befell those whose mates died. The Ancient Eald therefore decreed that should a surviving mate want their life forfeited it would be granted but not until then.

Zac may have told the Deoré something about finding a love that would never end, but it wasn't for him. He made a conscious decision not to fall in love, despite knowing that Faith was his. They may share the lust and give in to the attraction that ran rampant between them. He needed sex to satisfy his cravings and feed the Kinaré particularly during the days close to, during, and after the night of the full moon. He just refused to fall as his brethren did.

Chapter Fourteen

"Xavier, we have to go." Faith entered the room. Her mind was spinning. How did he know her full name? She was beginning to truly believe that he could read minds and that meant that he could read her sexual thoughts as well. Oh shit. Xavier's outburst broke her musings.

"Why, because he says so? No!" Xavier paced the length of the dwelling, his agitation and anger palpable. "What did he do to me?" He stopped to look at her. "He made me answer everything he asked when all I wanted to do was shoot him."

"You're not a killer, Xavier."

"I am."

"No," Faith reiterated gently. "You said so yourself. You still have scruples. A hardened killer wouldn't have batted an eyelash to kill me after I healed your brother. So you couldn't have killed Zac."

"That doesn't forgive what I've already done," he muttered as he shook his hand through his now lank hair. His shoulders slumped as though he carried the burden of the lives he took.

"No, it doesn't," Faith agreed. "But you didn't have a choice. El Jefe would have killed you and Felipe. Now that is a hardened killer." She jabbed her finger towards him for emphasis.

"Who is he, señorita? How do we know we can trust him?" Xavier's eyes clouded.

"I honestly don't know." *Only that he's the man who's made me wet and come like never before.*

"He's one of them, isn't he?" Xavier nodded vigorously. "He's one of the men who killed El Jefe and Los Tiradores!"

"No," Faith replied. "He's one of those who fought the group who killed El Jefe."

"Why didn't I see him? How did you see him?"

How could she tell him that though she didn't see Zac, she sensed him? It would bring about more questions which she had no answer to.

"What other provisions do you have, Xavier?" Faith walked to the other room, looking around for another bag. "Zac was there. You were just too engrossed with protecting Felipe."

"*Hermano?*"

"Felipe!" Xavier sat on the cot and took his brother in his arms.

Felipe grimaced.

"*Dios mío,* I'm sorry. Your wound!" Xavier laid his brother gently on the cot and lifted his shirt. He spun around to Faith. "What did you do?"

Faith's throat tightened. "I didn't do anything."

"You placed your hand on his wound." Xavier's voice was accusing. "You told me to leave. This room heated up and now my brother's wound looks as though it's been healing for weeks. Who are you? What are you?"

"You kidnapped me." She looked anywhere but at him. "Away from the medical mission I was a part of. Who do you think I am?"

"A doctor but also—"

"I am a doctor. You don't believe in curanderos, remember?" Faith said, finally staring him down and brooking no argument. "Let Felipe rest for a little longer and then we have to go." She tightened her hold on the clothes she wore. She needed to wash herself. It wouldn't help going around smelling like a beacon of sexual pleasure, not that she was worried about the brothers. She was more worried about the man with eyes that could capture her soul and make it his home. She wasn't so sure if she would be able to resist Zac the next time he came near her. Thinking of him brought a thrill pulsing down her spine and into her core, which was exactly the reason why she had to leave.

"I'm going to the pool," she said. "Do you know where I can clean myself in private?"

Xavier's eyes narrowed as though trying to gauge what she was hiding. In the end he nodded. "I'll take you there." Instead of leaving the room, he went deeper into the other room beyond. Sighing, Faith spun to leave and wait for him outside.

"Señorita!"

"Xavier, the name is Faith."

His eyes lit up. "Fe."

"*Si*." She smiled back.

"Here." He handed her a towel, a cotton T-shirt and soap. "You will need these."

"Oh my God, Xavier! Thank you!" Faith's eyes almost popped out in delight. She laughed. "How did you—"

"Don't ask." He turned beet red. "I'm sorry I don't have any woman's underwear."

Faith bit her inner cheek to stop herself from laughing.

"That's okay," she said. "I'll manage."

They went through a different passageway from where they first arrived, which was several metres away from the dwelling assigned to her. Xavier lit the unlit torch inserted in the sconce on the wall before entering the passageway, the light bouncing off the rock face.

"Watch your step," he warned.

Faith stifled a scream when she nearly lost her footing on the first rock hewn step, grabbing hold of Xavier's arm. Xavier waited for her to get her bearings before they continued. The stairs curved downward in a spiral. Every so often, Xavier stopped to light the torches hanging on the sconces. Just like the rest of the cave, they were equally spaced apart, lighting up the entire place.

"How long have you known of this part of the cave?" Faith looked around in amazement. "These torches are new."

"For a time now," Xavier said matter-of-factly. "Explored almost every part of it. There are places where it looks like there is silver along the cave's fissures, but I'm not so sure."

"Xavier, that could make you rich! You and Felipe could forge a new life!"

"Only if I have the equipment to mine them." His mouth curled to one side. "I will in time. This cave is mine."

They finally reached the bottom step where something like a cove lay in front of them. The pool's water ebbed and eddied gently on the sandy bank, whispering and inviting. This part of the pool was roughly ten by twenty feet in diameter. To the far end of the cove was a rock wall that reached all the way to the cave's ceiling, dividing the cove from the main pool. In the distance she heard water rushing to God knows where.

"Waterfall," Xavier volunteered. He pointed to the gaps in the rock wall ten feet away to their right. The holes looked like slits to nothingness. "I think the women and children bathed here while the men bathed in the main pool which we saw when we arrived. There must be a system in place where the pool is replenished from atop the mountain, but I haven't found it yet."

"It's beautiful," Faith breathed.

Xavier grinned. "Since I have decided that you are not my captive anymore, I will leave you alone. When you're done, we'll eat."

Faith felt the tension in her shoulders ease, and she laughed. "You never cease to amaze me."

"What is the saying, necessity is the mother of invention?" He cocked his head.

"More like necessity is the child of resourcefulness," she replied wryly. "Thank you."

Xavier flushed with embarrassed pleasure. "*Hasta luego*, Fe."

Faith couldn't wait to get into the water. She walked to the cave wall, placed the towel and clean T-shirt to one side and stripped down to her bra and panties, leaving her jeans and soiled shirt in a heap. Taking the soap, she made her way to the water, tentatively walking in. She made a sound at the back of her throat, delighted that she could finally become clean again. She waded deeper, goosebumps skittering her skin. As soon as the water reached her waist Faith dunked underneath, squealing and giggling as she surfaced. The coolness invigorated her and she could feel the dirt of the last several days leave her body. While she was in captivity, she was allowed to bathe, but with the lecherous eyes and grins of El Jefe's men, she only did the bare minimum. She cleaned herself, vigorously lathering the bar of soap all over her body and hair. She couldn't stop smiling at the dirty suds that left her, making their way through the gaps in the far wall. Satisfied, she made her way back to the shore only to leave the bar of soap. She was about to strike towards the other end of the pool by the dividing wall when she decided to remove her bra and panties. She craned her neck to make sure no one was around before getting out of the pool to let her underwear dry on a boulder. She hummed in appreciation as she swam, enjoying the water like silk against her naked skin. The pool was not too deep, dipping to about five feet the farther Faith was from the shore. While the torches gave the cavern a golden glow, the pool itself seemed to be illuminated from below. Faith couldn't find the source of the luminescence and at that moment she didn't care, allowing herself to drift away in relaxed abandonment. She floated on her back, letting her thoughts take her.

This was the closest to peace she had ever felt in a long time. Her life before the medical mission had been a mish-mash of anger and heartbreak, of fear and guilt. She had begun to feel as though she was being sucked into a quagmire that she couldn't escape until she received a call from her grandmother's lawyer.

She had always been wary of her ability to heal and she didn't know how she inherited it. She had several aunts who were healers, using traditional methods to siphon away illnesses from the sick. Her gift of healing was different. Her entire body heated up and when she touched the sick person, she was able to take the pain and illness away. She was a conduit taking it all in but she needed to be close to the earth so that she could pour the sickness out of her body and into the ground. But the last time, something went horribly wrong. The guilt that plagued her from the moment the child she tried to heal died made her lose her buoyancy and she sank underneath the waters. Faith closed her eyes, the deafening sound of silence surrounding her. She just wanted to stay inside this wet cocoon and never surface. No one would miss her. Not her family. Not even the man back in London she thought deserved her heart. He was never hers from the very start. Her lungs started to hurt, craving for air. Faith opened her eyes and willed herself to stay under. She wished she had the ability to breathe in liquid so that the silence could wrap around her, to buffer her from the recriminations of the world. But she couldn't, could she?

After all, she was just human.

She could feel her solar plexus hardening, at the same time wanting to burst out of her. With reluctance and eagerness in equal measure pouring through her she rose out of the water, crying out before sucking in huge mouthfuls of air into her starved lungs. The harsh intake of oxygen made her body hot and cold. Slowly, she swam towards the dividing wall, kneeling until the water reached her neck. As she turned around with her back against the wall, she froze.

Zac was descending the stairs toward her.

****

Telling the Ancients about his discovery about how the silver affected the Ancient Eald spurred Zac to find the *Specus Argentum*, the silver cavern. He also wished that the rest of the Cynn Cruors arrived soon. He checked his watch. It was T minus ten hours and counting. He could take the BGAN outside again and contact Roarke but those precious minutes were better used locating the cavern. The sooner he found it, the quicker the Cynn Cruor could protect and claim it.

The Ancients had given him directions of where to find it and as the Eald spoke, Zac noticed him weakening.

"My lord, you must rest."

"I am resting, am I not, Alaghom?" The Eald's mouth quirked to the side, his eyes twinkling with humour but also with discomfort.

The Deoré just rolled her eyes. "You have scaled down a lot but yes." She smiled ruefully at Zac. "He is."

Zac nodded.

"You don't believe me," the Eald stated.

"At the moment, sire, I am your doctor first, a Cynn Cruor second. Rest means sleep."

"No, it doesn't. Rest means not bloody doing anything."

"Sire, with the silver still inside you dissipating, you're as weak as stale scotch. The only thing that's stopping you from going into throes of agony like Graeme is because of your unique blood. So please, do as I say."

The Eald's eyes and mind probed Zac, who chuckled.

"I have nothing to hide." Zac arched his brow as he crossed his arms over his chest, deliberately keeping a tight cover on the secret he alone would know. "Do I have to treat you like a child?"

The Deoré laughed, her beauty radiating and anxiety leaving her. "Listen to him, beloved. Soon all will be well. I'll be here with you."

Chapter Fifteen

Zac left them to get his tanto, a shorter Japanese blade from his quarters. Taking a torch, he walked past several uninhabited dwellings to reach the passageway the Ancients said would lead him to the *Specus Argentum*, but when he got there the passage had already been lit. He entered the corridor until he reached an awning with a spiral staircase. He descended and saw that it led to a different and enclosed part of the pool.

And Faith. A very naked Faith.

"Bloody fuck," he swore underneath his breath. "Seriously?" Oh, it was serious all right because his cock took notice as it grew and hardened painfully against the confines of his suit.

It didn't matter that he wasn't in the shadows. Faith didn't notice that he was there as she glided and swam effortlessly in the pool. He growled softly at the sight of her breasts glowing like globes of fruit in the water for his taking and the sight of her bare core teasing him. He nearly fell to his knees when she spread her legs to kick the water, giving him a glimpse of the source of her nectar. She was his own private mermaid except that she had a pert bottom and shapely legs instead of a tail. Legs that he longed to encircle his waist as he entered her, pounding into her core until she cried out in ecstasy. Even after her first release, he'd continue to piston in and out of her, wringing out another orgasm until its wave buried him deeply inside her.

Deep and never leave.

The scent of lavender mixed with her essence

reached him, calling him by name to take her. His mouth watered remembering her taste, lost in the moment of being between her thighs. He could have stayed there for a long time, taking his sustenance from her because she was the source of his strength.

In more ways than he cared to admit.

Silver first! Keep your cock inside your suit and jerk off later.

Zac snorted at the way his mind took the moral high ground.

He watched Faith stay underneath the water longer than usual as he made his final descent. He waited, but she refused to surface. He was about to dive into the water and pull her out when she surfaced with a gasp and a splash. The cold that gripped him disappeared with relief that washed over him. Zac hadn't realized he had held his breath until then, and he closed his eyes.

Time was immaterial where his mate was concerned. Yet time proved too short to erase the stigma of rejection.

Zac heard Faith gasp. He knew she had seen him, but he continued to walk around the rock strewn sand as though he didn't notice her, despite the discarded clothes in a heap by his feet or her skin tone underwear drying on a flat rock. He knew Faith tried to make herself as still as possible, to not let the water ripple around her. She didn't know that it was immaterial since his enhanced senses could gauge even the direction of the current underneath the surface and his body attuned to her as it surrounded him, ratcheting his own hunger.

Zac had gone to many difficult quests through the centuries and dangerous missions as millenniums closed and the new ones began. But this mission to find the silver had to be the hardest and the most dangerous.

Not because of the silver.

It was because of Faith.

****

Faith pushed back as much as she could against the rock wall. No matter what she did, whether her chest rose and fell as she breathed, her minute movements made the tiniest ripples on the water but it didn't make a sound. It was the least she could hope for. The water rushing down in the crevices to join the waterfall outside of the cave became the roar of her blood in her ears. She wanted to inhale deeply, afraid that if she did Zac would notice she was in the pool and turn around to see that she was naked.

And very much aroused with her rosy peaks standing in attention and her core throbbing.

From Zac's clean cut dark blond hair, the shadow on his jaw, to the sinews of his muscled frame underneath his suit, he was a man Faith wanted to know. She salivated seeing his broad shoulders, her palms longing to feel his shoulders and chiselled stomach, her hand curling underneath the liquid surrounding her as it imagined itself holding his arousal in her hand.

What is he doing here?

Faith worried her lower lip, darting a glance at the undies she left on the flat rock to dry. Damn! She shouldn't have taken them off but how the hell would she have known he was coming to the pool?

You are in the same cave. What are the odds you don't bump into each other?

The pool had looked so inviting. Feeling sticky

and caked with dirt was a good enough reason to throw all caution to the wind.

Then Zac slowly undressed. Faith's breath locked. Zac pressed something by his collarbone and the front of the suit opened slowly, revealing the skin on his chest. He was Faith's own private striptease. He half rotated his body to pull his arms from the sleeves, his flat stomach flexing, the muscles in his arms straining for a moment. The more skin he exposed, the more Faith's sex moistened, the more heat engulfed her. When Zac's upper body was free of his suit, he stopped, letting the material hang low on his hips, showing the V that led to his shaft. Faith pursed her lips in frustration.

Zac walked toward the pool's edge to splash water on his face, his arms, his chest, allowing the liquid to glide down his stomach to his narrow waist and into that part of his body still hidden which Faith wanted uncovered. Before she could blink, Zac dove into the pool. Faith squealed before she could cup a hand over her mouth. Here she was, buck naked with a semi naked man, in a secluded pool. Trying not to move the surface of the water, she placed her hand over her mound and an arm over her breasts.

Please don't let him see me. Please don't let him see me.

Zac surfaced in the farther end of the pool opposite her, closer to the gaps in the wall. His forearms bunched with muscle when he raised them to wipe his face, water dripping from his hair, making rivulets down his neck and shoulders. Then his eyes opened, boring into hers.

"Hello, Faith."

Faith swallowed. She opened her mouth but nothing came out. She flushed at his cynosure, his eyes darkening with the gold flecks more pronounced, his lust reaching out to her across the glassy surface between them. Calm and serene on top. Heated with their burgeoning carnal hunger underneath. Faith's breathing became laboured. Even the water around her caressed her body as though it were Zac's hands touching her. Her lips parted as her lids closed, her pulse racing close to fever pitch. God! Why did she want Zac so much? Why couldn't her body be satisfied with just the kiss and when he touched her in between wakefulness and sleep? Why did she long to be in his arms, to hold her and never let her go. In the briefest span of time, why did she want to be his? But her flesh wouldn't be denied as though something settled comfortably inside her mind telling her that she belonged to him. That Zac was the man who had been made for her even before time began and the world spun on its axis. That he would be the answer to keeping her nightmares at bay.

So she opened her eyes, allowing herself to be drawn into the depths of his eyes that blazed with carnal hunger. Aching, watching, waiting. Her hands moved away from covering herself, a gesture of willing surrender.

Before she could utter a word, Zac crossed the divide with inhuman speed, pulling her up from the water to devour her mouth with his. The glassy silence erupted with water sloshing and bodies colliding. Faith immediately wrapped her arms around his neck, entangling her fingers through his hair, pulling him closer, both of them slanting their heads to kiss each other deeply. Tongues mated where core and shaft could not. Their lower bodies strained against each other, needing the feel of flesh against flesh. Faith moaned against Zac's velvet and expert tongue, submitting to him under the onslaught of his lips. He pinned her against the cave wall, her breast flattened against his muscled chest, yet so much alive. Her breasts begged for his touch again and her core's inner muscles squeezed involuntarily, needing him inside her instead of rubbing himself against her belly. Lord, what she wouldn't do to have him inside her mouth. She loved giving head, loved the feel of soft skin encasing a hard shaft that could bring her to climax. She loved the look on a man's face nearly begging but never there, always approving, deriving her pleasure from his own. Faith moaned when Zac cupped the underside of her breasts before his thumb made a wide circle against her globe, slowly swirling, tighter and smaller until it reached her puckered nipple, rubbing it again and again before taking it into his mouth. Faith leaned her head back against the wall as Zac feasted on her peaks, giving each one the same attention, his stubble grazing her skin.

"Yes..." She sighed. Each flick of Zac's tongue sent the same rippling sensation of need into her clit. Each suckle, a lick inside her sex. Her core was satiny wet amidst the water. Her moans and gasps echoed in the cavern. She looked down in disappointment when his mouth left her turgid nub but sighed when his tongue blazed a trail along the valley between her breasts, going lower. Faith watched Zac's tongue lick the water from her skin, leaving a trail of fire in its wake.

Then he moved away. Cold washed over her naked body and her cheeks flamed when she saw the tip of his arousal peeking as though desperately trying to escape the clutches of his suit.

"Zac?"

The heat of his gaze was more than enough to

stave away the cold.

"I don't think I'll be able to control myself with you." His voice was strained. "I'm holding on to a thin thread of control here. If you say yes, I'll take my fill of you, make you scream and remove all traces of any man lucky enough to be inside you in the past." His hunter green eyes glowed with sparks of gold.

She made a move forward, not bothering to cover herself, feeling her feminine power when Zac raked her body with his burning gaze. "I want to feel you inside me. I want what you do to me, making me forget and giving me hope for something much better. I want you, Zac. I want you to let go with me."

His mouth curled into a smile, both dangerous and sexy. Faith had the sudden urge to gyrate in front of him as though his eyes commanded her every move, her every want, creating a bond that allowed him to grant her every desire.

"Your blush radiates all over your body," he said, scouring his gaze down her naked form. "Rosy, wet, and hot. I tasted your pussy then like I want to do now. Will it also be the same?"

His words made her slicker between her legs. Faith felt her nether lips throb with anticipation, her core aching and longing to be filled, her juices trickling down her inner thighs.

"Faith?"

"Yes?" Her breaths were coming in quick gasps. Faith thought she would hyperventilate.

"I like eating you," he murmured, bringing his thumb to trace her jaw and caress her lower lip. "Licking you from your opening up to your clit and back again."

"Oh God..."

"I like spreading you apart enough to put my head

between your legs and drink your sweetness until you have no more left."

They were now less than an inch apart. Faith's breath was coming in pants. If Zac kept on talking to her like this she would come without even being touched.

"If I go down on my knees," Zac did just that, the water gently moving around him, "and put your leg on my shoulder, my mouth and nose flushed against heaven, will you let me take you? Will you let me use my mouth and fingers to fuck you? By the time I'm done and you've come, you will be ready to take my cock inside you. I will take you to where I've brought you before."

Faith looked down at him, mesmerized by his eyes, his angular face, his mouth.

And she was lost.

"Yes."

Triumph lit his eyes. And there was gratitude and humility as well.

She couldn't look away. Zac wouldn't let her either. She felt his thumbs against the outer folds of her sex, spreading her wider. Air locked in her throat at the sight of his tongue, and when Zac moved his head deeper between her thighs and she felt the first swipe inside her hole up to her erogenous nub, she came apart. But Zac wasn't done. He delved into her, his growl of satisfaction reverberating inside her core to spear her belly, the sensations flaring and igniting her body. He was voracious in his hunger, swiping at her bundle of nerves again and again that she held on to his head and shoulder to anchor herself. Then he took her clitoris into his mouth and flicked his tongue against it so fast that she screamed.

"So wet, Faith. All of this for me," Zac breathed

and Faith almost sank at seeing her cream on his tongue. Dear God, who would have thought she would get the best oral sex in the middle of nowhere?

"Zac! Oh fuck!" Faith couldn't stop the wave upon wave of orgasmic bliss assailing her. Her hips continued to buck against Zac's mouth and she whimpered when Zac placed two fingers inside her, her vagina clamping down on them. He brought then in and out of her, scissoring inside her while the water sloshed with the movement of his arm. Then he moved them inside, flicking them as fast as his tongue flicked against her clit and Faith came apart again.

Faith was in a whirlpool which she never wanted to get out from. Her body was on fire. Never had she felt such sexual decadence and exhilaration in her entire life. And this was just the start. No one had been able to wrench out the best orgasms she had ever experienced on this side of the world the way Zac did.

Zac stood and kissed her deeply, taking her moans into his mouth.

Her hand ran down his body, teasing, tentatively touching, making butterfly strokes against the valleys and hills of strength. Faith dipped her hand into the water, boldly bringing his suit lower to free and hold his arousal that pulsed stiff and hot. She curled her fingers around his girth, his length exciting her, pumping him and playing with the tip that she could feel oozed with his own juice.

Zac hissed against her mouth.

"I want you in my mouth, Zac," she whispered.

"I'd rather be inside you," he growled, holding her hard against him, causing her to arch her back.

"Señorita!"

Chapter Sixteen

If Zac could lash out and growl at Xavier he would, the haze their heavy petting made dissipating. A muscle ticked in his jaw, the only sign of his frustration and annoyance. His ramrod cock was hot, painful, and angry at the interruption, but his rational mind prevailed. He sent out a blast of energy, cloaking him and Faith from the young man's prying eyes. He didn't want Xavier to see Faith naked because he just might rip Xavier's head off.

"Holy shit!" Faith immediately dunk herself in the water.

"He won't see us." Zac watched the panic flare in her eyes and the flush of embarrassment colour her face. Ancients, she was beautiful.

"What do you mean?" Her eyes searched his.

"I can't explain it now," he said. "Just trust me."

"You keep telling us to trust you. How do I know you're not dangerous too?"

"Oh, I am dangerous when I want to be. Did your body think I wasn't to be trusted?"

"That's not the point!"

"It is, Faith," Zac said, his voice deep and husky. "And you know it. Otherwise you wouldn't have been willing to let me ravish you."

Delicate colour bloomed on her cheeks, and all Zac wanted to do was take her there and then.

"*¡Señorita! ¿Donde estas?*" Xavier's voice bounced against the cave walls. Faith looked at him in alarm. He was at the foot of the pool, looking around him. She saw Xavier look at their direction and didn't even blink an eye as he continued to scan the pool.

"Why can't he see us?" Her forehead pulled together in confusion. Her breath hitched. "What are you?"

"You'll know soon enough." Zac leaned forward, nipping at her earlobe before trailing his tongue down the column of her throat. A shiver of longing coursed down her spine to settle low in her belly.

"How can you do that to me at a time like this?" Her voice was less than a whisper.

"The more sex I have, the more I can keep the cloak up," he mumbled before licking the erratic pulse that beat at the base of her neck.

"Cloak? What cloak?" Faith's eyelids closed and she shivered. "I don't understand." She turned her head towards him, her cheek grazing his cheekbone, her hand revelling at the feel of the short strands of his hair against her palm. Zac raised his head, licking at the seam of her mouth.

"Xavier can't see us. As long as we pleasure each other, I get strength from you. So do you want me to stop so Xavier can see us? Or do you want me to continue to fuck you?" Zac's fingers parted her folds again to play and tease her, clit responsive, her slit flowing with liquid heat. His cock about to burst, the pleasure and pain mixing. He smiled against her throat, her moan vibrating against his mouth. "I need your answer, Faith."

"Señorita, please!" Alarm poured from Xavier. "Señor was right. We have to go. The people who killed El Jefe. They are on their way here."

"Fuck!" Zac whipped around to face Xavier, who immediately backed away and fell, landing on his bottom.

"Señor! How did you—"

"Now's not the time, Xavier." Of all the

convoluted things to happen! Zac was furious at himself. Where was the bloody logic he was known for when he needed it? "How do you know they are on their way here?"

"There is another passageway cutting through Felipe's quarters leading out of the mountain," Xavier answered. "I can see El Jefe's camp from there. *Hijo de puta*! How did you make me do that?" He pointed his weapon at Zac. "Where is Señorita Faith? What did you do to her?"

"Xavier, I'm here." Faith peeked out from behind Zac's back. "Go back to Felipe. I will be with you shortly after I dress."

"*Si*, I will go." The mention of clothing made Xavier flush. He scurried away from the shore, taking the spiral steps almost four at a time.

Zac raked his fingers through his hair and moved away from Faith. Damn his lust! God knew how much he needed a woman to strengthen him, but he hated himself for using Faith to do so. Now that Dac, the Scatha, and the werewolves were closing in, he needed to find the cavern and secure it fast. Zac looked at his watch. It was T minus five hours yet. Bloody hell! His mind clicked into mission mode.

"Zac?"

He clenched his hands underneath the water, his chin to his chest. What he wouldn't do to turn around and take Faith into his arms but if he did, he wouldn't be able to stop himself from taking her. God knew how much he wanted to do that now.

"I have to go." The farther he waded away from Faith, the tighter his chest felt. He grimaced at the inaudible gasp Faith made before the water moved. He later heard the trickle and splash, a sign that she was making her way out of the pool. He turned his head to look at her over his shoulder and clenched his teeth when he caught a glimpse of her round derriere before it was swallowed up by her jeans. She took her black hair in both hands and squeezed out the excess water before flinging it down her back. Zac's face hardened. Even from where he was standing in the pool, the waves of her humiliation and hurt hit him hard in the gut. Even as she stomped her way up the steps, Faith was still a sight to behold. Angry but beautiful. A spitfire he wanted to claim so that no one else could have her.

Who am I to demand that from her?

"Faith!" Zac turned fully to face her.

"Don't you dare come near me again." She stopped midway through the stairs, her body seething with anger, her eyes glittered with unshed tears. "By the way, thank you for that finger and tongue fuck. I did so need to come. When I get back to civilization, I'll let my friends know what a good man whore you are."

"Enough!"

Her brows rose. "No, I believe I had more than that." She continued up the stairs, disappearing into the carved out hallway.

Zac turned away, punching the water with his hands so that it made a huge splash, hitting him on the face. He clenched his fists so hard he thought his knuckles would pop out. He wanted to fly to Faith and hold her, to soothe the hurt he caused her, to tell her that it wasn't how it looked.

How exactly did it look? His mind taunted.

He scowled, his eyes narrowing in annoyance at himself. No, it was better this way. Faith would think the worst of him and he could move away from claiming her as his mate which he should rightly do. He donned the upper part of his suit and adjusted his still aching rod as he waded back to the bank. He grabbed his tanto and dove back into the water, this time into the deeper part of the pool, hoping that in the silent world underneath he'd be able to ease the ache of moving away from the one person meant for him.

****

Faith didn't know which was worse. Her heart thudding hard because she was fuming or her heart cracking because she was humiliated. After giving herself to him, he rejected her.

Story of my life.

Something brushed against her cheek and when she swiped at it, she realized that her anger had morphed into tears. She stopped short along the corridor and sucked in her breath. Now was not the time for self-pity. She was used to setting her pain aside which was exactly what she did and quickly made her way back to Xavier and Felipe. She didn't know how they would leave or escape this time, but she'd be damned if she stayed another moment with Zac.

The jungle outside felt safer.

Xavier was putting things into a rucksack when Faith arrived. When he saw her, he reddened. Felipe, on the other hand, stared at her in awe. He approached her and took her hand, pumping it up and down hard enough to possibly dislocate her shoulder.

"Thank you! Thank you!"

"*De nada.*" Her voice shook at the vehemence of his gratitude. She held on to his hand to take her own away. "Let me look at your wound."

Felipe raised the hem of his soiled shirt and gingerly touched the scar where his wound had been.

Faith looked at him and smiled, nodding. "It's healed well."

Faith looked at Xavier, who silently gave her another knapsack to fill. "There are bottles of water and food where you're staying. We can eat once we are away from this place. Don't fill it up too much so that it won't be difficult to carry." He finally looked up at her. "The path I showed you? I wasn't lying. We will take that path to get to La Nahuaterique."

"Xavier..."

"*No hay problema, señorita.*"

"Yes, it is," she insisted. "You can barely look at me."

Xavier flushed. "It's just that I am embarrassed that I saw you and...señor." He blew out a breath, looking anywhere but at her. "I didn't mean to intrude. I didn't even want to go to the pool when I knew you were bathing because..." He flushed again. "*Pero* those men. I just don't want to die. I don't want you or Felipe to die."

Faith raised her hand to squeeze his upper arm. "Thank you. Now," she moved towards the doorway, "I'll go to the other side and get what is needed. You said there was a passageway where you could see El Jefe's camp. Can we leave that way instead of through the cave's mouth?"

He nodded. "That's what we're taking. It will be a longer and a denser route so we will need to hack our way through. Here." Xavier gave her a machete that rested by the wall. "You will need this."

Thanking him, Faith went to get the food and water from her quarters. Freedom was within reach that she could savour it. Tasting it would come later. She sighed, a smile pulling at her mouth. She couldn't wait to get back to the city, and even if the cave was incredibly beautiful where she had the most glorious bath she'd experienced in a long time, her mortification and her body's yearning for Zac was more than enough to scare her to return to the mundane.

Suddenly she stopped and sat down heavily on the cot. Her face heated at the memory of Zac touching her for the first time. It was on the cot she lay on where she allowed him to undress her, to take her with his mouth and fingers, to make her cry out in ecstasy, allowing her to experience flying above the stars. She looked down at her hands. She really had to go. Everywhere reminded her of a man that frustrated her to no end, a presence she didn't want to be near to but couldn't bear to be apart from, and the only one who would be able to bring her to the heights of delight where no other man could.

Zac was her intimate stranger.

Finishing what she came for, she secured the rucksack on her back, took the machete and returned to the brothers. Before she could even leave the room, Xavier pushed Felipe inside. Felipe ran into the interior room while Xavier doused the torch.

"Xavier...oomph!"

He covered her mouth, stifling her voice.

What is it about men and their penchant for cupping a woman's mouth, dammit!

She wrenched his hand away, her eyes spitting fire but before she could open her mouth, ice froze her at his words.

"They're here."

Chapter Seventeen

Dac couldn't contain the smile that nearly filled his entire face. Not even the pain of going through a regeneration of his lost arm could compare to the elation of finding the place his human scientist refused to speak of. He looked at the mountain rising up almost a hundred meters above sea level. It was part of the Sierra Nahuaterique range that belonged to El Salvador that crept beyond its boundaries into Honduras. It wasn't any wonder that the location couldn't be found and the scientist had kept it a secret from the Scatha Cruor.

Some good that did after his head rolled on to his laboratory floor.

Dac inhaled the moist air, feeling it enter his lungs as the freshest air he had ever encountered in his immortal life. Revenge was such a beautiful thing and soon it would be his.

The Scatha and the werewolves spread out looking for an entrance to the mountain. Kamaria stood beside him slowly looking around, a smile on her mouth.

"You look pleased." Dac felt lust looking at her svelte figure. What he wouldn't do to ram his cock in both her holes and mouth.

Kamaria gave a sound between a laugh and a huff. "I didn't know this place was here. I should have."

"Why?"

"None of your business." Not sparing Dac a look she moved forward. Dac smirked, watching her hips sway. He'd do her ass first without her knowing it. The thought of hearing her scream of being unprepared tightened his balls. "There's magick here."

Dac's lascivious thoughts disappeared in an instant. "Magick. How can you tell?"

"By eating the shaman's heart." Kamaria's golden eyes pierced him with a stare. "I can do the same to you."

Dac laughed, unafraid at the growl that made her lips pull back from her teeth. "Eat my heart, Kamaria?" He chuckled. "I didn't realize you were so feisty. We can be so good together."

"Ugh! You stink."

He sighed, feigning nonchalance but that one phrase pricked his ego like no other. He prided himself in his appearance, his pheromones a come on to women who fell at his feet. He was an elixir of lust no one could deny.

They wouldn't last another hour if they did.

He watched Kamaria raise her hands, palms facing the cave, listening to the words tumbling from her mouth, clueless to what they were. The werewolves, still in human form, backed away, fidgeting, their eyes darting anywhere but at their leader. They closed in behind her as though waiting for her protective benediction. The Scatha, on the other hand, slowly changed into a host of huge teeth filled jowls and claws, inclining their heads as they watched with suspicion and curiosity. They felt her magick. So did Dac. It was an electrical current that lined the air and made the hair on his nape rise.

Kamaria walked forward. Her arms turned paws before she swiped them against the mountain's base, revealing the entrance into a cave. She turned to Valerian, her eyes glittering in triumph.

"Shall we?"

****

Swimming and cutting through the cover, Zac realised the cavern was immense, covering the entire pool's floor. The *Specus Argentum* could only be accessed through a narrow entrance now covered by moss. He now understood what gave the pool it's almost ethereal blue glow. Once the water hit particles of the silver a reaction occurred like a dull spark, causing it to flare, and because it was so minute, the flash could be mistaken for a glow. He wanted to remain in the cavern, explore it more. He could regulate his breathing under water and could stay for as long as an hour. All Cynn Cruors could. Being partly human, the natural buoyancy helped them stay afloat and not sink like a stone. He had taken more samples of the silver, the water around him enough to stave off the damage it could do to his skin if he used his bare hands to touch it. Looking around he found what looked like a broken earthen bowl edged between the rocks that dotted the cavern's bed. The ore was soft and easily broke away from the wall, floating until Zac secured it inside the bowl. Before he left, he covered the entrance to the cavern with more rocks from the pool bed, making sure that it didn't look disturbed. How it survived the ravages of time was something he would look into when the war was over.

Zac surfaced slowly from the pool and made his way to the bank and inhaled sharply.

Fuck! The Scatha are inside the cave!

Zac hated it when he had to be at the mercy of time. He zoomed through the corridor and stopped. He looked at where Faith and the brothers had been, then turned towards the opposite direction where the Ancient Eald was resting. His jaw hardened as he made his decision. He just hoped that Faith and the boys had been able to escape.

He swiftly made his way to his lab to leave the silver before preparing to warn the Ancients. He didn't have to bother. By the time he arrived, the Deoré's had morphed and the Ancient had two deadly swords in his hands.

"Sire!"

"You're not bloody going to tell me that I'm incapable of fighting, McBain," the Ancient Eald growled.

"Nay, Sire," Zac said, nodding his head. "How do you want to play this out?"

The Eald's eyes narrowed. He looked up at the cave's ceiling. "It's possible that we may be buried alive here."

Zac's heart squeezed inside his chest. The Eald looked at him, his face grim. "I need to stall them, Zac. I have read your mind. Roarke and the rest are on their way and they have alerted the Faesten here."

Zac forced himself to think of the impending battle and not the fact the Faith, Xavier, and Felipe might not have left. God knew how much he wanted to make sure. It didn't matter if he stayed buried with the Ancients. They would eventually get out. But Faith and the brothers wouldn't have a chance of surviving. He looked at his watch.

"It's T minus three hours, my lord."

The Eald sighed. The Deoré paced the ledge, keeping a sharp eye on the cave entrance to the city. "We have no choice."

"How much time can you spare, my lord?"

"What do you have in mind?" The Eald cocked his head to one side.

"The BGAN terminal," Zac said. "I need to leave it outside the mountain. If I keep it switched on, it will transmit a signal which Roarke and the other Cynn Cruors from the Faesten can zero in on."

The Eald nodded. "Thirty seconds."

Zac whizzed into his quarters and out to the opening he discovered earlier. He hooked the BGAN terminal to the laptop and switched it on. His gut plummeted when he saw that the laptop's battery was low.

Ten seconds.

He went back to get his microscope, placing it beside the BGAN terminal with five seconds to spare. He adjusted the glass towards the glare of the sun. If the BGAN didn't make it, he was hoping the Cynn Cruor would see the light flashing, but so would the Scatha. It was a risk he had to take. Zac returned to the Ancients.

"A second to spare, McBain." The Eald crooked a grin, then inhaled. "Is your mate still here?"

Zac didn't look at the Eald. No point in denying it either. "I wouldn't know, Sire. I told her to leave with the two mortals with her." It was no surprise that the Eald would have scented Faith on him. A Cynn Cruor's mate was unique for each Cynn Cruor destined to be theirs.

The Eald nodded. Zac was grateful that his progenitor didn't push. The Eald began to chant, one palm raised towards the cave's ceiling, the other palm pointed at the entrance to the lost city. Zac heard the crack first before the first of the stalactites fell over the entrance. Soon several pieces of the jagged rocks rained down on the entrance. The Eald staggered back from the onslaught of his magick but in less than two seconds, he stood, his stance commanding, the fatigue disappearing. Zac visibly relaxed, his mouth lifting in a lopsided grin.

"It's begun?" he asked.

The Ancient Eald's fathomless eyes bore into Zac, his smile wide. "It's begun."

****

Dread like no other fed the hysteria that threatened to swamp Faith. She couldn't move from where they were hiding. The falling debris made them stop running to look at what had happened.

"Oh my God," she whispered the same time Xavier exclaimed, "*Madre de Dios.*"

"*¿Hermano, quiénes son?*"

"*Soldados del diablo.*" He looked both at Faith and his brother. "They will not hurt us. They don't know we are here. We cannot use the path in Felipe's room. They will see us from there. There is another way. *¡Vamos!*"

Faith and Felipe followed Xavier through one of the numerous corridors, but this time they had to hack their way through the three roots that had seeped through the cave's ceiling. Faith suppressed the shudders when the roots clawed at her damp hair, brushing against her scalp in rough caresses. She thought of Zac. Where was he?

Why did she care? Why did she gravitate toward men like him? Men who pretended to care only to leave once they got what they wanted?

"We're here."

It took Faith a while to get her bearings. Having been inside the cave for a long while, she had to squint against the sun slowly sinking on the horizon. Her eye caught something glinting in the dying light. It was a laptop with a terminal and a portable microscope.

"What the hell..." Questions bombarded her. Did

these belong to Zac? The laptop was probably understandable but a microscope? Xavier had mentioned the silver. Was Zac after it too? Was that why they were in the cave?

"Señorita Faith!" Xavier hissed. "What are you doing? We have to go!"

"Xavier, isn't it dangerous to go now that the sun is setting?"

"I know this trail. I've been here before, remember?" Xavier sighed, adjusting the knapsack's strap on his shoulder while he had the assault weapon on the other. "Unless you want to stay because of Señor Zac."

"No." The word came out more vehemently than she wanted. She levelled her voice. "I forgot. You traipse all over the jungle at night."

"*Sí*, I do," he snorted.

They made their way carefully since part of the path was covered in lichen and moss. In order to get to the path leading to La Nahuaterique, they had to make their way down to the cave's main entrance. As they began their descent, holding on to overhanging branches to stave off their fall, they heard howling and cackling laughter that sounded in between a hyena's high pitched wail and the scratching of nails on a chalk board. Before they could return where they came from, Faith saw two men literally fly and land in front and behind them, and right before her eyes, they transformed. His hands elongated before turning to claws, all his teeth lengthened and sharpened, and his mouth widened, the jawbones breaking as it adjusted to accommodate his dental change. He looked as though he had the mouth of an angler fish. And his eyes...Faith's own eyes widened. They were glowing dark neon green.

Faith realized he was the same as the creatures she saw murder El Jefe's men.

"Nice, *chica y chicos*," he drawled. "Men, it looks like we're going to have some enjoyment even before the war begins."

War? What war? Faith's terror was garbling her thinking.

"¡Hermano!" Felipe grabbed Xavier's shirt as he cowered behind his older brother.

"Stay away." Xavier raised his weapon at the morphed man and his companion.

"Go ahead. Shoot," the creature said. Faith screamed when his claws sliced Xavier's weapon in half. His companion grabbed Felipe, who screamed, his claws slowly slicing into the boy's skin.

"Felipe!" Xavier threw his bags down to save his brother but the beast swiped him away. Xavier flew against the rock wall and fell in a heap, unconscious.

Faith saw red. Dammit! First she had to go through the trauma of a kidnapping. Next, she had to fight her way against these fiends. Then she had to deal with Zac's rejection.

She had enough.

"Come near me and I'll kill you."

The man laughed. "No mortal can kill a Scatha Cruor."

Faith bent her head and closed her eyes. This time she didn't rein the fury inside her but allowed it to curl over and over again until it was a huge fireball inside her gut. Her hands, previously clenched, loosened, the fire making her fingertips red underneath her skin. She felt the fire rising to her face and zero inside her eyes. She knew they would turn into orbs of lava, as though blood oozed out from it. This time, she didn't need to hold on to something so that the extra power she called forth did not harm or maim the person she was trying to heal.

This time she was going to kill.

Faith raised her head and opened her eyes. The creature who called himself a Scatha Cruor stepped back in surprise to see her eyes but grinned with malice as he stepped forward again.

"What kind of being are you?" he asked softly. "I wonder if you're a better fuck than a human."

Faith allowed him to come closer, swallowing hard to keep her roiling stomach at bay. His stench made her want to heave. When he was just a foot away, she raised her arms and placed both palms on his chest, giving the fire inside free reign. The Scatha's grin faltered, Faith's eyes latching on to his, never letting them waver. The fire inside her thundered through her veins from her solar plexus and into her palms, her fingers, her eyes. The Scatha's face slackened, shock replacing his confident smirk. He trembled, shuddered.

Then screamed.

Soon his body glowed, Faith's fire incinerating his internal organs, eating its way voraciously through every sinew, burning his blood, turning whatever was left into charred skin and bone. The Scatha fell in front of Faith, writhing in pain while his companion screamed in rage. The Scatha holding Felipe let go of him and hurled himself toward Faith. Faith raised her arms to brake his fall over her and as soon as her palms came in contact with his body, the fire greedily left Faith, incinerating him as well. Before long, three more men flew at her, transforming in mid-air.

"Felipe, stay with Xavier!" Faith didn't know how much fire was left in her. She never killed intentionally and the accident had involved a child. As it was, the fire inside her seemed satisfied with what it had burned. The fervour it had at the start, dispersing. She looked at Xavier's weapon which was of no use.

The macheté!

Faith turned to get the machete from the ground behind her but before she could stand up straight she was pushed to the ground. She fell to the side and hit her side on a sharp stone, the pain exploding in her hip. She was forced on her back, another Scatha astride her.

"What did you do?" he snarled. "You will pay for that."

Chapter Eighteen

Faith's heart plummeted but she was grateful. She wouldn't have to bear the burden of being reminded of those she killed. She thought of Xavier and Felipe. If she died, what would happen to them? She darted a glance at Xavier. He was still unconscious. Felipe clung to him, his face filled with terror as tears ran down his cheeks. Her mind was in turmoil. She wanted an end to her curse. She wanted to protect the brothers. Her death would only lead to the two boys being killed as well, or worse.

That's when she knew it wasn't her time to go yet.

Faith looked at the Scatha above her. She tried to wriggle her arms but they were pinned by his legs against her hips. He raised his arm, his claws elongating. Faith twisted furiously but to no avail. Before she could scream, the Scatha disappeared as ash rained down on her. She coughed violently as particles entered her nose and mouth. She turned away, spitting the abomination from her mouth.

Xavier! Felipe!

She knelt on one knee, the machete in her hand. When she looked at the brothers, there was a man with his back to them.

A very handsome man encased in a suit similar to Zac's, but instead of black, it was forest green. He was looking down at the ashes left by the Scatha that had been about to kill the brothers.

"You need to hack off the heads so that they don't regenerate." A female voice wrenched her from staring at the man. She looked up to see one of the most beautiful women she had ever seen. Her hair that flowed down her back was black, wavy and shone even in the dull light of dusk, as though she had just come out of a salon. She shouldn't be here, Faith thought. She should be in a studio doing fashion shoots of her hair. She wore a similar suit which had a crest embossed on the right side close to the shoulder. Faith took her proffered hand and was hauled to her feet. At that point, the man turned to her, giving her a devastating smile that had Faith had the hots for him, she would have melted. His broad shoulders, narrow waist and muscled flanks were moulded by the suit.

But the only feelings she had were for Zac.

The man pointed to the ground with his sword where the ashes of the two Scatha Faith had burned beyond recognition were the only evidence that they had been there.

"We don't have much time," he said curtly. "The Scatha are spreading out around the mountain and inside the Cave. We need to secure the Ancients inside. Bianca, stay here with her and the two boys. I need to get the Cynn Cruor to Zac before Roarke and the rest arrive."

"Understood." Bianca nodded.

"Zac?" Faith interjected. "What about Zac?"

"You know him?" The man's eyes narrowed before he inhaled deeply. His eyes held understanding before he masked it.

Faith hugged herself, suddenly feeling cold.

"The last time I saw him was by the pool inside." She couldn't stop the colour that stole up her cheeks. "He told us to escape while we had the chance."

"Which you didn't heed," he remarked. Faith's eyes flew to his, a retort on her lips, but there was an indulgent smile on his face that whatever she planned to say died.

"Don't mind my husband." Bianca rolled her eyes. "He loves to rile people. He says he doesn't, but I keep telling him that he does."

The man extended his hand. "Andrés de Alvaro. *Mi esposa*, Bianca de Alvaro y Berenguer." He looked at Bianca. "Hector will be here shortly. I better leave." He gave Bianca a hard and lingering kiss that had his wife melting in his arms. Then he was gone.

Faith blushed at the exchange, but she knew how that must have felt because Zac had shown her. And while she loathed him for using her, it would be something she would remember during the lonely nights that stretched endlessly before her.

She went to Felipe. He was cold, ashen, and unmindful of the blood that trickled down from the slashes on his forearms.

"He's going into shock," she said to no one in particular.

Just then another man catapulted himself towards them, landing softly beside Faith. He wore the same suit with the embossed crest as Andres and Bianca.

"*Por favor, permítame*." His voice was kind.

Faith moved away and let him speak to Felipe in that soothing tone. The boy continued staring into space before his eyes flickered, nodded once and fell asleep. Once he stood up, Faith placed her hand over Felipe's wounds with her other hand, face down on the ground. She did this with each and every slash on his arm until only red welts remained.

Now she was tired.

"That is some gift you have." Bianca helped her up. "This is Hector."

Hector nodded in greeting.

"I don't think of it that way." Faith gave her a brief smile. She looked at the forest and the sky. Dusk had settled. With the two brothers unconscious, there was no way she'd get to La Nahuaterique.

"I don't suggest we stay here exposed." Hector continued in Spanish. He had the most arresting dark eyes and lashes women would probably envy. His chiselled features almost looked hawkish because of his nose, but he had the kindest eyes Faith had ever seen. His physique resembled Andrés' body of all muscle, abs, and powerful thighs.

But he still wasn't Zac.

Why the hell am I comparing every man I see to Zac?

"We came through that opening." Faith, speaking in Spanish, pointed to where they came from. "It will lead us back into the mountain. Those creatures—"

"The Scatha." Hector volunteered.

"Scatha," she nodded, "won't see us coming."

"I've informed the rest of the Cynn Cruor," Hector replied.

"I'm not going to ask how you did that." She shook her head. "From what I've seen in the last several hours...?"

"We can talk some more later," Bianca replied. "Let's move."

****

Alaghom Na-om watched as Kamaria sauntered towards the pool before scanning the upper levels of the city. She had returned to her human form again. She loathed the smirk on her aunt's face and wished she could permanently slash her skin, her body, take out her heart the way her aunt had done to her father. How long had it been? Alaghom Na-Om couldn't even remember when it happened. She had been so overcome with grief that she remained in her werewolf form for a good number of years. She just wanted to erase the memory of seeing her own father, the Lycan Shaman being ripped apart because he refused to tell Kamaria where she was and how the Ancient Eald found the secret to stop the quickening. She had watched in horror as Kamaria dug into her father's chest cavity to pull out a still beating heart and drain her father's life force, drain the traditions and magick of their kind and fuse it with her own malicious intentions. Alaghom Na-Om would have remained a werewolf for good, not remembering her human part had it not been for the patience and love of the sorcerer who didn't need any magick to claim her heart. She had never expected to see her aunt again. Centuries had passed since she'd returned to the place where she was born, where her pack had existed. When she escaped with the Eald, the Lycan Shaman made her promise not to return, to make her way into the world and live peacefully with humans. Alaghom Na-Om did just that. She wiped all memory of the place of her birth, to move on to the point that she almost forgot she was a werewolf. But she wasn't completely one, was she? The Ancient Eald infused her with the Kinaré as well, which helped her prevent the quickening every month. It had instead increased her need to mate, to be taken by the Eald incessantly until she lost herself in the bliss of her mate's joining with her. The near death of Graeme Temple and the discovery of the silver from the *Specus Argentum* brought the painful memories back. She knew then that she would have to return to the place she would rather forget. As long as Alaghom Na-Om didn't know where Kamaria was it was fine, but when she sensed Kamaria, the remembrance of father's death came hurtling through her.

Her aunt would pay.

As Kamaria's eyes moved closer to where she stood, Alaghom Na-om sidled back behind the granite wall, which was the only barrier against Kamaria's sharp vision.

Alaghom?

I'll be fine. She cracked a smile as she turned to the Eald.

I've known you from the beginning of the best eons of my life. Do you still think I don't know what you're going through? I know you're not all right. The Eald caressed her face, thumbing her lower lip and cheek.

Alaghom Na-Om closed her eyes, leaning into his hand. *Yes, you do.* She opened her eyes, concern flashing in them. *How do you feel?*

Different. He frowned. *The pain is still there and I can feel the silver in my blood, but it's as though it's protecting it instead of destroying it. It's something Zac and I should look into.*

She nodded. *Speaking of Zac, what of his mate?*

The Eald nodded. *I sensed her as well in the clearing before we attacked Dacronius. Why he isn't with her is beyond me. Destined mates cannot deny the pull they have for each other. Not being together will tear them apart.*

Alaghom Na-om closed the gap, entwining her fingers in her husband's hair. The Eald's eyes flared, the gold flecks immediately surfacing in the pupils.

She took his lower lip into her mouth and sucked on it, causing the Eald to inhale sharply, to encircle his arm around her waist and flush her against his arousal.

Was that part of concocting the Kinaré? She mentally asked, their mouths locked, her breathing becoming heavy.

No, my beloved. I did not need to add that to the

mix. That bond is older than time itself. His tongue gained entrance into her mouth to begin their carnal play.

Yes it is, isn't it? She said before giving into her beloved's passionate kiss.

Because they didn't know how long before they could do so again.

****

Zac and the Ancients watched as Valerian and Kamaria told their followers to spread out. There were thirty Scatha and werewolves and counting. His heart thudded both in exhilaration he felt with every engagement with the Scatha.

And trepidation.

No doubt with the Ancients' more enhanced abilities they would be able to beat off the enemy, but it was going to be a close fight. The odds were three to one.

Zac lifted his head to smell the air. Faith's scent was no longer present. He nodded surreptitiously to himself. Good. As much as his body ached for her he found solace in the fact that she was safe from the Scatha.

And from him.

The Ancients looked like statues, stoic, unmoving, but he could sense their anger, their rage, each one lost in their own memories of Dac. How Valerian attempted to assassinate the Ancient Cynn was common knowledge. What Zac didn't know was what kind of deep wounds Kamaria left on the Deoré. Alaghom Na-om's body thrummed with rage. It wouldn't be seen by the human eye, but Zac could see how she vibrated like a taut violin string after it had been plucked.

"Search for the silver," Dac barked. "Come to me when you find it."

Is the Specus Argentum secure? The Eald telepathed.

Aye, my lord. It doesn't exist, Zac replied.
Good.

The only thing left to do was to wait for reinforcements and Zac hoped they'd arrive soon.

Now soon enough, McBain?

Bloody hell! Hamilton! Relief poured like a waterfall over Zac.

About time you arrived. The Ancient Eald's voice was wry with humour.

My liege.

The shadows moved behind Zac. Slowly he faced the movement, his wakizashi's tip to the ground, an extension of his right arm. He held his tanto on his left hand.

You better be behind the wall Dux, or whoever comes out of the shadows will remain part of it.

It's not death a man should fear, but he should fear never beginning to live it. The telepathic message came from the shadows.

Zac's face broke into a wide grin.

Well, fuck me, Temple! You're quoting Aurelius now? Zac was so overjoyed that he almost spoke. He placed his sword and blade back in the scabbards behind his back and extended his arm in the Cynn Cruor greeting. He clasped Graeme's arm. *So good to see you're back on your feet.*

Roarke came out next from the shadows. He, too, extended his arm in the Cynn Cruor greeting.

Graeme grinned. *I hate being in bed unless it's with Kate. So sorry, mate, I can't fuck you.*

Zac snorted in amusement before sobering. In less than a second, Graeme approached the Ancients and knelt before them.

My liege, my lady. I owe you my life.

Your situation was very unique, Graeme. We wouldn't have left Anglesey had it not been for the silver bullet you took, the Ancient Eald replied, extending his arm to Graeme to help him rise.

Zac said you have been shot with the same type of silver, my liege. Roarke crossed his arms over his massive chest, then inclined his head to one side. *You don't seem worse for wear.*

The Eald smiled. *That is something I will need to speak to the entire Cynn Cruor at length once this battle is over.*

Where are the rest? Zac waited for the rest of the Cynn Cruor to leave the shadows. *Finn? I saw Colin in the feed when we spoke.*

In sniper positions, McBain. Eleven and two o'clock, Roarke said.

Zac looked up and zeroed in on both Finn and Colin. *Looks like you're an adopted son of Manchester, Butler.*

In your dreams, mate, Colin drawled. *Leeds is too much in my blood. I'm just helping my less fortunate brethren. Craig's with me to help your sorry arses.*

On the mission, people, Roarke said.

Kill joy speaks. Colin Butler tutted.

Zac, I'll greet you when I see you. Finn's amused voice came through their minds before it sobered. *Dux, we have clear shots of everyone coming from the entrance.*

Roarke unsheathed his falchion—similar to a scimitar but shorter—from his back before looking at the Ancients.

Your orders, Sire. De Alvaro is outside. Forgive me, but we had to get the Trujillo Faesten to reinforce our numbers.

You wouldn't be Dux if you didn't know how to command and make judgement calls, Hamilton, the Eald said. *De Alvaro can be trusted. And from the looks of it, I'm glad you did.*

From their vantage point, everyone saw the Scatha and werewolves stream through the cavern's opening. The din the enemy was making was enough for everyone to speak without being heard.

"Three snipers may not be enough, Dux." Zac observed.

"Graeme is taking the lower eight o'clock," Roarke said. "Zac, stay with the Ancients."

"We are fine, Roarke," the Eald said before he and the Deoré transformed in front of Roarke and Graeme. Zac saw the stupefaction in his brethren's faces and knew exactly how they felt, particularly now that they saw the Deoré change into a werewolf. "Take down as many Scatha and werewolves. Dac and Kamaria are ours."

"Aye, my lord." Roarke nodded.

"There's one thing you have to know about the werewolves. They will roam in packs. You must not defend in a phalanx formation." The Eald's black red eyes looked at all of them. "Listen to the were blood inside you and let that knowledge rein the urge to hunt like a pack as they do."

Chapter Nineteen

Zac was ready for battle. From the moment Graeme was shot and he couldn't heal him immediately, this payback was long overdue.

"Here." Graeme handed him an Accuracy International sniper rifle. "That's loaded with silver flechettes instead of the normal bullets."

"Use those for the werewolves." Roarke instructed. "With their height and build it will inflict the most damage. Aim at the head. Graeme and Colin will pick out the Scatha."

Zac checked the chamber and noted the silver tipped bullets. "Will do."

Just then, the scent he longed for but hoped had disappeared drifted to him.

"Bloody hell!" he swore.

Faith was here.

"Hector," Roarke greeted the Honduran Cynn Cruor, who emerged from the same corridor. "You shouldn't have left Bianca alone."

Hector's kind eyes smiled. "You want my head to get chewed? Andrés won't like it either, but Bianca...well, she is Bianca." He looked at Zac, inhaling deep. "Rest assured, your mate is safe. Bianca is watching her and the two boys. They couldn't leave. The Scatha cornered them."

"Where is she?" Zac didn't mean for the question to come out harshly, but the thought of Faith being captured by the Scatha nearly paralyzed him.

"*Cálmate*, primo." Hector's eyes lit with amusement. "She's in one of the houses away from the firefight. She killed them."

"What?"

"*Sí*, burned them to a crisp. Andrés decapitated them." Hector looked at the activity below. "We can talk about that later. *Ahora*, let's fight."

Zac was stunned. Burnt to a crisp? His mouth straightened to a grim line only too glad that Faith had held her own. Admiration for Faith warmed his heart.

He just wished he knew how to let go.

Zac took his position thirty feet to the right of the cave's entrance. His vantage point allowed him to pick out the werewolves who towered at ten feet. He flattened himself, steadying his rifle with his arm underneath the chamber and against his right shoulder. There was a little static in his ear as Roarke's voice came through.

"Steady."

"Three...two..." Zac said under his breath.

"You counting again, McBain?" Finn's amused voiced came through.

Zac grunted. "...one."

"Fire!"

Outraged howls and bellows filled the cavern, causing some of the loose rocks to fall. Zac picked off several werewolves in rapid succession, his body minutely twisting to follow his target, whose heads exploded from the impact of the silver flechettes. From his side vision, he saw Graeme take down several Scatha, strafing their necks until they puffed in ash. Flechettes and bullets rained on them that many tried to back away from being hit. Those who managed to get away were taken out by Finn, Colin, and Craig, while those the Cynn Cruor narrowly missed were shot at by Roarke and Hector.

"The Ancients are moving in," Roarke shouted above the din. "Zero in on your targets, Cynn Cruor."

From his nine o'clock, Zac saw something hurtle into the fray, making him sweat ice. The Deoré barrelled into Kamaria, rolling them both to the ground. The Ancient Eald flew feet first, landing a bone cracking kick on Dac's jaw. Dac bawled in rage before transforming. The Cynn Cruor continued supplying covering fire, but Zac knew he and his brethren were dumbfounded at Dac's change, for they had never seen him do so. Admittedly, it was an awesome sight, but they couldn't stop firing. A millisecond delay was more than enough to turn the tide against them. The Scatha had the speed and agility of the Cynn Cruor, but they had an advantage. The werewolves were on their side.

"Wonders will never cease," he muttered.

"I heard that," Colin yelled.

"Mate, you're going to break my ear drum."

Colin laughed but didn't say anything.

Zac shook his head while he continued firing. Several Scatha and werewolves tried to avoid the hail by retreating but were blocked by the surge behind them.

It was a massacre.

Unable to retreat, the Scatha and werewolves scattered, taking their chances by separating from each other. Soon the Honduran Cynn Cruors emerged. Zac had never met Andrés de Alvaro, but he could see that de Alvaro commanded his men with military precision, leading the charge instead of letting his men forge ahead. He was a dynamo, hacking his falchion from left to right, a snarl on his face. Zac continued to shoot at his targets until he had no more ammunition left.

"I'm out," he shouted. "I'm going in."

It was time to enjoy the battle.

****

Faith couldn't keep still. Having made the brothers comfortable, she paced the length of the room. Bianca kept a close watch from the door, comfortably bracing her legs on silver heeled stiletto boots. It looked incongruous against her green body suit. Faith was able to study her at length, the torches fully lighting their temporary accommodation. Beautifully shaped brows arched over almond shaped dark brown almost black eyes. They were tinged with concern. She kept speaking to her ear piece, giving Faith an idea of what was happening. Her pert nose slightly flared every time she inhaled sharply, her beautifully formed lips speaking rapidly to the person she was communicating with.

"Cynn Cruors have boxed the Scatha in the first corridor." She stared at Faith. "Killing both Scatha and werewolves." Then she smiled in relief. "Andrés has broken through." She sank down to the floor with a huge sigh before chuckling. "I wish I was fighting with my husband."

"I didn't mean to keep you." Faith coloured. "I'm sure we are safe here. We're far away from the fighting."

"Oh, *cara mía*, I didn't mean anything of the sort. I apologize. Sometimes I can be tactless when I speak." Bianca spoke as she exhaled. "Guarding you is still part of my role as a Cynn Cruor mate. You are very precious."

"Me?" Faith stopped pacing and placed her hand to her chest. "Why?"

"You're a Cynn Cruor mate." Bianca looked at her in confusion.

"No, no." Faith shook her head. "You're mistaken.

I was kidnapped, wrenched from the medical mission that went to La Nahuaterique. When you saw us earlier, we were on our way to the village."

"But the Scatha arrived." Bianca nodded. "Andrés and Hector were giving orders to the men when we saw what the Scatha did to you. I have to say you handled yourself very well."

Faith looked away. "They were going to kill us. I had to do something."

"Hhmmm..." Bianca placed her arms around her knees. "You were very brave to do that."

"I only thought of getting away with the brothers. Survival instinct." Faith sank to the floor opposite Bianca. "It's hard to even begin to understand everything that's happened." She looked pointedly at the other woman. "Who are you, really? Who are the Cynn Cruors? The Scatha? There are werewolves out there! Figment of one's imagination that's come to life!"

Bianca didn't speak. Faith ran her fingers through her hair. Her heart dropped to her belly before returning to its usual place. If there were still more paranormal creatures out there other than those she'd seen, she'd make it a point to check herself into a mental institution. She wanted to scream in frustration, but laughter bubbled up her throat instead, throwing her at its mercy. She gazed at Bianca, who watched her with amusement. Faith gave in to guffaws until tears streamed down her face.

"It is hard to believe."

"You think?" Faith sobered.

Bianca smiled. "I grew up knowing they existed. I'm a Cynn mortal."

"Cynn mortal?"

"My father was a Cynn Cruor warrior and so was

my brother. There are no female Cynn Cruor warriors, but we are treated equally as the immortals."

Faith made a sound between a chuckle and a snort. Heat suffused her face. "Sorry."

"No need to be." Bianca waved her hand dismissively. "It was the reaction I expected. No harm done. I can tell you more."

Faith rested her head on the wall behind her before looking at Bianca.

"Elucidate me."

****

This wasn't how it was supposed to happen. If there was another word that went beyond fury, rage, and the absolute desire to annihilate the entire world, that was how Dac felt. The Ancient Eald came after him blow after blow, but every laceration inflicted healed even before the next swing. Nothing he did as Caesar's general prepared him for this. He cursed himself, something that was redundant because he was already cursed. With reluctance he had to admit that he had become soft. Gnaeus Valerius Dacronius soft! But here he was, straining against the Eald's punches. The Kinaré inside him yowled in anger.

"You have caused enough mayhem, Dacronius. It's time you die."

Dac cackled. "Die? Only the Council of Ieldran can dictate whether I live or die."

"I am Ieldran." The Eald's glare was furious.

For the second time in less than forty-eight hours, Dac was afraid. He howled in pain at the deep slash inflicted diagonally across his chest, blood flowing in rivulets down his torso. He loved pain but this was different. This made him think that his death was near.

"The Council answers to me."

Another shattering scream tore from Dac's throat. He arched his back like a taut bow when he felt another deep cut diagonally across his back.

"You will answer to me."

Before the Ancient Eald could douse him with another blow of magick, Dac barrelled into him, smashing the Eald's jaw before his claws embedded themselves in the sides of the Eald's body. The Eald roared in pain but before Dac could administer the coup de grace, he was knocked off the Eald's body.

"You've done enough!"

The Deoré was behind Dac, a hairy arm in a lock hold around his neck.

"Not quite!" He raked his claws over her arms. She screeched but instead of letting go, her arms tightened. He couldn't break free. He could feel his strength ebbing. A sharp crack reverberated around the cavern like a clap of thunder. The sounds of battle stopped immediately.

Dac's neck had been broken.

Alaghom Na-Om stood, her chest rising and falling with exertion. She knelt down and took out a doubled edged serrated dagger from her boot and lifted her arm.

Then she screamed.

The dagger fell from her had as the silver bullet speedily entered her blood stream. She looked up to see Kamaria with a triumphant smile, holding the gun. Doggedly, she tried to stand, but staggering to do so pushed her and Dac into the pool. As the water closed in on her, her last though was of the Ancient Eald.

Pandemonium broke. The Scatha, undecided. The werewolves, jubilant.

"Alaghom!" The Ancient Eald didn't even finish

roaring her name before diving after her.

"Cynn Cruor on the mission!" Roarke barked instructions. "Hack any fucking Scatha and werewolf polluting your way!"

"You heard him. ¡*Vamos!*" Andres commanded his men.

Manchester and Trujillo contingents fought as one. Slicing, slashing, decapitating. Ash rained on everyone as though a volcano had imploded and sent its ash fall inward instead of blanketing the green forest grey.

Roarke's heart bled for his leader. Even from a distance he saw the desolation clouding the Ancient Eald's face before he dove to retrieve his beloved. Roarke knew of the indescribable pain of loss when he thought Deanna had died in the battle of Hamel Dun Creag, and he thanked everything he held holy for returning Deanna to him. Never again would he allow that to happen. The next time it did would be their last on Earth.

****

Finn stood from his kneeling position having just beheaded a Scatha and werewolf a mere second from each other. From the second level of the cavern, he had watched the Deoré come to the Ancient Eald's rescue and saw Kamaria shoot her. He saw how the Deoré sank beneath the waters, her blood weaving a dark ribbon in the luminescent blue pool.

"Fuck!" he swore softly. He thought of the time Eirene came to his rescue. Eirene, his sexy, stubborn, beautiful mate. She had been told not to follow him when the Cynn Cruors raided Dac's night club *Dare You!* It was a good thing she did because she had saved his life by giving him blood so that they could keep him alive and transport him back to the Faesten. Finn's gaze narrowed, and he jumped to the ground level of the cavern, killing the Scatha and werewolves that blocked his path. He continued hacking through them, slicing them vertically, horizontally before beheading them, even though they were already running away from him. The bloodlust in his veins ran rampant at the sight of the Ancient Eald's grief until he stopped dead, his face hardening in shock at the horror of what he was doing. His eyes refocused as though coming out of a stupor. A werewolf lay at his feet, fear and defiance clouding its golden eyes. Finn had enough. All he wanted to do was return to Eirene.

"I'm granting you your life," Finn said with barely suppressed fury. "My quarrel isn't with you, but if I see you again with the Scatha, your mangy arse is mine and it will be dead."

The werewolf jumped on all fours with a low growl, its teeth bared in a snarl before it whimpered and loped away. Did Finn see respect and gratitude flicker in those gold depths? He shook his head.

My imagination is going haywire.

All around him, the leaderless Scatha were retreating. Kamaria had laughed after shooting the Deoré, then ordered the werewolves to leave. But Finn's focus wasn't on them. He stood beside Roarke while he grimly waited for the Eald to resurface.

When the Deoré fell and the Eald dove after her, Graeme instinctively followed into the water, his oath as a Cynn Cruor foremost on his mind. The water on this side of the pool was deep with boulders and jagged rocks buffering the sides like a mouth filled with uneven teeth. He kicked towards the Eald who had the Deoré partly in his arms. A ribbon of blood faded into the water from the Deoré's bullet wound, turning the water a tinge of dark purple. Graeme knew what it felt like for silver to enter his body, for it to burn through without let-up that he had wanted to die than to go through the agony of healing.

Graeme, Alaghom's foot is stuck. The Eald telepathed.

Graeme nodded, finding the offending rock and throwing it with one hand. Once freed, the Eald gave a forceful kick to bring them both upward, Graeme trailing behind them. The Ancient Eald's terror of losing his mate rang through Graeme, tightening his chest. He didn't want to go through that. He didn't what that to happen to Kate.

Fighting a battle without Kate by his side was a bitch.

He wouldn't have it any other way.

****

Colin retreated to the shadows, reconnoitring the area for Scatha and werewolf stragglers. Though he was one of the best at what he did, his mind wasn't on what he was doing. His mind was on Finn as he swathed a path through werewolf and Scatha fleeing from him until Finn had stopped as though he realized what he had done. A werewolf lay on the ground. As if on hindsight, Finn spared the werewolf's life.

Colin took a moment to lean against the cave wall. He closed his eyes and was transported to a dank cell where a person lurked in the shadows. He knew this person. He was the one who placed him there. Since that moment, no amount of cajoling or threat could make the person come forward. It would just be so easy to enter the cell and speak with the man in the shadows, but Colin didn't. Because if he did, and the man decided to kill him, Colin would be willing to have himself killed. If the Cynn Cruor knew who killed him, the person responsible wouldn't have a chance in hell of living and Colin wanted him to live. He owed him that much and not a day passed without him being eaten up by guilt. It was exactly because of the Cynn Cruors' single mindedness of purpose that Colin had kept this secret all through the centuries.

A secret that was his fault.

"You need to tell them, you know." Craig stood beside him, breathing heavily. They both watched the scene below them unfold. "They won't take that against you."

Colin's mouth straightened, nudging his chin at Finn's direction.

"If this battle is anything to go by, I'm not so sure anymore."

Chapter Twenty

Roarke watched the two figures swimming up to the surface of the pool with the Deoré between them. He turned to his left, watching a sombre Andrés and Hector approach.

"My men are scouring the forests," Andrés said. "They will deal with any Scatha or werewolf they see."

Roarke nodded. "See to your mate, de Alvaro. I know you want to be sure she's safe. The Eald with understand," Roarke added quickly when he saw Andrés was about to object.

"*Gracias.*" Andrés smiled with gratitude before leaping to the second level of the cavern, running through one of the darkened corridors.

The Eald broke through the water, then the Deoré. Graeme surfaced at a respectful distance. Zac sheathed both his swords into their scabbards behind his back before taking a step forward.

No, Zac. Roarke's voice entered his head. *I know it's your duty as a healer, but this is the Eald's duty as the Deoré's mate. Let him ask for help if he needs it.*

Zac deferred to him. Roarke knew the Ancients more than him. The Hamilton, Roarke's father was one of the Ancients' trusted advisers and enforcers. Roarke knew what he was talking about. Zac also knew the implications of touching someone else's injured mate. The bond between immortal warrior and mate was a strong one. If they were both wounded, they both had to heal each other. The Eald's wounds had already closed, but the Deoré's was still open, blood and water trickling from the small hole that held the very thing that could kill her. Any gesture of help could be construed as interference and could lead to unnecessary fights because of the almost feral desire to protect. He had seen it with Eirene and Finn, Roarke and Deanna, and the growl that gurgled from the Ancient Eald's throat was enough for those assembled to take a step back.

"Dux, I'm going back to check for Dac's body. It's time for him to stand for his crimes." Graeme looked at Roarke.

"Do that and watch your back." Roark nodded.

"Always, Hamilton." Graeme entered the water again.

The Ancient Eald mouthed an incantation, his eyes closed as he threaded water. The Deoré's body slowly lifted, levitated above the rippling surface as excess water fell from her unmoving form before it was gently laid on the rocky ground.

"Zac."

"Aye, my lord." He swiftly checked on the Deoré while she shifted into human form. The Ancient Eald catapulted himself beside and knelt next to his mate.

"Vitals are weak."

"Thank you." The Eald nodded.

Zac and everyone else watched as the Ancient weaved his magick around his mate. It looked like an aural wave pulsing from his palms. The Deoré stirred and opened her eyes, slowly blinking to focus.

"Eald?"

"Yes, Alaghom. I'm here." He held her hand.

"I'm glad." She smiled before she lost consciousness again.

****

The Trujillo Faesten sat atop one of the mountains

over the city, facing the Caribbean Sea. The half-moon lent its light to the waves that whispered its secrets and sighed its laments to those who cared to listen to stories of mariners long gone. Faith inhaled the sea's essence, taking it into her lungs as the breeze wafted against the thin curtains.

She was given a room that faced the sea. Red tiled floors were cool on the soles of her feet. Muslin draped the antique wooden four poster bed that if closed would give the person inside her own private world. On both sides of the bed were two reading lamps that added to the soft light of the room. There was a chest in front of the bed that doubled as a seat with colourful throw pillows. A black iron chandelier hung in the centre of the room. Underneath it was a round mahogany table where remnants of her meal had been left. She hadn't realized that she had been so hungry until her stomach growled in glee at seeing the food laid on the table. The bathroom, made of marble, had a shower stall with monsoon shower heads that could fit half a dozen people with room to spare. She couldn't complain. This was more than what she was used to. Even after entering into wealth she never thought existed, she still maintained her simple living with just a few token luxuries.

The flurry of activity that came after Andrés arrived to tell them that the battle was over for the moment didn't give Faith the chance to talk with Zac. She could sense his presence always as though he was near. When she looked around, the only people she saw were the rest of the Cynn Cruors, who had the unenviable task of seeing to the dead.

People. Faith gave a sound between a laugh and a snort. Yes, they were partly human. As Bianca told her the Cruors' story, of how it became the Cynn versus the Scatha, her logical mind rejected every notion with a protracted sense of disbelief, while her own knowledge of the esoteric accepted their existence. No amount of literary imagination could have conjured what she had seen, had witnessed in the hands of Dac Valerian, whom she now knew as the man who killed El Jefe. She would have relegated what her eyes saw as a figment of her imagination if she also didn't have the fire inside her. Science could explain it as internal combustion or something similar. Point was, it didn't kill her. Science would be unable to explain how her eyes changed whenever the fire consumed her when she started healing.

Or when she killed.

Faith, Xavier, and Felipe were whisked away by helicopter and brought to the Faesten. She was given the room while the brothers were given a bungalow on the grounds of the compound.

A soft knock broke Faith's thoughts. She turned to open the door, the sleeveless red dress Bianca gave her to use billowing against her legs.

"Come in, Bianca." She smiled.

"I hope everything is to your liking." Bianca walked to the centre of the room before she turned to beam at Faith. Her hair shone like a black silk curtain that flowed down her back. She had changed to a colourful skirt with Mayan patterns that cinched her already small waist, and a terra cotta off the shoulder blouse. On her feet were high heeled terra cotta coloured sandals.

"Everything is perfect, thank you." Faith replied. "When can I join the medical mission I was with in La Nahuaterique?"

Bianca leaned her head to one side, a flicker of confusion on her face that quickly disappeared.

"The Cynn mortals are checking on them now. As soon as you are able, you are free to go."

"Thank you. And thank you for the dress. As soon as I get back—"

Bianca waved her hand. "Keep it. It looks very good on you. If there is anything good that came out of your ordeal, let it be the dress."

And Zac. Faith thought. Her mouth curved instead as she nodded.

"I know it might not be any of my business, but Zac McBain isn't going to take his eyes off you when you come down for supper."

Heat rose from Faith's chest, creeping to her neck, then to her cheeks. Her pulse started to race.

"I doubt that," she said.

"*Cara mia*, you don't see how beautiful you are." Bianca approached Faith to put her hands on her shoulders. "The blood red colour of your dress compliments your tan and your dark hair." Then in a softer tone, she added, "I can understand why he chose you."

"Bianca." Faith licked her dry lips, her belly doing somersaults at the knowledge of Zac being in the same house as her. "Please don't take this the wrong way, but what you think happened between Zac and me." She shook her head. "There's nothing going on between us."

Bianca's tinkling laughter filled the air. "I said that before when Andrés pretended not to pursue me. But when Fate decrees it, we have no choice but heed its call."

"If we don't?"

"Would you want to find out?"

Faith turned her face away.

"We are getting into something philosophical that

needs more time for discussion. I don't think you want that. Forgive me. Come! Let me take you to Xavier and Felipe." Bianca smiled as she entwined her arm around Faith's arm and they both walked to the door. "I'm sure they're both quite anxious to see a familiar face."

"Are they all right?"

"Yes, they are. You seem to have developed an affinity for your kidnappers, *cara*." Bianca made a frustrated noise. "Ahh! *Lo siento*. I sometimes talk before thinking!"

Faith smiled. "It's okay. I have. It's good to be able to talk to someone about their plight." She then went on to tell Bianca about Xavier and Felipe and the hard life they've had to live.

"It is sad. They're no different from others who live the same way. The only difference is that you have brought them here and now the Cynn Cruors have an opportunity to help."

"You will?"

"But of course! The Cruors were created to help humans until Valerian corrupted several of the warriors. Just because there is a war is not enough reason not to help them."

They continued walking along the white washed hallway lit by wall lamps that looked like eighteenth century lanterns. Along one side of the hallway was a long narrow tapestry depicting a war. It was encased in non-glare glass and nearly stretched from one end of the corridor to the other.

"What's this?" Faith stopped in awe. "It's dangerously beautiful. And the stitching, it looks handmade."

"That's the visual history of the Cruors and when Dac broke away from them."

Faith looked at the intricate embroidery. "I can only imagine how long this took."

"*Sí*. All of the Faestens have this to remind us of the sacrifices we have to make to keep as much evil out as we can."

The Trujillo Faesten consisted of the main house and several bungalows spread all over the property. Bianca and Faith took the staircase just outside of the hallway to the ground floor before making their way to one of the bungalows where a Cynn Cruor warrior stood guard.

"Señorita Faith!" Xavier stood up immediately as soon as they entered. Felipe, on the other hand, launched himself into Faith's arms. They had changed into clean clothes, the tell-tale dampness of their hair and the scent of clean soap giving evidence of their bath.

"You don't seem to be worse for wear." She teased, ruffling Felipe's hair. Twin beds with colourful spreads were placed side by side against one wall. In between was a bedside table with two lamps. Flushed opposite the beds was a sofa and matching armchairs the colour of latte. It surrounded a coffee table where remnants of meals were left behind. Faith smiled happy that Xavier and Felipe had a decent place to stay. They wouldn't have to live in the streets anymore. They would always have warm food in their bellies, soft beds to sleep in instead of the hovels they were used to. Most of all, the life Xavier wished for himself and his brother could finally come true.

"Señorita, what will they do to us?" Xavier's eyes darted from Faith to Bianca.

"No harm will come to you," Bianca answered in Spanish. "Though I understand you kidnapped Faith."

"We needed a doctor." Xavier defended, swinging

his arm towards Felipe. "My brother had been stabbed."

She nodded. "You had to do what was needed to save your family. I understand that Felipe is the only one left."

"It still doesn't answer my question."

"Xavier!" Faith chided.

He spun away from them while Felipe's brows knitted.

"All will be well," Bianca replied gently, addressing Xavier's back. She looked at Felipe, who still clung to Faith. She pointed to another door at the opposite end of the bungalow. "That is a game room. You are welcome to use it."

"Xavier! *¡Vamos a jugar!*" Felipe ran to grab his brother's hand, pulling him towards the door.

Faith approached Xavier and faced him. "They know what happened to you and why you had to do what you did. I vouched for you. Call it Stockholm syndrome of the blandest kind, but if you are given a chance to change your life, don't throw it away."

Xavier looked away.

"Have I ever let you down?" Faith slanted her head to search his eyes.

He reluctantly shook his head.

"And I never will." She assured him with a smile. "You have a good heart and you're a good person, Xavier. Don't harden yourself to the point that you lose that complctcly."

"Xavier. *¡Por favor!*"

He looked at his younger brother, his mouth quirking to a fond smile as he rolled his eyes. "My brother needs me. Again."

Faith laughed. "I will come back before I go."

"You're leaving?" The alarm was back in his eyes.

"It was never going to be permanent, was it?"

Her mouth lifted slightly to one side. "I have to get back to the medical mission."

He sighed in agreement. "*Hasta mañana*." He gave in to his brother's prodding by allowing himself to be dragged to the game room.

As soon as they left the bungalow, Faith saw Zac stride towards them. She sucked in her breath, her heartbeat becoming a staccato pulse inside her chest. He had changed to low slung denims and a white shirt that hugged his muscled torso. His clean scent of sandalwood and vetiver almost made her swoon. The closer he came, the more her body became aware of his presence. It was as though it knew who its master was with the quivering in her belly and the tingle that moistened her folds. His words caused liquid heat to rush out of her.

"I need you."

Chapter Twenty-One

Zac wanted nothing more than to check on Faith and see if she was all right, but with the turmoil caused by the Ancients being wounded and the need to transport them to safety, he had been kept occupied. Now that the battle was over the thought of the Scatha accosting her made his blood boil.

The Ancients, the rest of the Manchester and Leeds Cynn Cruors and Andrés de Alvaro got into the Eurocopter EC 155. Zac understood from Andrés that Bianca had gone ahead with Faith, Xavier, and Felipe. Once they landed in the Trujillo helipad, they were immediately rushed to the Faesten's hospital. The Eald and Zac worked on removing as much of the silver from the Deoré. With her unconscious, they had no other recourse but to insert a drip into the Eald, who stayed in another bed beside the Deoré's and insert the cannula into the Deoré's carotid artery.

"Zac, wait." The Eald sat upright from the bed.

"My lord, we're wasting time."

"No, we're not. He stood from the bed and walked to the Deoré. "I have silver in my blood. It's part of me. Part of the Kinaré in me. Alaghom is a pure werewolf. What do you think adding more silver into her bloodstream is going to do to her?" The Eald's eyes clouded with distress. "How can I heal her when the very thing she needs is what can kill her?"

Zac stayed his hand, frustration coming out as a huge sigh. Yes, what could happen to the Eald's beloved? Determination pinched his mouth, his eye narrowing at all of the possibilities. Zac could give her more of the serum, but she wouldn't heal as quickly as with her mate's blood. The Eald's life essence was more potent.

Even if there was silver in it.

"Sire, we don't know how it's going to affect her now that the silver from the *Specus Argentum* is inside you. We thought that you would die from the bullet Valerian shot you with. You didn't. The only thing I can give you is hope. Hope that because of how it's affected you, it will do the same to the Deoré."

The Ancient Eald was silent, his hands balled into fists.

"It's your decision, Sire."

Zac watched the emotions flit through the Eald's face and his chest tightened. He didn't want to go through that indecision. To heal or kill the woman he loved.

"We have to at least try," the Eald said quietly. "If she dies then we know I have failed."

"Sire—"

"I made the decision to inject her with my blood, Zac. Not you. It won't be you who failed." The Eald returned to his bed. "Do what you have to do, Cynn Cruor. I hope we all come out of this without regrets."

Zac inserted the tube into the Ancient Eald before gently inserting the other end into the Deoré. He made sure that his patients were comfortable before he left the room.

Aye, my lord. Without regrets.

****

The visiting Cynn Cruors were each given a room in the main house despite their protestations that they could all stay in one room or bungalow. Andrés, coming from a long line of hidalgos who arrived with

Hernan Cortes, wouldn't hear any of it. With a flourish he billeted them in some of the best rooms in the Faesten. They were given time to rest and shower off the vestiges of their cave battle. They would all meet in the Faesten's agora afterwards.

Zac set the bag containing his minilab and his samples on the round table in the centre of his room, his footsteps sounding like bullet spits against the polished mahogany floors. The chamber given to him was in hues of grey and white. It had with a huge canopied bed with filmy grey drapes all of a sudden seeing Faith lying on it.

"Blood hell," he swore. He couldn't get her off his mind.

Zac placed his swords on top of the huge mahogany chest that was converted into an upholstered love seat at the end of the bed. He started to undress as he walked to the bathroom.

The warm shower did wonders to cleanse the dust of battle and the Scatha and the werewolves' remnants from his body, watching the dirty water swirl down the drain. He closed his eyes and said a prayer. Some of those remnants may have belonged to the Cynn Cruors who died. He thought of those they left behind. He thought of the mates who joined their husbands fight that day. He thought of the children who would now be orphans. While the Cynn Cruor zealously guarded, cherished, and protected the Cynn Cruor offspring, whether mortal or immortal, they would not be able to shield them from the pain of losing their parents. It was something Zac couldn't empathize with after having been given away by his mother who refused to have anything to do with him.

He thought of Faith. The mate he refused to take. What if he died in battle? What if she? What if they had children they would leave behind? Would they understand? Or would they be too young to know how their parents lived and gave the ultimate sacrifice? Would they be resentful of the call of duty each and every Cynn Cruor had to adhere and respond to? But if only for one moment, one brief moment of his immortal life that translated into a lifetime for a human, he could experience that indescribable feeling of joining, of loving, or sharing everything, of cherishing one woman fated to be his, he would with her. He wanted to feel what it was like, to experience what Finn, Roarke, and Graeme had found. A sense of security. A sense that despite the battles they still had to fight, things were much better.

As the steam rose from the water, Faith's scent wafted up his nose. The water wasn't taking it away. Her smell was imprinted on his skin. It was just a faint scent, a smell that latched on to him when he tasted her. Thinking of her mound against his mouth, her sweet heat against his fingers and on his tongue sent signals down to his phallic receptor. With a groan he fisted his shaft and squeezed his balls, bracing his legs apart as he did so while the monsoon shower heads rained down on him. He imagined Faith's soft kisses against his groin. He looked down at the shiny bulbous head of his cock, pre-cum oozing from the slit. In his mind, he saw Faith taking his shaft in slowly, all the way to the root, sucking him until it reached the back of her throat. His hand slid up and down, pumping harder and faster, the drops from the shower making his sensitive shaft tingle. He concentrated on his head, pumping the sensitive tip, hissing at the pleasure that swirled inside him as he massaged the ridge, adding to the ecstasy building down his spine until his balls tightened to shoot his impending load.

"Faith!" Zac hissed her name as trails of his seed hit his chest and part of the shower wall. He removed his hand from his balls to keep him up while his other hand continued to stroke himself. His black haired spitfire with her luscious curves, delectable pussy, and kissable mouth refused to let go of his mind.

****

By the time Zac arrived in the agora, almost everyone was there.

Unlike the Manchester Faesten's main hall which was a former ballroom, the Trujillo's hall was in a sprawling room with several French windows that were wide open, allowing the cool evening air to circulate. Zac heard the whisper of the leaves in the trees and the tell-tale sign of crickets completing their mating ritual. Several sofas and comfortable leather armchairs faced a huge glass coffee table. They formed a semi-circle, facing a wall where the Trujillo Faesten's crest was displayed. Apart from the wolf and the griffin that were the symbols associated with the Cynn Cruors, the Trujillo's crest had an anchor with a plain ring called an annulet around it. Not only did it symbolize de Alvaro's maritime origins and his descent from knights, it also meant hope and salvation, two attributes the Honduran Cynn Cruors also stood for.

"Where's Colin and Craig?" Zac thanked Andrés for a drink, taking a sip. "Damn this is good! What is it?"

"Vino de Mora." Andrés' mouth quirked in amusement. "I'm glad you like it. It's made of blackberries. Smoother than your scotch, no?"

Zac grinned.

"Scotch is in a league all on its own," Finn piped

in wryly. He raised his glass. "This is wine. Scotch is...scotch."

They all laughed, the tension of the last several hours easing off for the moment.

"Colin and Craig had to leave," Roarke spoke.

"They got word that several children have gone missing and the police have arrested a few people suspected of grooming them for prostitution," Graeme spoke up from the pillar he was leaning on.

"Never ending." Zac shook his head as he looked at the purple red liquid of his drink.

"Indeed."

Everyone stood as the Ancient Eald came into the room. Like the rest of the Cynn Cruors, he had also changed into his regular get-up of khaki coloured trousers, sports shirt, and boat shoes.

"At ease, Cynn Cruor. I'm not too fond of pomp and circumstance. I was once just a plain alchemist before I became your leader. So let's get to work, shall we?"

"How is the Deoré?" Roarke inquired.

"Stable," the Eald replied. "Prognosis, Zac?"

They all looked at him.

"The silver that hit the Deoré isn't the same as the one that was used to shoot Graeme and the Eald. We have taken out as much as we could of the silver in her system."

"Alaghom Na-om has never been hit by silver in her life, knowing how deadly it can be," the Eald interjected.

"However, it's possible that even though she also has the Kinaré inside her, her dominant werewolf DNA may not be able to take it," Zac said quietly.

That news sounded like a death knell. The silence in the room was louder than a cannon's boom, the distant sound of the sea and the rustling of the leaves outside oblivious to the tension inside the room.

"Cynn Cruors, I am not afraid of the Deoré dying. I would know it in my heart if she was. She is strong and has enough latent magick inside her being the Lycan Shaman's daughter. But she has never felt the need to probe the gift she has when what I have is enough for both of us."

"You both used magick to heal me," Graeme spoke, his eyes mirroring his concern.

The Eald nodded. "What she used wasn't even the tip of the iceberg. In fact, she can be more powerful than me."

"Sire, the silver," Finn said. "Roarke said that you would tell all of us."

The Eald placed his hands inside his pockets. He looked searchingly at Graeme's face. "When you were shot you felt extreme pain like no other."

"Aye."

"Zac was already with us en route here when you recovered. How long was it before you left the Faesten's hospital?"

"Two weeks."

Zac's mouth straightened, but he didn't say anything. Now that he had his evidence, he knew that it was part of the process.

"Did you feel weak afterwards knowing that you had silver in your blood stream?" the Eald continued.

Graeme nodded. "It didn't last long."

"Explain."

"Well." Graeme shifted his weight to his other foot. "When I fought Bar du Daegal, I expected to be less agile, not strong enough to do battle as I used to before I was shot. But the more I fought, the stronger I became. Invincible even. I knew there was something changing inside me. When Du Daegal shot me with silver, I thought that was it. That I was finally going to die. Instead, my body absorbed the deadly effects of the bullet and repelled it. It was as though my body developed an internal shield from the silver. It still hurt like hell, though."

"And that, Cynn Cruors, is your answer." The Eald grinned in triumph.

"I still don't understand." Andrés' forehead puckered. Then his face became bewildered, disbelieving. "Are you saying that Graeme is now immune to silver?"

"I was shot with the same kind of silver," the Eald said. "Unlike Graeme, I healed quickly. But if I get shot again? My body will repel it. What did you tell me, Zac?"

"You and Graeme have the silver from the *Specus Argentum* and it has fortified your blood. Except for decapitation, you can never be killed by silver at all."

Chapter Twenty-Two

The implications of what the Ancient Eald and Zac said fell over everyone in a thick blanket. Mouths agape, drinks forgotten, pairs of eyes narrowed in various stages of disbelief, making their expressions comical that Zac had to bite the inside of his mouth to stop from grinning. Hell, that was exactly how he must have looked like had there been a mirror inside his makeshift lab in the cavern.

"De Alvaro, the cavern. Is it secure?" The Eald's voice cut through the shock of Andrés de Alvaro.

"*Si*, safe and secure." Andrés broke from his semi-stupor and ran his hand through his hair. Determination settled on his face. "And all the more so must it be protected now that we know the werewolves and the Scatha know its location. Hector was left behind with a few of the brethren to make sure everything was protected. As of now, they are still looking for all of the ingress and egress into the mountain. They will permanently seal them. We will need your advice, Sire, on the kind of security you wish."

"Mmmm...agreed." The Eald rubbed his chin. "Magick will be needed."

"Does Valerian know how it affects us? How it can affect him?" Roarke queried, his arms crossed over his chest, his eyes narrowed.

"It doesn't appear so," Zac replied. "If he did, he wouldn't have tried to shoot you with it."

"Now that we know you're invincible, Temple, don't get cocky." Finn ribbed.

"In your dreams, Qualtrough." Graeme snorted. "Still hurts getting shot, you know."

Finn chuckled. "Is your mate resting, Zac?"

"I haven't seen her. I—" Zac stopped. Pairs of amused eyes were on him, including the Eald's. "Nice try, Finn." He got the bottle of vino de mora and poured himself another drink. "She isn't mine."

"So we all say," Andrés drawled, joining in the fun.

"Not me." Roarke shifted in his seat as he crossed his ankle over his thigh. "I knew the moment I saw Deanna that she was meant for me."

"No!" the Ancient Eald suddenly roared, his face harsh with pain. A heat wave surrounded him and he was gone.

"Bloody hell!"

"What the—"

"*Hijo de—*"

Oath's followed the Eald's disappearance.

"Not your fault, Hamilton," Zac replied curtly, setting his glass down. "It's the Deoré." He zoomed out of the hall, not waiting for his brethren to follow.

****

The Cynn mortal doctor looked at Zac with sad eyes when he arrived. Zac made his way through the crowd that gathered by the Deoré's door. When he entered, the Ancient Eald was by the side of the Deoré's bed, watching the life slowly ebb away from his beloved. Before Zac could close the door behind him, the Eald spoke.

"Call Hamilton, De Alvaro, Qualtrough, and Temple."

When they were all in the room, the Eald spoke, "I won't be alive for long at the rate the Deoré is doing." He turned to Zac, his torment apparent. "It was my choice."

Zac looked away. The rest waited for him to continue.

"You and De Alvaro have to tell the Council what happened," he told Roarke. "It has to be recorded. Before I go I'm going to choose who takes my place because the Council of Ieldran will need someone higher to break a decision deadlock."

"Your father was brilliant Cynn Cruor tactician, de Alvaro. Hernan Cortes was lucky to have him by his side. He served the Council of Ieldran well and would have continued to stay in the Council had it not been for his demise."

"*Muchas gracias, señor*. It's an honour to hear you say that about my father."

"Roarke, The Hamilton has never left my side and has always been my staunchest supporter eschewing the Council's decision when it wasn't good for our kind. He kicked my arse several times as well." The Eald's attempt at humour fell flat in the midst of the gravity of what the entire Cynn Cruor race was about to face. "He will know how to break the deadlock when the time comes. So I choose him to take over my mantle."

Roarke's eyes widened in shock.

"You will tell the Ieldran of my decision. All of you." He looked at everyone in the room before setting his gaze on his mate. "All of you are my witnesses."

"My lord, this is not the end. If I talk out of turn, then so be it."

"Look at my mate, Hamilton. She's between her human and werewolf form! The silver is too much for her wereblood to take. The Kinaré is weak."

Zac took a step forward but was stopped by the Eald's growl, his eyes beginning to change colour.

"I need to check her, Sire. If I can save her I will do so."

It still didn't stop the Eald's upper lip curl into a snarl.

Carefully, so as not to disturb the Deoré, Zac placed his hand on her skin and gritted his teeth when heat hotter than fire greeted his fingers.

"She's fighting the infection," Zac said. "Her inability to shift means that her body doesn't know how to repel what's inside her." He looked at the Eald, whose eyes were blazing. Zac held his ground. "She's between healing and succumbing. Her fever needs to be taken out of her."

"How do we do that?" Finn asked, his face harsh as though bracing himself from the inevitable.

"Only one person can help her," Zac said.

"Who?" Graeme asked.

Zac turned to his brethren.

"Faith."

****

"Excuse me?" Excitement wasn't exactly supposed to suffuse Faith at Zac's words, but it did. How could he say that in front of Bianca when she just told Bianca that nothing had happened between them?

"I need you. I need your help." The lights from outside the house and the bungalow threw the garden path into its crosshairs. Faith noticed the flicker of desperation in Zac's eyes. She, too, was also exposed to his scrutiny and hardly thought he wouldn't see her blush. But what she wouldn't show him was how disappointment crawled up to her chest at the real reason for him to say those words. She looked down for a moment and took a deep breath.

"What do you want me to do?"

"The Deoré isn't healing. Her fever is trapped inside. I need you to take it out of her."

His requests splashed like cold water over her. So, this was the second time Zac was going to use her, she thought dully. Her disappointment curled into an aching void inside her gut.

What the bloody hell did you expect? You were both thrown together. You pleaded with him the first time, gave in the second time. You enticed him.

Yes, she did, didn't she? Maybe her curse just attracted men she should avoid like the plague.

"Show me where she is." Emotions had no place.

They followed him through the open patio of the ground floor and made their way to the other wing of the house. The warriors, some of whom she saw in the cave nodded to her before they parted like the Red Sea to let her, Zac, and Bianca to pass through.

"This way." Zac opened the door. Three men who dressed differently from Andrés' men nodded at her with slight smiles, as though they were privy to some secret.

Bianca placed her hand over her mouth as she saw the state the Deoré was in. She immediately moved towards Andrés, who flushed her against his side. She touched his face, their gazes lovingly caressing each other while they talked softly. Bianca bowed her head, placing her hand and her cheek on Andre's chest. Faith sucked in a breath when she saw how the Deoré looked. She had never seen anything like it. Part of the Deoré's body was furry, the other half remained human. Her face contorted in pain between wolf and human form, half of her mouth curled in a snarl while she whimpered. Another man watched her, his eyes flicking to her every move. Faith felt danger exude from him but it was as though he was controlling it.

"Faith," he said her name softly.

She swallowed through the dry lump inside her throat. Her hand balled into fists to stop herself from hyperventilating.

"I am the Eald," he said, his charm emanating from his handsome features. He held out his hand. Faith looked at it.

"I will not bite."

She blushed. *Does this man read minds too? Is it any surprise?* She slowly lifted her hand and placed it on his. His hand was warm, soothing. A feeling of peace settled over her.

"Zac said you might be able to help my beloved."

Faith licked her lower lip. "I can..." She cleared her throat. "Try. I can try."

"She's unconscious." Zac's breath by her ear sent sparks down her spine. She inhaled sharply, her hormones waking at Zac's deep voice. She inclined her head towards his mouth and was rewarded with a brief kiss on the shell of her ear, but that was enough to set her heart beating like a congo drum and wetness coat the apex of her thighs. She nodded and gently took the Deoré's hand in hers.

"Oh my God." Something inside her clicked. She threw the blanket covering the Deoré's body away and removed the intravenous line from her wrist, causing the Eald to hiss.

"Stay away!" the Eald roared, about to blast Faith with magick. Zac growled and pushed Faith behind him, his eyes starting to change to colour of battle.

Faith moved forward, ignoring the sounds coming from both immortals. The Eald pulled back in astonishment. Faith knew that he could see the fire in her eyes, but she didn't give a shit.

"If I stay away, she'll die," she retorted. She turned to Zac. "I need to be near the earth. I cannot remove her fever without it." Faith swung her head to face the Eald. "She's burning too much inside and she can implode."

The Eald immediately scooped the Deoré. Andrés and Bianca opened the sliding door leading to the gardens.

"Take her there to that clearing." Faith instructed, pointing to a part of the enclosed garden where a huge patch of earth had been cleared. The Eald breezed ahead. She was about to run when she squealed as Zac lifted her and swept like the wind towards the place, placing her down in less than a few seconds. Briefly she saw that the rest of the Cynn Cruor who had waited outside of the room had filtered through watching them from the sliding doors.

The Eald laid the Deoré down gently. She started breathing hard, as though the air couldn't pass through her throat.

"Eald," she wheezed.

"Whatever I do, don't come near me." Faith held the Eald's gaze with her own, brooking no argument. "I need to be alone with her."

The Eald's jaw clenched, but he nodded.

A sound that was between a human wail and the growl of an injured wolf broke from the Deoré's throat. Faith knew it was pointless to speak to her. The Deoré wouldn't be able to distinguish reality from hallucination. She took the Deoré's wolf limb, hissing at the heat that singed her palm, seeping into her skin and bloodstream. If she didn't have the curse inside her, her hand would have already blistered, but the heat she carried would eventually heal her.

Her other hand clawed at the earth to anchor

herself and allow her curse to take hold of her, feeling the cool soil enter her fingernails and soothe her hand. Faith thought she would die from the intense heat. She felt her blood thicken, become sluggish before it thinned and rushed through her system, causing her to moan and gasp at the onslaught. She gritted her teeth as the fever seemed to wrestle with her blood, waiting for it to take on its role as conduit. Her blood soon recognized something foreign joining it. She felt it pulse through her like red tendrils, her life essence absorbing it and hurriedly transporting it through her veins and out to the ground. She saw the same tendrils enter the soil, burning it, baking it. She felt her forehead pucker, the sweat beading and trickling down her temples.

Just a little bit more, Faith. Say your name. Keep going.

That voice in her mind was her constant companion whenever she healed. The sound soothed her, allowed her to continue.

She heard the Deoré whimper and cry out, but she kept hold off the shifter's arm. The ground below her heated, almost breaking down the soil around her into dust, baking the earth. The soil she gripped solidified, the moisture from the ground changing to wisps of vapour. Faith moved her head from side to side, her eyes remaining closed as she probed the Deoré's body for remnants of the fever. Her mouth thinned, feeling her energy dissipating.

"Almost there..." she muttered.

Finally, she felt the Deoré's fever drop.

Faith opened her eyes, her sight blurry. She blinked several times and looked around. The earth around her and the Deoré was like a miniscule wasteland. She noticed that the Deoré fully returned to her human form. She was looking at Faith with golden orbs of thankfulness.

And respect.

The last thing Faith heard was Zac yelling her name before she fell to the ground.

Chapter Twenty-Three

The Cynn Cruors cheering nearly drowned Zac's shout. He reached Faith before her head touched the shrivelled ground. The Eald scooped the Deoré in a crushing embrace. His mouth found hers and she welcomed it, holding on to him tightly.

"Faith," Zac whispered, closing his eyes. "Come back to me."

There, he said it. He voiced what he felt but was afraid to accept. He spoke words he thought he would never tell anyone, opting to remain alone, afraid to feel rejection again. Seeing Faith take on something that was beyond what any human could bear, take it as her own before spewing it to the ground entailed strength and the courage to be a vessel of healing. It also scared him shitless seeing her glow much brighter than when she healed Felipe. Her skin thinned and he could see how the Deoré's fever run like quick flowing lava through Faith's veins, swirling in protest before it disappeared through her hand on the ground. Zac couldn't even imagine how it felt like. He carried Faith gently in his arms close to his chest. He felt the residual heat of her body. Not just heat.

Fire.

The Cynn Cruors parted so that he could pass, their heads bowed in reverence, relief, and respect, and Zac's heart swelled at the thought of his mate being the reason for it.

Bianca opened the door to Faith's room for Zac before she left, closing the door behind her. He walked to the bed and laid Faith gently atop the bedspread, brushing away the dark tendrils of hair from her face.

She was the most beautiful woman he had ever set his eyes on.

Her dress suited her. Red, like the fire blood inside her. Like the passion he had coaxed out from her. Her hair splayed around her, her skin had regained its natural colour and was translucent. Her soft dusky rose lips parted while she slept, her lashes sweeping down across her cheekbones. She was soft and delicate as she slept, a part of her that she hardly showed the outside world. And the more Zac saw her vulnerability, the more his need to keep her safe strengthened.

He crossed to the open balcony windows, breathing in the tropical night's air. Massaging his neck to relieve some of the tension he looked up. It didn't matter that he saw the moon waxing. He already knew that. His body was starting to feel the pangs of lust that came with the increasing size of the white orb in the sky. Many of the Honduran Cynn Cruor had already left for the town of Trujillo to see who would bed with them willingly. Many would also take a nip of their sex partner's blood to see if they were possible Cynn Cruor mates.

It was their circle of life.

A rap at the door made him pivot to see who it was. The doorknob opened and the Ancient Eald stepped in.

"My lord." Zac turned to face him fully.

"How is she?"

"Still sleeping." Zac returned to the side of the bed. "It happens after she heals someone. The first time I saw her do this was inside the cave. She healed her captor's brother. Somehow, I knew that whatever she has, whatever she calls a curse would heal the Deoré."

The Eald inclined his head in agreement as he

clasped his hands behind his back. He looked at Faith's sleeping form.

"You never told me your mate was a fire binder," he murmured.

"Fire binder?" Zac's eyes narrowed.

"Someone who can generate incredible amounts of heat and make huge balls of fire from within. It's a gift and it's a curse. It can heal as well as kill. For us, blood transports oxygen throughout the body. After all we are part human. It's more for your mate. Faith's blood becomes both the conduit and the vessel for her cleansing fire. Her blood thickens to absorb the illness before her body calls the cleansing. She transfers it to a medium that can take the intense heat of the fire, carrying the illness out of her body."

"That's why she needed to be close to the ground."

"Yes."

"What happens if she can't find a container for the illness?"

"It goes back to its original host, but it's not just that. The fire used as the medium is also taken in by the sick person. That's when the fire binder kills."

A gift and a curse. Zac now understood her burden.

If only she would let him in. If only he was strong enough to go through it. Telling her to come back to him while she was unconscious wasn't necessarily a gauge of his resolve.

Why the hell does something special happen when she's bloody sleeping?

"I sense prevarication, Zac."

He darted a glance at the Eald. "I'd like to say I don't know what you're talking about, Sire, but that would be stupid."

"No." The Eald let loose a soft laugh. "That's

being human."

Zac gave a low gruff noise before he ambled to the balcony. He knew that he was about to get a lecture. The Eald was like Roarke, or should that be the other way around, he thought. In battle, the mantle of leadership sat firmly on their shoulders, but when the dust settled, they were all brethren. He thought that being part of the Ancients' contingent, he would feel uncomfortable. After all, he only saw the Eald from a distance the first time. The second time was when they made a trip to Manchester from Anglesey to assist him with saving Graeme. With what he found out from looking at remnants of the Eald's blood under the microscope, he had every reason to worry. Yet, here he was as comfortable in the Eald's presence as he could be.

The wind stirred behind him before the Eald stood by his side, studying the waters of the Caribbean in the distance, twinkling in the moonlight. Zac inhaled the scent of the profusion of blooms in the night air, a bold sweep of colours in a Cynn Cruor garden that would never surpass the beauty of the woman lying on the bed.

"The first time I met the Deoré, I was in a dark place. I had latent magick in me. I could feel it in my blood. I could feel it stir in my mind. Growing up, I knew I was different and so did my parents. They treated me with a reverence that I did not want. Respect that was meant for the elders and not for a boy of five moons. They believed I was a gift from the gods, much to my brother's chagrin. But they loved me equally as they did my brother. I was younger and I thought that it was normal for older brothers to detest their younger siblings. I saw how this hurt my parents, saw it in their eyes. Yet all they could do was to shower us with their love. We were nomads, moving from one place to the other before the ground broke apart to what it is today. I had a thirst for knowledge, a word that hadn't existed then."

The Eald suddenly chortled.

"My father became so annoyed with all of my prodding because he couldn't answer them, so they allowed me to roam, knowing that I would come back to them. No matter how far I explored, I always found my way back. They were my constant, the two people who loved me without question and I didn't know any better until they died. They were victims of an illness that almost decimated the tribe. I hadn't realized that the respect the tribe accorded to me was borne out of fear of what I could do to them. Something which even I didn't know I could do, which never even crossed my young mind. One night, whoever was left of my tribe including my brother beat me within an inch of my life, leaving me for dead as they continued to travel to the gods know where." He turned to Zac, his eyes hollow. "How could a boy of five survive on his own before the dawn of time?"

Zac watched the Eald sit on one of the chairs that faced the balcony.

"It took several days for another tribe to find me. A woman who had lost her son, took me as her own and helped me heal," the Eald continued. "She was the tribe's wisewoman, and like my parents, she knew I was different." He paused. "But she was different too. I wasn't healing fast enough. I had lost so much blood. Do you know how she cleaned my wounds? She licked them clean, savouring how my blood tasted like. Wherever she licked, the wounds closed. They healed. Her saliva had healing properties and whatever my body had absorbed became part of my blood too. It was all too good to be true until I found out she wanted to heal me only to kill me for my blood later. They also didn't travel during the day, preferring to travel at night. They never aged as long as they had blood. Their teeth were jagged, their incisors more so. They hunted at night, returning with their mouths dripping with blood. Some carried empty animal skins with them and returned with it overflowing with the same fluid. I knew then that my time was running out. The day before I was to be sacrificed, I killed the woman who saved me, slitting her throat to drink her blood to fortify my own. Vampires."

Zac plopped down on the other chair. "But you can walk in the sunlight, just like me."

"Not too much like you Zac." The Eald's mouth curled to one side without humour, then snorted. "You can take the sun's beating. I can't. I must have drank too much of her blood that when the sun is basking the earth, I will burn."

Zac bit the inside of his cheek. The veritable Ancient Eald, snorting? This was something he'd tell the Cynn Cruors. Correction, not Roarke. Just Graeme, Finn, and Blake. Thinking of Blake Strachan, another Cynn Cruor who left Manchester, brought a dull ache in his chest. Blake had just left without any explanation. When Zac saw him visit Graeme, he believed in his heart that Blake would stay, but he had left. The young Cynn Cruor who had been so full of life was starting to become a husk of who he was, and Zac believed without a doubt that it had something to do with the Cruor wars.

"Go on, Sire."

"The enhanced blood that I had in my veins allowed me to travel faster, like the wind." The Eald's eyes glazed over at the memory. "I covered my tracks, making sure that I left traces of my blood in so many directions to make them run in circles."

"How did you do that?"

"Magick." The Eald shrugged.

"Figures." Zac's mouth lifted in a lopsided grin.

"Eventually, they gave up and I was free, but I was lonely. I missed the warmth I had with my parents and for a time I even missed the vampire who cared for me. I thought that if I affiliated myself with a tribe and used my gift in exchange for companionship I would be all right. That was the first time I came across a tribe of fire binders too. But tribes were always suspicious of outsiders. That started my descent to hell. The constant beatings and treatment as though I was lesser than an animal spurred a hatred for others I never thought I had inside me. I plotted my vengeance by learning. Constantly and voraciously learning until I could strike it on my own. I was losing my humanity."

The Eald took a deep breath, exhaling slowly. "Knowledge was my companion. Trustworthy, unfailing. It would never betray me. I became attached to things—no, concepts, abstracts that wouldn't have a chance to hurt me because they were intangible. I brushed away every good memory as immaterial, every way of revenge as absolute. It became the reason for my existence. Because I was different, whatever smidgen of altruism shown my way that could have come from the gods as a balm for the pain the world caused me became an aberration in my eyes. Without my parents, I made myself believe that I was not a person anyone could love and accept. Until Alaghom Na-Om."

The Eald's eyes softened. Zac sucked in a sharp breath before leaning forward, his arms resting on his thighs as he clasped his hands together.

"What do you know?" Zac kept his head down, feeling the flush rise to his face.

"I don't know anything other than what you show me, Zachary, and I see your pain. I see your indecision. I see your fear of rejection."

Zac gave an imperceptible nod.

"The opinion of others shouldn't hold you back to find your own happiness. You're letting them win if you do. Even after they have already left this mortal plane."

"And you say that you don't know anything." Zac swung his head slowly towards the sea as the Eald stood.

"Never said I didn't have my omniscient moments either." His progenitor winked before walking towards the door. "Alaghom Na-Om and I will thank your mate after you're done with what you have to do."

"What's that?" Zac shot over his shoulder.

"You'll know."

The door softly clicked with finality.

****

Zac remained by the balcony long after the Eald left. What his liege lord said smarted. It was an alien thing to feel more than lust for a woman or extreme fondness for others. He had built a buffer around his heart for hundreds of years so that no pain would scar the muscle beating inside him ever again. Was he a coward? Probably. Then again, not everyone was immortal and that was a bloody long time. He had always been satisfied with the Cynn Cruors' camaraderie and brotherhood. It had been enough.

Until he stumbled on a clearing and sensed the woman he knew could make him whole.

Who would have thought he'd find his mate in the middle of a battle? After making Faith believe that he had used her, would he have a chance at convincing her he wanted her? Because that was the unvarnished truth. He craved her unlike anything he wanted in his life. He wanted her in his arms, holding her, embracing her, and to never let her go. Didn't she know that she had him wrapped around her like glue and he would do anything for her? He knew he had treated her shabbily. She called him a man whore, told him not to touch her again. That had sliced through him worse than the slice of a sword with silver. But her body knew otherwise, knowing that his touch could ignite a different kind of fire inside her that could take them up to stratospheric ecstasy.

A different cleansing fire he hoped would heal his wounded and weary heart.

He walked to the light switch to bathe the room in darkness and returned to the balcony. The moon's gentle rays shone through the open doors to cover Faith's body with its mantle.

Tomorrow would tell him if he still had a chance to be purified by Faith's fire.

Chapter Twenty-Four

Faith's hand automatically swiped at something tickling her nose. Her eyes moved beneath her lids, waking her up from slumber. Strands of her hair played peek-a-boo as she inhaled and exhaled. She brought her hand to her face to remove the offending strands, lifting herself on her elbows. Dawn was waking like she was basking the Honduran sky in blush pink over thick mountain foliage, edging the now pastel purplish hue of the night higher so that the sun could eventually take centre stage. Sighing, Faith lay down again, snuggling back into the covers, her hands underneath her cheek.

Then her eyes snapped open as memories of what happened the night before jumped in front of her mind's eye. She was still wearing her dress and the bed spread had grains of soil stuck to the fabric. Her forehead knitted while she brushed the dirt off the bed. Who carried her back to the room? Wait! The Deoré? How was she?

Faith climbed out of bed and rushed to the bathroom, quickly doing her ablutions. She looked at herself in the mirror more intent on raking her fingers through the tangled mass of her hair. She returned to the room looking up, and brought her hand to her mouth to stifle a scream.

"Zac! What the hell are you doing here?" Her initial fright gave way to annoyance, her heartbeat thumping erratically from fear to a gradual thrill knowing the man who could leave her breathless and wanting all the time was in the room.

"I wanted to make sure you were okay after what

you did for the Deoré, for the Cynn Cruors."

She licked her suddenly dry bottom lip, her body thrumming in response at Zac's low growl.

"As you can see, no harm done, I was about to go and find out how she was." She cracked a small smile. She pivoted to open the bedside lamp, anything to distract her from the way Zac was watching her, the willing prey. His green gaze was enough to put her hormones on overdrive.

"At this time? She'll still be asleep." He smiled. "All Cynn Cruors, except for Bianca and the warriors' human mates will be in their rooms. They'll be staying away from the windows when the sun reaches its zenith. It isn't exactly forgiving in this place."

Faith sat on the bed. "I still can't believe it. This is still so surreal, but I'm living it." She shook her head. "Yet I'm no different. Bianca told me the Cynn Cruors were part vampire. And the Deoré is a werewolf. If I hadn't seen it with my own eyes..."

"She also has the Kinaré in her but her were blood is stronger than whatever little protection the gene could offer."

"And you." She faced him. "You're a Cynn Cruor. The sun will soon rise. You better go."

"The sun doesn't affect me. I don't burn even at high noon."

"Why?"

Zac shrugged. "I have a recessive gene that allows me to walk like any human, day or night."

"I see." She nodded. "I'm sure you'd like to rest."

"I don't need too much sleep."

"Then be where you have to be."

"I already am."

Oh shit. Zac delivered that one line with a low sexy voice that would make molasses come out of the sugarcane. His eyes had those gold inflections that glowed against its hunter green colour. Hunter. Yes, it was such an apt description. He was the hunter, she the hunted. The predator and the prey.

A very willing prey.

Zac stood, his every step a direct line to increasing the sound and tempo of her heart.

"We didn't finish what we started," he said softly, cupping her cheek before ghosting his thumb over her lower lip. Faith heated, her spine straightening so that her hardening peaks brushed Zac's chest, causing his gaze to flare with the same heat simmering inside her. "I pushed you away and I hurt you."

"Reading minds now, are we?" she spoke on a sigh. It was her attempt at a quip, not a sexy whisper, but she couldn't help it. She was so attuned to the heat emanating from Zac's body, at the possessive way his other arm snaked around her waist to bring her flush against him. She was aware of his scent that sent her pulse running, whetting her carnal appetite that her mouth watered. God! What she wouldn't do to give him head.

"I do a lot more, Faith." He leaned into her, the stubble on his jaw against her cheek making her shiver with suppressed delight that coated her thong, as he whispered in her hear. "I want to show you more." He nipped at her earlobe, causing Faith to gasp before he sucked and licked the sting away. Faith moved her hips against his hard on, her eyes closing. Her lips parted, her hands slowly travelling up his biceps to encircle his neck.

The nip zinged and made a bee line to the south, causing a gentle swell of pleasure between her folds. Both a moan and sigh escaped her lips when Zac's mouth ghosted along her jaw to the column of her throat to lick at the hollow between her neck and collarbone. She leaned her head to one side, giving Zac more access and gripped the back of his head when he sucked. Her forehead furrowed at the slight pain, but it only elicited more heat to flood from her core.

"Damn, I liked that," she murmured. "More."

She felt Zac's mouth curve to a grin before taking her lips in his. A sweet chaste kiss that nipped, licked at the seam. A gradual burning kiss that made her slant her mouth against his to deepen the ache she knew could only be fulfilled with him inside her. A hungry kiss that made his tongue break through the barrier so that it could mate with hers. Swiping, teasing, demanding, Zac's torrid possession consumed her. Their hands greedily tore at each other's clothes. He growled before immediately taking a hardened nipple into his mouth while cupping and playing with her other breast, pinching her tit.

"Yes!" The roughness of his possession only fanned the flames inside her. Faith could feel the heat building, a different kind of heat that she welcomed. A fire that could bring pleasurable death. The mixture of pleasure and pain caused her core to throb and ache inside. Her heart thundered as erotic waves threatened to bring her under. Zac's hand grazed her mound, parting her thong to plunge two fingers inside her while his thumb played with her clit. She cried out, then watched Zac's mouth and tongue devour her nipples, her hips seductively moving against his fingers while he toyed with her centre, her essence coating his hand. Ripples of desire ascended to suffuse her body.

"I like how wet your pussy is, Faith," Zac rasped when he lifted his head to look at her, never letting up with petting her. "Wet, wild, all mine. I could dine on you over and over again. To hell with food. I'm going to eat you and make you cum so hard you'll forget yourself."

He didn't wait for Faith to acquiesce. She didn't need to because she was already putty in his hands. Zac tore the flimsy barricade and knelt, taking one leg to put over his shoulder and dove in, gently lapping her cream and taking her entirety in his mouth. A strangled cry escaped her mouth as she threw her head back again, her hands holding on to Zac's hair, pulling to her mound, to slowly hump his mouth. He sucked at her outer and inner folds, speared her bundle of nerves and flicked it rapidly to bring her to the edge of her release, only to stop when she was about to fly. He tongued her, laved her with his flat tongue from her hole to her clit and back again before stopping. She growled in frustration and looked down, but her heart and insides trembled at the way Zac's eyes glowed, the gold nearly dominating the green. Zac widened her opening with his thumbs, his face glistening in the lamplight. His tongue licked her cream from his lips before he returned to her opening to put his tongue inside. Faith's knees buckled at the onslaught, her vaginal walls clenching while whimpers upon cries tumbled out of her throat. She crumpled on the bed, unable to remain standing. Zac continued without let-up, his possessive growl vibrating against her quim and radiating through her body. Faith writhed underneath his expert mouth, panting at the way Zac swirled his tongue inside her opening, thrusting in and out.

"Oh God, I'm coming...more! Please!"

Zac took out his tongue to insert two fingers inside her, hooking them and flicking them inside before he latched his mouth on her clit. The combination of fingers and tongue flicking her clit from side to side brought Faith's climax crashing through her in a scream. Her back arched, her head dipped against the bed, and her hips bucked against Zac's mouth as curls of bliss beckoned her to lose herself. Before she came down from her climax, she felt the tip of Zac's arousal nudging her entrance.

"I can't wait, Faith," he rasped. "I should have taken you in the pool."

"Take me now." Her voice was breathy, putting sucking kisses against Zac's throat, his chest, and his nipples. "Don't hold back." Never in her life had she pleaded to be thoroughly claimed. God! She was delirious with need.

Zac didn't give her time to get used to his size and Faith didn't mind. He tipped her chin to claim her mouth with a kiss of possession at the same time he thrust into her. Both their mouths parted, their eyes locked, their breaths mixing in a cloud of hunger. His tongue slaked against hers, giving her an erotic taste of herself. The desire and ache inside her called strongly for her to be taken, and as her inner muscles stretched to accommodate him, rapture rippled through her from her core. She held on to his taut buttocks as she lifted her legs to hook them against his arms.

"Oh dear God, that feels so good," she whimpered against his mouth, feeling her pussy flood with more liquid heat. Her mouth opened in a silent scream of bliss when Zac sat himself to the hilt and he sucked in his breath when Faith's inner walls fluttered around him. She finally got what she wanted. Zac inside her. The thought made her heart swell and for some reason she felt as though she had come home. She bucked underneath him. She could feel the tide cresting. Her body was screaming for her to give in and she knew that if she did, Zac would follow.

"Not yet, Faith." His breathing was harsh. "Don't make me come yet. Fuck, you're so hot and wet." Zac licked her mouth and she angled her head to catch him, but he evaded her. He chuckled at her growl of frustration.

"Dammit, Zac." She clamped around him and grinned when he hissed. "Now we're even."

"I don't think so." He withdrew and thrust deep, causing her to suck in her breath. He withdrew again.

"Harder," she said softly, basking in the heat of his eyes.

"It's the waxing moon, Faith," he spoke as he continued pistoning in and out of her. "Soon it will be full. You know what that means?"

Faith moaned.

"It means that we fuck hard. And when we fuck hard, we fuck more than good." Zac nipped at her shoulder before moving to her neck to suck at the pulse beating there. "I will fuck you so hard that no other man, mortal or immortal can compare. Your pussy is mine. You are mine. No. One. Else's. Say it."

"Yes...yours," she cried. "Always yours."

More moisture flooded her, bathing them both as Zac gave her what she wanted. Something inside her mind wanted to explode and cascade around them.

"Yes, Zac! More. Rock me now."

Zac captured her mouth in a hard kiss, his tongue possessing hers as he plunged in and out of her, increasing the tempo. The burgeoning desire ran uncontrollably through her bloodstream, making her wrench her mouth away from his to focus on how his length pleasured her, hitting her sensitive nerves, angling his entry to rub against her nub.

Suddenly Zac raised himself and lifted her legs, bending them against his chest before leaning back down.

"Oh God!" She was wide open, her juice flowing and bathing Zac's cock with her lust. She grabbed on to the covers, her hands fisting the material while her pleasure built. The friction of their joining sped up. His balls slapped against her upturned derriere. Faster, unbelievably faster. Skin against skin slapped, moans tore from their lips over and over again.

The fire inside her glowed. Faith could see it in her mind's eye. It heated and enveloped them, intensifying their carnal hunger.

"Ancients! We're burning up," Zac uttered. "I like it." He fed the pleasure, quivering from her core. "Bloody hell, Faith, I love the way your quim sucks me."

Faith couldn't hold it any longer, the flame ratcheted her pleasure beyond belief.

"Zac! Oh God! Yessss!" she cried, her eyes closing at the sheer ecstasy rolling through her.

"Ah, Faith! Faith!" Zac came with her name spoken like a prayer. Faith felt him spurt ribbons of warmth inside her, her sex still quivering with tiny orgasms that made it longer for her to come back down. She continued to milk him, causing him to groan as he fell on top of her, her legs falling to the sides of his body. She whimpered when she felt his mouth and tongue on the pulse on her neck, wrapping her arms around him, giving him access to her flesh. Zac remained inside her and she wouldn't have it any other way.

She opened her eyes. Against the back drop of the coming day, a thin opalescent flow surrounded them. She lifted her arm.

"Zac?"

"Hmmm?" He continued to lick her neck, moving

to her collarbone, down to the swell and valley of her breasts. Faith almost forgot what she was going to ask.

"Can you see this? Zac...please...oh...stop...just for a second." She was drowning again.

He sighed and grinned, raising himself on one elbow to look at her arm. His lazy grin disappeared. He inhaled sharply before slowly easing himself out of her, both of them sighing at the loss of connection.

Faith's heart squeezed to the point of aching as she looked at the man who thoroughly shifted her world.

"Are you leaving me again?"

Chapter Twenty-Five

Zac didn't answer. Instead he gave her a hard kiss that removed all doubts of what he wanted to do. He lifted his head and braced himself on one elbow. He kept his eyes locked with hers as his hand slid down to the indention of Faith's waist, moving to her hip and thigh before reversing direction to cup the underside of her breast and brush her nipple with his thumb. He grinned at seeing the areola pucker then harden. Her sigh made his blood stir once more.

"You're a very responsive woman," he murmured. He felt his cock begin to stand, nudging Faith's hip.

"So are you...a responsive man, I mean." Faith's soft laughter hit him hard in the chest. He gathered her in his arms and kissed her, pouring in all that he felt. His tongue didn't allow any barrier to get in his way of her sweetness. He made his way down to swipe his tongue on her breast before taking the hardened nipple into his mouth.

"Oh, Zac..." She sighed, sliding her hand up and down his arm. "I like what you're doing to me but please, look at this."

Reluctantly, he let go, Faith's nipple popping out of his mouth. He moved away from her to scoot back towards the headboard before opening his arms so that Faith could lie beside him. God, she felt good in his arms, the way she placed her head on his shoulder while her hair covered the pillow like black silk. Warmth from a deeper emotion imbued him in the way she placed her arm over his body to lightly brush her fingers against his skin. It was in the way she laid her leg over his thigh in total abandon, her sex exposed to him if he wanted to have her again. She was perfection.

His perfection.

"I will tell you what that is but before that I want to know what has Bianca told you?" His fingers trailed down her back.

"A lot and still can't get around all of it." She sighed, her breath tickling the hair on his chest.

"But she hasn't told you how mates are chosen."

She looked up. "Uhm...no. She said—"

He grinned at her blush. "What did she say?"

"She said I was your mate," she blurted before hiding her face.

Bloody hell, she was adorable.

"Yes, you are."

Faith looked up, almost hitting his chin. He laughed softly as he evaded being butted.

"How can that be? I didn't even know you before I got kidnapped."

Zac expelled a deep breath as he looked up at the ceiling. "I can't answer you how. All I know is that even before I touched you, even before I tasted your blood, I knew you were mine."

Faith stiffened.

So did he.

"Is that bad?" He looked down at her head. Wouldn't it be ironic to realize that when he was opening up she would reject him? Uncertainty plagued him like the dry rustling of dead leaves.

"No, Zac. It's not bad at all," Faith replied so softly that no human would have heard her.

A sensation originating from his spine to travel to his belly and expand to his chest was something he hadn't felt before. It settled in his bones and it felt so right.

Peace.

"So where does this come from?"

"It comes from when we have sex." Zac watched the opalescent glow hover less than a millimetre over their entwined bodies.

"I don't follow."

"In a nutshell, there are three stages that a Cynn Cruor and a potential mate go through. First is when he stamps his mark on her."

"How?"

"His scent will be with her and only her no matter how many women he beds."

"Oh..."

"Jealous?" He teased.

"Should I be?" She shot back, her voice amused.

"We tend to taste a little of the blood of the woman we are with," Zac answered instead. "Your blood is the first that's ever called to me."

"Ever?"

"Yes."

"How old are you?"

"Over six hundred years."

"Geez, you put a whole new meaning to the word DOM."

"Dominant?"

"No, dirty old man."

Zac barked with laughter before pinning her to the bed. She grinned, but it soon disappeared when he nudged her opening. "I rather like the word dominant."

"Yes you do." Her eyes softened, desire lighting them up. "You did that earlier."

He nudged her legs apart, his shaft's tip covered with her wetness. "Did you like it?"

"Yes."

Several moments later, coming down from their

joint highs, the tropical breeze cooling their heated skins, Faith spoke again.

"The glow around us is thicker, I think."

Zac didn't need to see it to know that it was. His heart was still racing after taking Faith again. A smile formed on his mouth. She liked it rough, for him to ride her hard and the more she urged him on, the longer and thicker he became. When he shot his seed into her, he thought he would pass out. *Petit mort.* Bloody hell, he wouldn't mind that again.

"It is," he said simply.

She chuckled softly.

"What?" He gathered her close to his side.

"It's a good thing I'm on birth control."

"You don't need birth control. I don't shoot blanks either," he quipped.

Faith's tinkling laughter warmed his heart. "Shoot." She started laughing again and Zac's shoulders shook with his own mirth. Ancients! If Faith willingly came to him, telling him she'd gladly be his mate, what a wonderful existence it would be. She could take herself seriously and yet had a joie de vivre he found refreshing.

"Okay, that laughing trip felt good." Her mirth receded, but she still had a smile on her face. "I gather that it's a Cynn Cruor thing not to get women pregnant."

"Not exactly. Children are precious to us and so are our women. It's also a joint decision. Both warrior and his mate decide together if they want to have children or not. Since the Kinaré inside us increases our libido several times over before, during, and a little after the night of the full moon, just imagine if the woman gets pregnant and we have to go to war not knowing if we will ever come back."

"That's a sobering thought."

"It is," he agreed. "The only time a couple can conceive is the night of the full moon."

"Bianca said she was a Cynn mortal."

"There are no female Cynn Cruors."

Faith propped her chin on his chest. "Then how do you differentiate?"

"There are only certain times of the year that a Cynn Cruor and his mate can sire an immortal. The times coincide with the full moons during the equinoxes and solstices. The Ancient Eald has made it so. The mortals are conceived during any other full moon. There is no difference in the way Cynn Cruor mortals or immortals are treated. Only our life span sets us apart."

"And the mate, if she's human?"

"She becomes immortal as long as her warrior lives." Zac played with the strands of Faith's hair. "If he dies so does she and if she goes ahead, he will follow."

"Mate." Faith lay back on the bed, not bothering to cover her breasts. "Wow."

Zac placed his hand on her stomach, stroking her skin before trailing his finger underneath her breast and over to tease her nipple, delighting in the way Faith quivered at his touch. "Even if the woman has been chosen, nothing will happen until she willingly comes to the warrior. We do not force them to stay with us. I can't force you to stay with me."

Faith's cheeks bloomed as a ghost of a smile settled on her mouth.

"Have you come across any warrior who had a mate reject him?"

"The women always see our side in the end."

"Zac, come on, I'm serious." But the sides of

Faith's mouth lifted.

He sobered. "If she refuses, then the immortal has to live a life alone. He won't take anyone else as his."

"No pressure then," she quipped. "And the third?"

"Blood exchange when they come together."

"We didn't do that." Her gaze caressed his face.

"No we didn't," he agreed. "Only when you decide that it is so, it will be so." Zac kissed her hair. A different anxiety pulled at him. For the first time in his more than six hundred years of existence, he wasn't looking forward to another six hundred years of emptiness. He wanted someone by his side.

He wanted Faith.

He wasn't deluded to thinking that what he was feeling was love. Or was it? He wouldn't know because he didn't know what love was anymore. It was all lust for him. Roarke, Finn, and Graeme found that elusive emotion that became personified in the women they chose, smitten from the very start.

So were you, his mind taunted.

Zac inhaled deeply.

"I can hear you thinking," Faith suddenly spoke, looking at him beside her.

"Really? What do you hear?"

"It's all jumbled up," she jested.

"Ahh, Faith." He cradled her body to his side, holding her as though he never wanted to let go. "There are still so many loose ends."

"Yes, there are." She sighed. "I need to get back to La Nahuaterique to check on the medical mission."

Zac thought he had been punched in the gut. Was his old wish coming true? Would fate let him live a life alone as he wanted before this incredible woman by his side came into his life? His mouth thinned. He'd be damned if he gave up so easily when he'd spent his entire adult life not giving the Scatha even a smidgen of an inch.

"I'll take you to La Nahuaterique."

"You will?"

"Faith, you're my mate. Before that you were kidnapped. I'm not taking any chances of you being kidnapped again," Zac said firmly. "The Cynn Cruors know about you. We will forever be in your debt for saving the Deoré's life. The least we can do is protect you."

"But the war...the man who killed El Jefe..."

"We're meeting again later at dusk to continue where we left off before the Reaper tried to take the Deoré." His mouth curled to one side. "Did you know you were a fire binder?"

"Fire binder?" Faith's eyes mirrored her surprise before she frowned. "That's the first time I've heard of that."

"The Ancient Eald came over last night to see how you were. He said you had a rare gift."

Faith laid her cheek on his chest again. "It can't be a gift, Zac. Two years ago, I killed a child using what you call a gift. Yesterday I killed two Scatha."

"Sorry to hear about the child but good on the Scatha."

She leaned away and swatted his arm, scowling. "I'm serious, Zac."

"So am I." He defended, placing his hand on his chest. "Much as I never wanted you to be caught up in the war between our kind, you happened to be in the wrong place at the right time."

"I'm glad someone thinks so." Faith got out of bed and went to the bathroom.

"Faith! Bloody hell," Zac swore softly, chagrin eating him up. He should have been more careful. He understood her abhorrence at killing someone. The guilt of ending someone's life gnawed at him the first time he had to do so. Centuries hardened him to killing to save the human race. Faith didn't have that luxury of time. He had become so used to walking the line between life and death that he gave the same level of dedication to healing someone and killing the Scatha. Faith didn't. Zac lay back on the bed.

Bloody stupid, McBain.

Zac got out of bed and sauntered to the bathroom, hearing the shower running. His eyes narrowed and his cock started to harden at seeing Faith bathing, her body glistening under the soft lights of the bathroom. Her hair lay black and sleek down her back almost down to her waist, the water cascading to her pert bottom. She was oblivious to his presence, but he wasn't, particularly his raging hard on that bounced like a dousing rod after a pool of desire. He entered the shower, encircling Faith's waist from behind. She stiffened for a moment before sighing, relaxing, and leaning back against him. Lust flared inside him when she wiggled her behind, his shaft nestled between her cheeks.

"I'm sorry," he whispered, nipping and licking the skin between her neck and shoulder. "I keep thinking of what you have as a gift. You think of it as a curse. I was tactless to congratulate you for killing the Scatha." His hand skimmed her shape, slowly palming her belly, all the while rubbing himself against her before dipping his finger between her folds to find the spot that drove her wild. His blood roared through his veins, the Kinaré craving her essence. However, this time wasn't about him, what he wanted. It was about Faith, to appease the hurt he caused her.

"Tell me how to make it up to you." He sucked at

her shoulder, eliciting a moan from her that went straight to his cock. "Tell me."

Faith turned. He never thought he could become harder, but he did when he became trapped in her limpid brown pools. Her mouth lifted to one side in a smile that made his heart race and excitement beat a path to his shaft. She tiptoed to take his mouth in a languid kiss, her tongue sweeping inside. Damn! He liked Faith taking the initiative. He could feel some of his lust seep out of his slit. Bloody hell, he didn't think he'd ooze as much as he did because of a kiss. He grabbed her waist to flush her against him, but she stood her ground and stopped her own sweet intrusion. Her mouth ghosted against his jaw to his ear.

"I know how you can make it up." Her tongue twirled against his earlobe the same moment her hand encircled his girth. "Oh, Zac, such soft skin covering a hard, hot cock."

"And it wants inside you." He nipped at her mouth, licking the bite when Faith shuddered. "Is that how I can make it up to you? Because my cock wants the slick walls of your pussy to swallow it."

"No." She sighed.

"No?" He slightly angled away to look at her.

Faith placed her other hand on his chest, the teasing light still in her eyes.

"I like sucking cock. Can I suck you, Zac? You can make it up to me by allowing me to give you head."

Zac thought his balls would explode and he'd come that very second. His jaw clenched as he refused to give in to a climax. If this was how Faith wanted reparation, then by the Ancients he would suffer blue balls only for the moment. He was like a randy teenager about to experience his first blowjob. Her eyes never left his as she knelt in front of him, sliding her hand up and down his member.

"Your eyes are turning gold again." She swiped at the tip, making him shudder before giving his head a noisy kiss.

"Because of you." His harsh breathing drowned his words.

Her mouth curved into a seductive smile before her tongue licked his tip again. Zac hissed at the butterfly strokes.

"Ahhh..." He threw his head back, the water cooling his face and soaking his hair while the heat built below. Faith flicked her tongue against the underside of his dick all the way to the base, swiping against the thick vein pulsing along his erection with her tongue and lips. She continued to pump him, first with one hand, then with both, gently twisting his member while she sucked his glans, before taking his balls into her mouth.

"Ahh, fuck!" Zac braced his hands against the wall, the shower pelting them with soft rain and steam, the heat generated by their bodies adding to the mist. He couldn't stop his lids from lowering to half mast, his lower extremities enjoying Faith's mouth. His legs strained as Faith continued to pamper his sac before her tongue made tiny flicks against the line that divided his sac all the way underneath it.

"Oh fuck, Faith. Where the hell did you learn to do that?" Zac gritted, a breath coming out of him in sheer pleasure.

She popped his balls out of her mouth, pouting while she continued to pump him in earnest. "Shhh, just enjoy me sucking you."

Zac growled and immediately groaned when Faith finally covered his shaft's head with her mouth, the warmth of her sweet cavern almost undoing him. She held on to the base of his shaft, so even if Zac wanted to blow, he couldn't.

He was completely at her mercy.

And he loved every second of it.

Then she let go, her hands gripping his hips now, her head moving back and forth, alternating between quick and slow, the water and her moist mouth lathering and fuelling his climb. Damn, but she really loved it! Zac saw her eyes close, her mouth devouring him, spoiling him. She teased, laved, made her mouth a vacuum that tightened around his shaft in an erotic vice. Then she took him out and just sucked on his head over and over again that the sensitivity her lips gave brought bolts of lust radiating up and down his spine. His butt clenched at the sensations centering on his groin. He twisted her hair around his hand to stop her moving so that he could fuck her mouth. Faith opened her eyes briefly and looked at him and moaned. Zac hissed, feeling her tongue swirling around his arousal as he went in and out. The coil of his release tightened inside him, firing up his spine, his belly, the inside of his sac. The sounds from the back of Faith's throat reverberated through his cock, edging him closer, taking him higher. Then Faith stopped and took him all the way inside her mouth until Zac felt the back of her throat. His tip touching flesh broke the dam and he roared his climax as his seed jerked out of him into Faith's throat in streams. He couldn't think. He thought he'd died when his heart palpitated. White light flashed before his eyes as he continuously came undone, joyously falling into the heat of Faith's fire.

Chapter Twenty-Six

Zac moved stealthily through the house. French doors that were flung wide open the night before were closed shut to keep the glare of the sun away. He peered through the flowing drapes. Cynn mortals patrolled the grounds while their immortal brothers slept. He opened one of the doors and the moment the Honduran mortals saw him, they gave him a wave before continuing their patrol. News had already spread that he was a rare Cynn Cruor immortal who could walk in the sun. The rest of the Cynn Cruors had been surprised at first but easily accepted Zac's uniqueness.

He made his way to the brothers' bungalow because for all of what Xavier had done, this was their chance to move away and build a new life. The Cynn Cruor would take good care of them. Humans who desperately needed a way out to make things better. Humans who were continuously put down by their fellow humans just because they didn't come from the correct social stratum. It infuriated Zac and the Cynn Cruors to no end. Still, it was the same human genome in his blood that tempered his bloodlust. It was the genome that allowed them to feel altruism, allowed them to appreciate humanity.

"Zac."

He pivoted slowly to see the Eald outside the Deoré's hospital room shielding himself away from direct sunlight. Zac changed course, greeting his liege lord with a curt nod.

"The Deoré?"

"Is much better than I've ever felt in my life." The

Deoré emerged from her room wearing a skirt and blouse not dissimilar to what Bianca wore the night before. She looked healthy, the fever having left her. Her eyes were shining and her Cleopatra smile made Zac's heart stutter.

The Eald chuckled. "Happens every time."

Zac bowed his head, a flush creeping up his neck. The Deoré's beauty was timeless, but she didn't hold a candle to Faith, who had his heart, mind, and soul.

"How is she?" the Deoré asked.

"Asleep, my lady."

"You must have tired her." Her eyes twinkled.

"No more perhaps than the Eald tiring you," Zac quipped. "You're positively glowing."

The Deoré laughed. "Touché."

Zac grinned before sobering. "Faith wants to return to La Nahuaterique. I'm going with her."

The Eald nodded. "De Alvaro will send Cynn mortals with you. It's unlikely that he wouldn't as we are his guests. When?"

"As soon as possible," Zac replied. "She wants to find out what has happened to the medical mission she was with. It's been five days since she was last seen. She doesn't want them to fear that she's dead."

"Let's check with Hector. I understand that they also scoured La Nahuaterique for stragglers." The Eald turned to walk through the hospital room with the Deoré and Zac following. "He's in the nerve centre checking on the Scatha's whereabouts."

They moved through the ground floor corridor of the mansion before the Eald led them down the stairwell to the nerve centre located in the old cellar. The lower they went, the cooler it became. The wide corridor was well lit. Underneath the stairs was a small bar with liquor and coffee making appointments. A mahogany top was nailed to the wall and underneath it was a row of high mahogany stools. Two leather couches—one located directly below the stairs and another that sat as a divider from the corridor—completed the setting. Some of the Honduran Cynn Cruors in the café stood when they saw the Ancients, but the Eald gave them leave to relax.

They continued along the corridor to the end where glass doors opened to let them into the nerve centre. The set-up was no different from what the Cynn Cruors had in Manchester. Monitors of close circuit cameras slowly swung from one area to the other, covering the entire Trujillo Cynn Cruor compound. A huge LED screen on the red brick wall was divided into four quadrants that showed intermittent feeds of the rainforest surrounding the *Specus Argentum*.

"I'm glad that Honduras has started setting up security for the cave," the Eald said to no one in particular.

All of the Cynn Cruors, including Hector, turned. Andrés, Roarke, Finn, and Graeme were there as well, nursing mugs of coffee. The aroma of the brew permeated the air.

"Señor, we didn't hear you arrive." Hector grinned with a bow. He swivelled his head to look at the monitors. "It still needs a few more adjustments and it will be good. Several Cynn Cruors and their mates have volunteered to live in the caves."

"Arreglado," the Eald replied. "Thank you. Make sure those who volunteered—"

"Have no children," Hector finished for him. "*Sí, señor*. They don't."

"I made sure of it," Andrés said. "They will be rotated between mortals and immortals."

"Those who died, I want to preside over their ceremony," said the Eald, his eyes sad. "As with any battle, it's difficult to separate the Cruors, but we were never meant to tear apart. The Scatha's ashes will not leave the ground. No amount of magick I call can carry the weight of their abomination. They cannot enter the Cynn Cruors' pantheon." He looked around at the assembled. "I'm sure all of you have seen that after a battle during the ceremony to send our dead to rest in peace."

They all gave a moment of silence before Zac walked towards his brethren.

"No sleep?" he asked, grinning. "You all don't seem worse for wear."

Finn chuckled. "Good thing we stayed here after your mate healed the Deoré. I can't sleep without Eirene beside me."

"I stayed up talking with Deanna on the phone," Roarke remarked before taking a sip of his brew. "At least she knows where we are."

"How's the charity and Deanna's foundation?" Zac crossed his arms over his chest. He remembered the first time he met Eirene, Finn's mate. She and Devon, a solicitor, had established a charity called Kids Come Home. Eirene had stumbled upon Dac Valerian's whereabouts, which brought her to Finn. Roarke's mate, Deanna, created the Haven Foundation for the women she rescued from the Scatha.

"Deanna's busy putting it back together." Roarke replied. "After it was trashed by the Scatha, she made sure that the building she transferred the headquarters to had state of the art security. She will not let the Scatha get to the women ever again."

"With the Cynn Cruors protection, the Scatha will think twice." Graeme added.

"So," Zac smacked Graeme on the side of his shoulder. "You've found your mate. Congratulations. How did you meet?"

"Remember what Eirene said about Graeme meeting his mate by the community bin?" Finn asked, his eyes twinkling in amusement.

"No shit!"

"Not exactly, shite mate," Graeme grumbled good-naturedly. "She parked close to the garage door, and I had her car clamped."

"You're cruel."

Graeme shook his head. "Good thing I did. She led me to my nemesis, Bar du Daegal. He was using the name Elliot Hammond."

"How's she connected to him?"

"She's a freelance journalist. She uncovered du Daegal/Hammond's human trafficking ring. Now that Hammond's dead, she's been helping both Eirene and Deanna with locating the missing women and children. It seems to have blended nicely," Graeme spoke. "With Kate's connections, they're able to cast a wider net. Henry Heaton is helping out."

"You won't believe what else has been uncovered." Finn spoke.

"What?"

"There is a female Cynn Cruor."

"No way. That's impossible!" Zac's eyes widened.

"I'm afraid it is," Roarke spoke quietly. "I'll speak to the Ancients about her. Something must have happened to make her who she is."

"Her name?" Zac was still disbelieving.

"Adara Kerslake."

"There are so many revelations it's doing my head in." Finn's shoulders shook with slight mirth. "The Deoré is a werewolf. There's silver that can stop all silver that can kill us. Adara is a Cynn Cruor immortal. What else will there be?"

Zac looked down and immediately shut down his line of communication. When he looked up, Roarke was eyeing him curiously. At the mention of the private investigator's name, Zac changed the subject. "Any news about Penny?"

They all shook their heads.

"Bloody Hell."

"That's exactly what Devon is feeling," Finn agreed. "It's also frustrating for Eirene because she promised Devon she'd find his daughter. We can talk about that later." Finn placed a hand on his shoulder, squeezing it. "What I want to know is how goes Cupid's latest victim?"

Zac grinned ruefully before he shook his head. "Too early to tell."

"Why?" Graeme asked. "Her scent's all over you, mate."

"But she's not come to me willingly yet. She needs to make up her own mind." Zac brushed his already tousled hair. "I'm going with her to La Nahuaterique. She was with a medical mission when she was kidnapped."

Graeme blew out a breath. "We've got our work cut out for us. Now that we're all together, I'd like to go with you. Dux? That okay?"

"Let's all go." Roarke nodded. "We'll back you up, McBain."

"Do you think you can convince your mate to wait until dusk?" Finn enquired.

"I'll try."

They joined the rest of the Honduran Cynn Cruors and the Ancients.

"The *Specus Argentum* has been secured, right?

There's another pool behind the main one. That's where you can access the cavern." Zac volunteered.

Hector nodded. "Thank you." His eyes held his amazement. "Unbelievable. And from what I've seen this is something the Scatha can't have."

"And they won't," Andrés said.

"Any trace of Valerian?" Graeme asked as he walked towards the monitors.

"None."

"Bloody hell." Graeme bowed his head in frustration, his hands on his hips. "How could he escape?"

"There's an underwater current close to where the silver cavern is, Graeme," Zac replied, his arms loose across his chest. "He could have been siphoned into one of the crevices underneath. As a Scatha, he won't have the buoyancy we have. He's likely to drown."

"Then why can't we find the body?" Graeme spun, his face darkening.

"Ease up, Temple." Roarke admonished. "It's not your fault."

"It's no one's fault, Cynn Cruor." The Eald interjected before Graeme could reply. "We are at war. We win. We lose. The Deoré only broke his neck. He wasn't beheaded."

"The war isn't over yet." Zac sighed. He faced Andrés. "Faith needs to go to La Nahuaterique. She was with a medical mission before she was kidnapped."

Andrés' face tightened. Zac arched his brow. "Problem?"

Andrés looked at Hector.

"Is there anything I should know?" Zac frowned and placed his hands on his hips, his legs braced apart.

****

Dac blinked, his body seized. He couldn't see. He blinked several times and still couldn't make out the shapes, but he could hear voices whispering. He could feel the soft undulation of the waters underneath him.

By the gods, how he hated water!

"You're awake." Kamaria's voice sounded disembodied.

Silence.

"Can you hear me, Valerian?"

He nodded, the pain shooting up his skull. What the hell was wrong with him? He should like this pain he was feeling, but he wasn't.

"It looks like I've saved your sorry arse again."

"And you enjoy reminding me of it." He blinked again, his head following the direction of the voice. His heart raced to almost three beats a second. He swallowed the rising panic compressing his gut.

Kamaria chuckled. "You owe me big time, Dac. You could have drowned completely in the three inches of water I found you in, could have chopped your head off and end this conflict."

Bloody hell, the pounding in his head was getting worse, like a hangover a hundred times its normal effect. *Why am I thinking of hangovers when the Cruors never get drunk? You've been through hell and back, Dacronius.* The shapes were clearing, sharpening. His sight returned but not as much as he wanted it to. Dac didn't care that he released a huge sigh of relief in front of the woman fixated on any sign of weakness from him.

This wasn't good.

"Why didn't you?" he asked through clenched teeth.

"Because I need you."

The bark of laughter that should have come out of his throat became a stifled groan. "I'm useless, Kamaria. You should've killed me."

"Wow," she breathed. "I don't believe what I'm hearing. What did you do to the notorious Dac Valerian? Are you his doppelganger?"

"Shut the fuck up."

"Okay. He's there somewhere then. Licking his wounds." There was a rustle of cloth from someone walking, then the swish of air as a door opened. "I'll leave you to your pity party. You'll probably feel better once you barf all of that water inside your miserable lungs."

Dac didn't have to wait for the door to close before he attempted to empty the contents of his stomach into the bucket he just knew was there.

Kamaria smiled. Euphoria built inside her that she thought it distended her stomach, but when she looked down her belly was as flat as ever. At long last, Alaghom Na-Om would soon die or if not had already dead. No werewolf survived silver running virally through their veins. Her niece would soon disintegrate, her internal organs atrophying before they shut down, hardened, and turned to dust. Her only regret was that she didn't get the chance to eat Alaghom's heart. That would have made the magick she absorbed from her cousin complete. She should have thought of the silver bullet. No point in dredging magick that could kill her.

Silver. Kamaria's triumphant smile faltered, replaced by the thinning of her lips and the low growl from her throat. One of her men who passed her immediately whimpered at the sound, his head bowed low, his legs bowing out from underneath him. He remained in that uncomfortable position until Kamaria disappeared around the corner. He suddenly fell on all fours and with a hurried swing of his head loped away as quickly as he could.

She entered her state room. It was heavily brocaded in deep burgundy and gold to the point of stifling, just how she wanted it, thick, warm, cloying. A huge circular bed dominated the chamber, big enough for a number of her werewolves to pleasure her. For just one moment, they could dominate her, take her in every way possible. The werewolf who made her scream her release the loudest was gifted with a miniscule amount of the magick that flowed through Kamaria's veins. A taste of heaven, of power, of invincibility. It only lasted for a moment, giving the werewolf such a high that he had no choice but to lie down either on the bed or on the floor as Kamaria took him in her mouth. To pleasure and be pleasured. A cycle Kamaria was happy with.

But sex wasn't on her mind at that moment. It was the baneful metal that caused this current battle to erupt. With Dac falling into the pool and the Scatha rudderless, she took the reins of leadership and told everyone to retreat, costing her the loss of the silver high ground. She had to plan. She needed that silver to cement her rule, not only over her pack but over the entire Lycan race. It was like having the only nuclear bomb in the world. Everyone would have fallen at her feet under the threat of being shot through with that special silver. She'd had her experience with being wounded by silver and she'd thought she would die, but the magick she had inside her had staved off the worst of the effects, allowing her to survive.

She sat on the thickly upholstered burgundy chaise lounge, looking out of the open deck. She lifted her nose, inhaling the scent of the sea in the breeze. She extended her tongue. Salt. It wasn't too salty because it wasn't refined. It tasted just right. Her ears perked. Somewhere in her yacht, her werewolves rode the females enamoured by the men's bodies, pleasured by their long tongues and shafts, little knowing that in the rare occasion that they got pregnant, Kamaria would know. She took the children, killed the mothers and raised the offspring as her own, adding to the Lycan race.

If she was going to attack the cave she would need to call in markers to ask the packs for their strongest werewolves. Unlike Valerian, Kamaria didn't delude herself that she could take on the entire Cynn Cruor. Grudgingly, she admitted to herself that she would need to share leadership of the Lycans. Temporarily. No one knew she had magick in her, making sure to keep it to herself. When the Cynn Cruors in the Honduras had been dispatched, it would take a few days to send in reinforcements. That was enough time for her to wrestle the Silver Cavern from them. With Alaghom gone and the Sorcerer wallowing in grief, he would be incapable of leading them.

Yes. Kamaria's mind churned as a plan formed. Her mouth watered at the taste of victory that would finally be hers.

She closed her eyes, her head falling on the pillows behind her. In her mind's eye, she saw herself over the body of the Sorcerer who defiled her niece, his heart in her hand, envisioning herself sucking the magick out of it.

Chapter Twenty-Seven

Faith woke to find Zac gone, but his scent lingered on the sheets. After their torrid shower, they continued where they left off back in the bedroom. Zac continued to love her in every way until she was hoarse from the number of orgasms he gave her. Through her lust glazed eyes, she saw how the opalescent glow thickened around them. The more she and Zac came together the denser the glow became, wrapping both their bodies in some sort of cocoon. She also felt something else. Her gums started to itch. She was astride Zac, rocking against him when her tongue licked at her teeth and felt her incisors had sharpened. The more she licked the stronger her pleasure became. She leaned forward and started to lick Zac's chest, whimpering as Zac bucked his hips hard and fast as he thrust into her. Something primal inside her told her to bite into Zac's chest in that spot by the side of his heart.

She didn't do so.

Because she was afraid. Afraid that it was too good to be true. Afraid that if she gave herself completely to him, he would break whatever was left of her heart. Afraid because she knew deep down that she was falling for him.

Her uncertainty had disappeared when she felt the familiar ripples of an orgasm coming and when she pushed over the cliff with Zac joining her a split second later, she gave into the onslaught of pleasure before she succumbed to a much needed slumber.

She groaned as she stretched. God, she was sore and wouldn't have it any other way. A blush stole up her cheeks, and her mouth lifted to a wide smile before she curled and hid her face in a pillow, squealing and laughing. She turned towards the balcony and judging from the sun, it was nearing the afternoon. She sighed before sitting up and climbing out of the bed. She needed to get to La Nahuaterique and connect with her mission team. She still didn't know how she was going to stay with the team and with Zac. She had no intention of pulling him away from his own duty and neither did she want to abandon her raison d'etre for coming to La Nahuaterique. After all, she was the one who funded the mission coming over to Honduras from her inheritance which she never knew existed. Her face puckered to a frown and she winced. Yes, she would need to take it easy because of Zac, but thinking of him started the excitement to pulse inside her core again.

She had just gotten out of the shower and was drying her body when she heard the door open.

"Faith?"

"In here," she called out. A grin formed on her lips. They were beginning to sound like a couple. The thought made her warm all over as she took out the new set of lace underwear Bianca had generously provided her and was just about to clasp her bra when Zac's hands took over. Faith gasped at his touch before she leaned back, the heat of his knuckles warming her spine. He caressed her arms and shoulders before kissing the sensitive spot behind her ear. Faith shivered, need pulling at her.

"We need to talk," Zac whispered.

Faith turned around to face him. "Are you okay?"

"Yes, I am." He smiled, hooking his arms around her neck to bring her closer for a kiss.

"Why do you look so serious? Is there anything

wrong?" Faith nearly forgot what she was going to ask after that kiss that teased her tongue, sending new lust signals to the apex of her thighs.

"Why don't you dress and I'll take you to the nerve centre." He kissed her forehead.

"Nerve centre?"

Zac kept quiet.

Faith couldn't understand the uneasy feeling in her gut that flicked on her rile switch. There was no rhyme nor reason. Zac wasn't going anywhere, was he? He did say that she was his mate, that he would protect her. He offered to join her back to find her medical team.

The team.

Her heart knocked about her chest as she sucked in a deep breath.

Dear God, don't let the team be in danger.

"What the hell is going on, Zac? Don't hide anything from me. I don't need the damn Cynn Cruor around me when you drop the bomb or whatever the hell you refuse to say."

Zac walked away from her. Quickly donning the new set of jeans and T-shirt left for her, she walked barefoot back to the bedroom.

"Zac, please."

"You don't have to go to La Nahuaterique."

"Why not?" Faith swallowed. Her heartbeat was racing so fast in her temples that she thought she would pass out. "The medical team—"

"Isn't there anymore," Zac said quietly. "They left the day you were kidnapped."

Faith reeled. "Excuse me?"

Zac regarded her. "Andrés dispatched some of his men to find the medical mission so that they could be told you were alive. When the men got there the people in the village said the team had left as soon as they found out you'd disappeared."

So many possible scenarios raced through Faith's mind. However, there was only one possibility why her team had decided to leave.

She sat down on the bed, stunned, not bothering to look at Zac when he sat down beside her. Yet, she wasn't that surprised, was she? She knew that no matter what she did, someone would always botch it up.

Always.

"Is there something you want to tell me?" Zac placed the stress on 'you.'

Faith shook her head. "No, there isn't." She stood up and shoved her feet into a pair of dainty sandals. "I'm going to Xavier and Felipe."

"Faith."

"Please, Zac." She took a deep breath to stop herself from tearing up. "I need some time alone."

She went to Xavier and Felipe. One look at Xavier's face and she realized she couldn't disturb them. The lines of tension and stress on his face had eased. Instead of lines of fatigue that crinkled the sides of his eyes, they creased with the laughter and joy he was sharing with Felipe.

They creased with youth.

"Señorita!" Xavier stood when he saw her.

"I can see you're enjoying."

"*Sí*." His smile lit his face. "I have never had so much fun in my life. Hector also passed by earlier and played with us."

"Good." She grasped his shoulders. "They will take care of both of you, Xavier. They gave me their word."

"As Hector gave me his," he agreed. "I still can't

believe this to be true."

"Believe it." Faith smiled. "They don't take their *palabra de honor* lightly."

"So, are you going already? Is that why you came here?" Xavier's eyes lost their spark.

Faith shook her head. "It appears that I won't need to go back to La Nahuaterique after all."

"Why?" Xavier's eyes rounded.

"It's nothing for you to worry about," she replied, evading his question. "Xavier, I need to ask you something."

"Okay."

"When you kidnapped me, how did you know I was a doctor? Did someone tell you specifically who I was?"

His face scrunched. "El Jefe gave us a picture of you."

"How did he get it?" Faith stared at him in bewilderment.

"*No sé*. My uncle had a lot of contacts. Spies even. He knew his men and my brother needed a doctor, so I guess that's the reason."

Faith didn't ask how they got her picture anymore. There was no point. She tamped down the growing anger that could consume her. She needed to find out what happened before she blew. There must be some explanation.

It was an explanation she knew she would like.

"Is there anything else, *señorita*? Are you still angry with me?"

"Oh, Xavier, of course not! It's something I'll need to look into when I return to England. And I just wanted to see if you were both okay." She darted a glance at Felipe, who was oblivious to her. She gave a shallow smile before bringing her attention to his older brother. "I'm going to Trujillo. I need a break."

"Do you want me to come along?"

Faith shook her head. "I'll be fine. I'll ask Bianca to join me."

****

Faith needed to think and being by the sea would do her good. Instead of taking her to the city, Bianca took her to a private beach which belonged to the Faesten.

"I need to get a few things from town," Bianca said. "I can come back for you in a few hours. Will you be all right?"

"I'll be fine." Faith nodded. "Thank you."

Before Bianca left, she made sure that a meal was prepared for Faith, whose stomach growled in anticipation of getting food inside it. But despite the delicious meal of sopa de caracol or conch soup and fried yojoa fish served with pickled onions, red cabbage, and deep fried sliced plantains, she couldn't eat as much as she wanted to. A few hours later, she was still sitting on the beach facing the Bahia de Trujillo, her arms around her knees. She had been too engrossed to see who had lit the torches, so when she turned to look at the house, flames dotted the property with its light. It didn't detract from the start of a beautiful sunset, something Faith was able to enjoy. She had walked the length of the private beach, her feet gently sloughed by the warm white sand as the waters washed and receded from the shore. The air was filled with the scent of flowers and exotic plants that bloomed around the beach house. Heliconias that looked like birds of paradise blended in profusion with a variety of hibiscus, wild orchids, and ferns, making a natural barricade from prying eyes. The sound of the sea whispering and coasting in the breeze was enough music to make the place a haven from the rest of the world. A place of solitude. But Faith couldn't find solitude in the paradise she was in.

She snorted. Why did her team abandon her just like that? Was it so easy for them to believe that she had succumbed to the rainforest? Why didn't they call the police? Before she left the Faesten, Faith placed a call to her solicitor. He was shocked but elated to know that she was alive. She was told the team had returned saying that she had been killed. How could they have known that when they hadn't even waited to hear what had happened to her? Something was going on, but until she returned to London she wouldn't know what it was. Now that her solicitors knew she was alive, they would stop the process of transferring her fortune and wait until she returned.

She thought of Zac and her chest tightened. She could just throw it all away and be with him, be his mate. She could take that great leap into the unknown with the new found knowledge of a supernatural world that would welcome her, would consider her curse a gift that was rare, to be a healer who was respected and treasured. Didn't her grandmother wish for the same thing before she'd finally decided there was no point in using her gift? With Zac, she had a chance to explore what she had to repress, what she had to use surreptitiously for fear of reprisal from those who refused to understand. All she wanted was to be accepted not shunned because of her ability, to be loved not derided.

A wisp of her hair landed in front of her face. When she swivelled her head to remove it, she saw Zac walking towards her. Her heart raced at seeing his denim clad figure ambling towards her with the confidence of a jaguar, his body hugged sensuously by his dark collared shirt that was open at the throat. And his eyes, those hunter green eyes that looked at her with so much adoration now.

And concern.

Her gaze returned to the sea. She swiped her cheek against the left sleeve of her T-shirt.

Zac sat down beside her and before she knew it, curved his hand around her nape, bringing her mouth to his. Faith closed her eyes, sighing against his lips, opening herself up to him, her barriers already asunder around the man who seemed to be hell bent on capturing her heart in a short span of time. His tongue teased hers, its velvet smoothness exploring the inner recesses of her mouth. Zac gently tipped her back on the sand, his mouth never leaving hers as he nestled his body on top of her between her legs. This wasn't a rough dry hump between them. This was a slow burn, slow sensual moves that reignited the pleasure that lay ready and waiting between her thighs to flush her sex with liquid heat. Faith delighted in the feel of his short hair, waking the sensitive nerves of her palms, his male scent, the hardness of his body pressed against her softness. Her hips bucked against his arousal, one thigh raised against his hip, and she moaned when Zac's erection hit her covered hole, her thong soaked and her sex aching with need. If only Zac felt more than lust for her, maybe she'd consider giving in.

"Are you okay?" he asked as he trailed his tongue against her ear before splaying open mouth kisses against the column of her throat, blazing a path down to the pulse at the base of her neck.

"Now I am." She sighed, bringing his mouth to hers again, taking the initiative to plunder his that he growled.

"If you're as daring as you are in bed, I'm game here on the beach." Zac prodded her jeans clad sex. "My cock wants inside you. Always."

Faith laughed softly, trying to bring the sensual temperature of their tryst down. "Maybe someday but not now."

Zac leaned up and arched an amused brow. "Someday. Are you saying we're going beyond where we are now?" His hand crawled inside her T-shirt to stroke her belly before cupping her breast, his thumb teasing her laced covered nipple. Faith closed her eyes at the trail of electricity his digit caused.

"Yes." She opened her eyes. "We will." She sucked in a deep breath, about to say something, then she stopped.

"Faith."

She looked up at the sky, the stars beginning to appear in the comforting blanket of the dark. "Lie down with me, Zac."

"Come here." He cradled her to his side. "This is where you belong."

Faith sighed, nestling her head on his shoulder, her hand on top of his heart. Her eyes started to mist. Again. She thought she had exhausted her tear ducts earlier, but the warmth and strength emanating from Zac made her feel that someone truly cared for her. Loved her? She didn't know. Lust her? Definitely. Was she warming up to accepting herself as his mate? She wasn't exactly sure. Who knew what the next few days would lead to? Both of them had been thrown into a situation where passions ran high, making them grasp every moment given, to grab every chance of coming together, to make it memorable because of a future marred by uncertainty.

"Don't talk, we'll fuck." His voice rumbled underneath her ear.

She playfully pinched his side, making him jerk chuckling. "You're crude."

"And you like it," he drawled, then his voice changed. "C'mon, Faith. Talk. You need to get whatever is bugging you out in the open." He combed his fingers through her hair. She hummed. Damn, it felt good.

"The medical mission was something I organized at the spur of the moment. She sighed as she began. "I came into a lot of money. My inheritance is from my grandmother, but it wasn't always like that. I didn't know that I had that kind of wealth because I was close to living in penury almost my entire life."

"Why?"

"My grandaunt."

Zac kept quiet.

"My grandmother had invested wisely in stocks and companies that experienced an explosion of profit. She invested in almost anything that would make her money work for her. Until her sister took it all away." Faith left Zac's embrace to lie flat on the sand and look at the stars. "My grandaunt said she was going to invest it in several companies that would bring my grandmother more wealth. See, although my grandmother was wealthy and I was the only grandchild, she didn't spoil me."

"What about your parents?"

"They disowned me."

"What?" Zac braced himself on his elbow, shock tinging his tone. "Why?"

"Because of my curse."

Chapter Twenty-Eight

"Bloody hell." Zac lay back on the sand, his chest heaving as he raked his fingers through his hair. "Where are they now?"

Faith shrugged. "I have no idea."

"Wouldn't your gran know?"

"She would have, but she didn't say. She's dead now. I think she thought it was better that way because she too was what you called a fire binder. She was ostracized for a lot of her life. She never practiced blatantly, but everything I know, I learned from her. She was the one who suggested that I take up medicine so that when I used my curse…"

"Faith." Zac looked at her sternly.

She sighed. "All right. My gift."

"Good."

She shook her head ruefully. "Used my…gift, no one would be the wiser. When that boy died..." She looked out to sea. "There were a lot of complications which also led to the child's death, but he died on my watch. The hospital I worked for made it abundantly clear that they didn't want me working there, so I left. I couldn't find a decent job anywhere. No matter how good the references were, nada. Until a small hospital in north London needed a temporary doctor for their Accident and Emergency department."

Faith sat up.

"I got a phone call from a law firm two years ago. I was scared shitless. I didn't know what it was all about. Were they representing the boy's parents and was I being sued for malpractice? The letter I got didn't say why they wanted to see me. I decided to bite the bullet and go. I worked Accident and Emergency, and I had to rush to the solicitors' office. After the niceties, I thought they were preparing my head for the chopping block. It was the other way around." She looked at the immortal beside her. "In less than an hour, I had become filthy rich. I was twenty-three when my grandmother died. Two years later I received that call from the solicitor. My grandmother had kept a bulk of her wealth in an offshore account and named me her sole beneficiary. I didn't have to work unholy shifts anymore or worry every day if I'd still have a job the next week, but the desire to heal was too ingrained in me. So I set up medical missions. Sometimes I went with the missions, but most of the time I didn't. This time I just had to leave. There was so much drama in my life and I wanted out."

She huffed, her voice tinged with sarcasm. "The problem with having too much money? People pretend to be your friend and use you. For as long as you have the moolah, you're the "it" person of the moment.

"Even after my grandmother's death, her sister insisted that she was owed huge sums of money. Since I now had money at my disposal, I had her investigated and found out that she had embezzled so many people. I didn't bother to sue her anymore. She was living a horrible life without me having to add to it. I did tell her that the moment she contacted me, I was going to throw her in jail."

"And the medical team? I gather that's why you left. You wanted to know why they didn't look for you?"

She hesitated before nodding. "Among other things. I have a strong suspicion that my grandaunt is somehow involved in this. I still don't have any proof, but I'll find it. Before I left London, I made my will. In the event I died, all of my money was going into a fund to support medical missions in dire need of medical help. Now, there's more I want to do. I'm changing my will when I get back. When I saw how Xavier had to belong to an evil group in order to keep his and Felipe's body and soul together, I vowed that I would set up a fund for their education and enough money for them to start a new life somewhere else. I was able to inform my solicitors that I was alive so it's just a matter of setting up the fund for them and deciding where I go from here."

"British common law isn't going to allow anyone to touch your money until after seven years." Zac brushed his hand up and down her spine, making her sigh. "What happens then?"

"It will go to my next of kin."

"Which could be your parents."

"If they're still alive or whoever my relations are, or worse, my grandaunt, unless she kills me, in which case she forfeits any claim."

"Ancients, Faith!" Zac sat up, putting an arm around her shoulders. "I'm so sorry."

"Shit happens." She sighed, shrugging. "That's why we have toilets."

Zac's roar of laughter startled several of the birds that nested in the trees. Their squawks indignantly cut across the peaceful sound of the sea. He turned away from her, curling in mirth.

"Well, I'm glad I made you laugh," she remarked dryly but started giggling herself by watching Zac, the fearless immortal in the cave, the passionate lover in bed, roll around in the sand seemingly without a care in the world. When most of his mirth was over, he stood up before extending his hand to help her stand. His eyes still sparkled with amusement. His smile was the most devastatingly handsome smile Faith had ever set her eyes on.

"Bloody hell, Faith, I'm going to enjoy loving you."

Faith's breath caught in her throat, her heart swelling inside her. She found it hard to swallow through the lump in her throat. Dear God, was Zac going to say the words she wanted to hear? Her breath started coming in short puffs, the excitement swirling in her belly near to unbearable.

"Zac..."

Zac cupped her face in his hands, bracing his feet on the sand. She held on tight to his forearms. "You heard me." His eyes glowed in the firelight from the torches that surrounded them. There was an emotion that Faith saw fleetingly when they came together, but now it was as flagrant as the sunset.

He kissed her forehead.

"I."

He kissed the tip of her nose.

"Am going."

He kissed her right cheek.

"To enjoy."

He kissed her left cheek.

"Loving you."

He placed a gentle kiss on her mouth.

"Because I do." Zac's arm encircled her waist while he cradled her head. "I love you, Faith. I really love you. I have lived almost six hundred years without anyone to call my own. I don't want to spend the next six hundred alone now that I know there's someone in this world for me. I refused to acknowledge it. I refused to let anyone in. I was content with the love and friendship of my brethren until I saw you and the comradeship wasn't enough anymore. I don't want to live the rest of my immortal life without you by my side, Faith. I know it's too soon. Ancients! Roarke, Finn, and Graeme fell for Deanna, Eirene, and Kate in so short a span of time. I couldn't believe it, didn't want to believe it." He chuckled. "Until I got hit too."

"Zac, I—"

"I'm not asking you to say the same thing if you don't feel the same way I do, if the only thing you feel for me is what happens between us in bed, or in the water." Zac's attempt to lighten things fell flat at the fleeting pain that lanced his gaze. "I'm just asking to let me do so. Let me love you the way I know how to."

"Why are you in a rush?" Faith asked softly, her eyes drinking in his features, the uncertainty in those depths that could melt her, could make her blush, could make a wanton. Propriety be damned.

"Because we don't have much time," he murmured, closing his eyes before touching his forehead against hers. "I don't know how this battle is going to end. I said I won't force you, that you would have to come to me, and I still won't." He placed a gentle kiss on her lips. "But it won't stop me from showing you how much I want you to be mine."

"Oh, Zac." She caressed his cheek with her own before kissing his throat. "That's not what I meant."

He stiffened and raised his head.

"Don't you see?" She cupped his jaw, tears misting her eyes as he nuzzled her palm, her other hand over his heart. "So many things played in my mind when I found out the team had left. I realized that everything around me, no matter how much I try to make it permanent, doesn't really last. I lost my anchor when my grandmother died. I've cast it out so many times in the hope that when it latches on to something, it would keep me from floating away. But everyone let go. They cast me adrift, making me believe there was nothing out there for me, until my anchor latched on to someone that at first, I could only sense, not see. And when I saw him I wanted to leave, but the anchor bade me stay."

"Oh, God in heaven." Zac was so soft and incredulous, but Faith could feel his heart thunder beneath her palm.

"So I will follow what my anchor bids me to do. I will stay." A tear slipped down to her cheek.

Zac inhaled sharply.

Faith smiled through her tears. "With you. I'm willing to give up everything for you because there's nothing left if you're not with me too."

Zac took her mouth in a mind blowing kiss, taking her breath away. She bade him enter as elation filled her heart. He crushed her to him that Faith almost couldn't breathe, gasping and laughing against his mouth.

"Bianca—"

"Told me you were here," Zac said between heated kisses. "She's gone back to the Faesten and said to stay here."

"Holy crap, you Cynn Cruors know how to move." Faith giggled, then moaned when Zac blazed a trail of open mouth kisses down the column of her throat to the racing pulse on her neck, gasping when he sucked hard on it and felt herself getting wet.

"Yes, we do. And Faith?"

"Yes," she said huskily. Zac sucking on her neck was causing sparks to ignite inside her body.

"You do belong to me. Your blood tells me so. It will be the only blood I will drink from now on. You are a Cynn Cruor mate."

Faith sucked in a breath when Zac carried her in his arms, reaching the beach house's bedroom with unbelievable speed. They fell onto the low bed, the sound of the waves lapping against the shore drowned by the roar of their blood running through their veins, their heated breaths and groans. Zac undressed Faith in less time that she could remove his clothes. Naked they splayed kisses over each other's bodies, their tongues frenziedly licking, their teeth gently nipping. Zac held her hair and gently pulled her head back to feast on her throat, causing her to moan and her heart to beat faster. Faith fisted his arousal, moving her hand up and down, the heat of his shaft causing her sex to crave him. She cried out softly as Zac gently fondled her breasts before taking one hardening peak inside his mouth while he rolled his palm over the other before covering her breast with his hand. Faith's head was spinning with desire. Zac growled in satisfaction against her breast, sucking, licking, nipping at Faith's hardened peaks when she continued to jerk him and play with his balls. Then she opened up to Zac, raising her leg so that she could lave his arousal with her heat.

"Ancients, woman," he rasped.

"No foreplay, Zac." She kept pumping him. "I want you inside me. I can't wait."

Zac settled between her legs before kneeling in front of her. Faith moaned, her back arching, her hands holding on to the sheets underneath her when Zac lubricated his cock head with her cream, teasing her opening when he allowed only the crown to enter.

"Zac, please!"

Zac's face hardened, his abs straining before he gave in and thrust into her completely to the hilt.

Bliss vibrated from her core all over her body. Faith's heart stuttered as though wanting to fly at that very moment. Indescribable pleasure took hold of her when Zac moved.

"Oh, God," she whimpered as her body heated. She opened her eyes and sucked her breath at the golden glow of Zac's eyes, which dominated the green. Her hips bucked with his every thrust, welcoming him into her heat. It felt so good to feel Zac piston in and out of her, his hips teasing every sensitive nerve of her sex. He leaned down, his mouth and teeth grazing her throat, sending more erotic signals down to her core that caused her to squeeze her walls around him.

"Oh fuck, baby. Do that again...yes!" Zac's tongue darted to lick her ear before he sucked on the sensitive spot behind her earlobe. Then he took her moans into his mouth, to her gasps of bliss down his throat. Faith's breaths came in soft gasps as her ecstasy began to build, Zac rotating his hips to increase her pleasure. She whimpered, begging for more, her body boneless against his onslaught.

Then she felt her gums itch as before. She heard Zac hiss and look down at her mouth. He smiled with all the feeling he had for her before he swiped his tongue against the fangs slowly peeking from her mouth. Faith shuddered at the intense sensation his tongue made that her vagina clamped around Zac's shaft again.

"Oh, fuck!" Zac uttered.

Faith was in a whirlpool of heat that consumed her from inside, her climax building more than she could ever imagine. Cries and sobs fell from her lips, her eyes closed, her whole being centred on the pleasure of Zac's lovemaking. She felt her incisors tease her lower lip, drawing blood at the same time increasing her rapture. Then as though she knew what she had to do, she gripped Zac's torso and opened her eyes.

"Zac," she whimpered.

Zac bent down again and touched her fangs with his tongue again. Faith screamed and raised her head up, burying her fangs by the side of Zac's chest. Zac gave a guttural cry as her teeth pierced him and they both climaxed. Zac's body shuddered over her, his thrust short and hard as his shaft bathed her womb. Her orgasm came out as a throaty moan. Zac's warm blood entered her mouth. She thought she would gag, but his blood was the most delicious thing she had ever tasted and she drank from him. She was voracious in her hunger that she felt Zac's warmth bathe her again. As she continued to take from him, Zac's life flashed before her eyes, the life he lived with the monks at Inchmahome Priory to the moment he met his mother, the length of time he wandered earning a living by healing until he was taken in by The Hamilton. Faith saw the moment Graeme was nearly killed through Zac's eyes and the desperation he felt when he couldn't heal the Cynn Cruor. She saw many more turning points in his life.

And saw the secret he hid.

Then her gums slightly opened and her own blood flowed into Zac, feeding him, nourishing him. Zac groaned as she mewled, her palms sliding up and down his body, his back, his shoulders. The coppery scent and taste of his blood mixed with her own made her heady. Faith knew that the passion she felt when she climaxed had heated her life fluid and for a split second she was afraid that Zac would not be able to take the fire from her veins. But he was strong, an immortal. In her mind's eye, she could see how her blood mixed with his, how the licks of fire in her corpuscles readily blended with Zac's own life essence, how their cells joined together so easily as though the two fluids were waiting for each other.

Her immortal.

Zac rolled to bring her on top of him.

"Ahh..." he groaned when Faith's fangs receded. He gripped her buttocks and eased out of her with a sigh as she licked the fang marks closed.

Faith looked at him, the opalescent glow surrounding them thicker and softly sparkling like the multifaceted colours of the fire opal. She smiled, propping her chin on Zac's chest as he sensually stroked her back.

"Your mother was wrong. She may have brought you into this world, but she didn't deserve to be blessed by you. Any woman would be lucky to have you to love. I'm glad you chose me because I choose you. I love you, Zac."

Chapter Twenty-Nine

Zac slowly smiled. The peace he longed for, which he knew he would find with Faith, settled in his bones. The emotion he had blurted out on the beach, seeping into his skin. He was overcome with sentiment that he whooped out loud, making Faith squeal. She laughed with him as he splayed kisses all over her face, her neck, making her gasp when he sucked hard at the concave hollow of her throat where her pulse beat in tandem with his. And that did it. Every time he got a taste of Faith's body, the Kinaré roared to life, his body flaring with need to claim Faith over and over again until both of them were spent. For the very first time, he allowed the walls to chip and crack, giving them permission to tumble down in a heap. He didn't need them anymore to protect himself. As long as Faith was with him, he would be all right. Zac breathed deeply, inhaling Faith's essence that had mixed with his, smelling the orchid and neroli scented wash she used that day prior to leaving the Faesten.

"Ancients, Faith. I can't get enough of you," he muttered as his hands explored the satiny softness of her hip, her waist, her back. His tongue trailed down the valley of her breasts before swirling his tongue around one turgid peak. "I just want inside your skin. I don't want to go anywhere. I want you always with me."

"And I will be." Faith gasped, her hips bucking against his, her head tossing from side to side. "Holy crap, Zac. I need you inside me again. Please."

Zac raised his head. Faith's deep brown eyes now had the same gold flecks his eyes had when he was aroused. Her mouth, swollen from his kisses were softly parted and slightly lifted in a sensual smile.

How could he say no to her?

He spooned her, kissing her back, between her shoulder blades. Faith's head rested on the pillow. Zac would never admit to understanding how love could bind someone, how its bonds were unseen but felt. Here was the woman who was that bond, who bound herself to his heart for as long as they lived their earthly existence. And from the knowledge imparted to him by the monks eons ago, he knew that leaving the earthly plane should he die in battle, would never break the bond between a Cynn Cruor and his mate.

He raised Faith's leg and placed it on his hip before gently entering her from behind, his cock hard and hot again, needing to thrust into her quickly. But Zac tightened his jaw with his effort of taking it slow. When Faith closed her eyes and asked him for more he pressed himself inside her to the hilt and almost came. Then they rocked, each knowing when to push and pull. Zac took Faith's lips in his. She was sweet, pliant, and soft to his firm, hard, and masculine. He increased the pace, one hand holding her thigh slightly elevated so that he could piston in and out of her, while his other hand curled under her thick locks to cradle her head.

"Zac," Faith whimpered.

He watched as the gold flecks in her eyes gradually grew and dominated her pupils, her lust matching his, making her vaginal walls tighten her hold around his shaft. He grunted, his hunger feeding his cock into Faith's sweet heat, feeling her velvet walls suction his member like her mouth. Sweet hot satin. His hips bucked again and again at the same time his pleasure built layer by layer. The tingling that whizzed up and down his spine started to centre by his buttocks, her fire stoking him, claiming him as hers. The small sounds that came from her throat drove him to distraction, fuelling his lust, increasing his desire. His thumb reached for her distended clit, swirling it.

"Oh God, yes! More," she cried.

"Oh yes, baby. Oh fuck," he growled. His cock lengthened and thickened and her pussy gripped him. Her cream covered him, making his thrusts slick and fast. His balls tightened to the point of pain. Then he withdrew.

"Zac!" she wailed.

He turned her to face him, raised her leg again and thrust back into her.

"Yes," she whimpered.

"Faith," he growled and he roared when he felt his fangs descending. Faster he fucked her, Faith's body arching and taut like a bowstring, her cries of rapture bringing him closer to the precipice until he exploded and his fangs sank into the side of her heart. She screamed and sobbed as she held on to him. Zac felt Faith's orgasm ripping through her as his warm seed entered her womb. He uttered small groans as her sweet blood filled his mouth and he greedily drank from her, the sweetest blood he had ever tasted. Between the coppery notes of her life essence was the scent and taste of jasmine. Tangy and sweet, just like the woman from whom it came from.

To whom he belonged.

Zac gently laid Faith on her back as he continued to drink from her, stroking her belly, caressing her waist. He held her tightly as he saw her own life flash through his mind. How her parents left her with her grandmother saying they would return for her but never did. How her grandmother taught her to heal, told her stories of their relatives who were healers too, but who weren't fire binders. How in the blink on an eye her grandmother lost everything and how she died leaving Faith all alone. Zac saw all these and more and his heart ached for her. Then he gently opened his gums so that his own blood rushed through the puncture wounds into her heart. Faith gasped and trembled, but she held on to him and Zac could feel her accepting his blood, welcoming his life force in her veins, into her system. Her blood was now a conduit for the fire that burned in her and for the fire of his love for her.

He continued to feed her, the glow around them strengthened, binding them for all eternity, the sea and waxing moon their witnesses.

Now they belonged completely to each other.

They were now irrevocably Cynn Cruor.

****

Zac's eyes snapped open. He looked down at Faith snuggled beside him.

Something was wrong. It was too quiet. Even the rush of the waves sounded muted as though he was under water. He scanned the room, his sharp sight assessing everything in the room. He was relieved to see that no one was inside. He glanced at the windows through half lidded eyes.

There!

Glowing pairs of eyes tried to look inside. Gold and dark neon green.

Werewolf and Scatha.

Immediately, he sent a blast of power, altering their perception of reality. The sex he and Faith had was more than enough to keep it up and still fight.

Faith.

She stirred but didn't wake.

Faith, baby. Wake up. Don't make any unnecessary moves.

Zac knew she was awake when she stiffened.

Zac?

Yes, Faith. You can hear me in your mind. I think we have company, but we can't let them know we sense them. Do exactly as I say, okay?

Okay.

Zac lay on his back, his eyes easily picking up his jeans in the dark. He leaned over to get Faith's T-shirt and jeans, pretending to slowly stretch.

Crawl over me. Pretend that you have to go to the bathroom. When you get there lock the door and get dressed.

No.

Zac scowled. *Why the hell not?*

I will fight beside you, Zac. I won't let you out of my sight.

Bloody hell, woman. You're possessive.

Look who's talking.

There was a thud outside of the bedroom door.

"Shit."

CHAPTER THIRTY

Zac grabbed Faith's hand and he sped them both inside the bathroom. Faith dressed immediately only in her jeans and T-shirt. Zac put on his denims, his shirt left behind on the bedroom floor. He wore a thunderous scowl.

"I'm sorry, Zac," she said in a small voice. "Stop frowning."

He gave her a hard kiss to quieten her and nearly gave in when her body moulded itself to his. He ended it slowly. "I'm not frowning because you didn't do as I said. Cynn Cruor mates can be as stubborn as hell. I'm frowning because you don't have a bra."

"Oh, for the love of God." She rolled her eyes as she moved away from him. Damn, she looked sexy with her mussed hair.

She looked thoroughly fucked.

"Stop thinking with your dick, Zac. I can read your mind now, remember?" Faith smirked.

"How can I forget?" Zac shook his head as he fished his cell phone from his pocket. His ear piece was still inside, but the distance between the beach house and the Faesten was too big.

"What's out there?" Her eyes clouded with worry.

Zac didn't get to reply when Roarke answered his call.

"McBain."

"Roarke, we need extraction," Zac said quietly cupping his hand over his mouth. Faith leaned towards him to be able to hear what the Cynn Cruors were telling Zac.

"Where are you?"

"The Trujillo's beach house."

"Zac, you're on speaker phone." After three seconds, Roarke spoke again. "How many?"

"I haven't got a clue. I haven't been out. Faith is with me."

"Understood."

"*Primo*," Andrés spoke. "We keep some weapons under the bed and in the walk-in closet just off the bathroom. There will be some amorphic suits in there also." There was amusement in Andrés' voice. "You and your mate will just have to be one of the Trujillo Cynn Cruor for the time being. You'll have everything you need there."

Faith's brow rose. She walked over to the closet. An array of suits similar to what Zac wore the first time they met was neatly lined in a row.

Call it a Cynn's intuition to know that the bedroom and bathroom are two of the most important rooms in the house. Zac gave her a crooked grin.

"There's a secret door that leads out to the beach," Andrés continued. "Just turn the closet handle and it will open."

Removing her clothes, Faith turned away from Zac to put on the suit closest to her size. Bloody hell, if they weren't in the middle of a battle Zac would have preferred Faith to be buck naked. Jealousy bloomed in his chest at the sensual way the suit hugged her curves.

"McBain, CCTV counts about twenty Scatha and werewolves surrounding you," Graeme spoke. "Shite, make that forty."

Zac reluctantly dragged his attention away from his mate and zeroed on the situation they were in. His heart thundered behind his ribs. The kill call stirring inside him was only dampened by his worry that Faith was with him.

"How did they find out about this place?" he asked.

"A transfuge." Andrés' voice was filled with quiet fury. "He will be dealt with accordingly."

"Zac, we're just suiting up. We're taking the EC 155. The Ancients are tagging along. Our ETA in five."

"Aye, Dux." Then as an afterthought, he added, "The Specus Argentum—"

"The place is secure. Andrés has made it so. Trujillo has sent reinforcements there," Finn replied. In the background, Zac heard several weapons being locked and loaded. "We did think that this might be a diversionary tactic."

"Good," Zac said, relieved, pausing before speaking again. "De Alvaro, I'm sorry about the transfuge."

"*Yo también, primo.*" The Trujillo Dux's voice was grim. "*Yo también.*"

"Radio silence after this call," Zac said, his face hardening, then his mouth quirked. "And hurry. You're going to miss all the fun."

****

Kamaria threw the glass against the mirror and screamed. Broken crystal and shards of polished plate littered the carpeted floor. She screamed again, her body straining, her muscles tightening as she transformed.

This was not how she planned it. Alaghom could not have survived being shot by silver. She made sure of that. But the traitor in the Cynn Cruors' midst had reported otherwise. It didn't matter if the sorcerer tried to heal his mate because she would have succumbed eventually. Creatures infused with both vampire and werewolf blood were more susceptible to the poison silver posed, but someone had stopped Alaghom from dying.

A fire binder.

Her eyes narrowed to slits. This was the first time she had heard of someone having the gift of fire healing.

She would make a very good addition to her Lycan empire. If this woman, this newly minted Cynn Cruor whore refused to join her, Kamaria would kill her.

For keeping Alaghom Na-om alive.

Kamaria would next kill her niece, the sorcerer would finally follow. No. Let Dac Valerian have the pleasure of killing his nemesis. As long as she was allowed to take out the Eald's heart and drink his blood from the beating muscle, the Scatha leader could do as he wished. Nobody would get in the way of her ambition of ruling the entire Lycan race. Not her niece, the Cruor leaders, or the ongoing war between them.

The door to her stateroom slammed inward. She immediately turned with a snapping growl.

"Why the fuck aren't we going for the cave?" Dac roared, his eyes a dark glowing green. "We had an agreement."

"And I will honour it once I tie up loose ends." Her wolfen jaws snapped. "Your precious Deoré is still alive."

"She's not my precious Deoré. She's the Eald's slut," he shot back. "I want that cave!"

Kamaria waved her hand nonchalantly. "And I want the woman who helped Alaghom survive. If I get her, she can be a valuable bargaining chip for both of us, to my eternal disgust." She spared Dac a disdainful look. "The Cynn Cruor value their mates and will do anything in their power to get them back. Kidnap this woman, then we go to the cave. If we go for the cave now, it will be a phyrric victory. I don't want that." She paused, arching her brow. "Do you?"

Dac's face filled with rage. His mouth curled in a snarl. Kamaria unconsciously took a step back. She felt the lycan inside her flatten her ears and hide her tail between her legs. Dac approached her steadily, his fury palpitating like a sonar beep locked on her. Kamaria's legs nearly bowed, but she balled her fists and locked her knees to remain standing. She would never bow to a Cruor. Cynn or Scatha.

"If you were anyone else I would have already flayed you alive and used your fur to make stools for my bar," Dac said softly. "Be careful how you flaunt your power, Kamaria. You don't know the meaning of what it really is."

"Stay away from me," she growled.

"Let's get this Cynn whore, then we return to the mountain." Dac spun to walk out of the room, not bothering to close the door.

Kamaria's fur rose as her rage consumed her. Dac had just successfully turned the tables to make her do his bidding.

****

Zac suited up, the material immediately conforming to his muscled body. Faith swallowed, salivating at her mate's form. No lights were needed. She saw clearly in the dark since imbibing Zac's blood, had sharper hearing, and a compelling need to be by Zac's side in a fight. The fire inside her rested, like a small dragon in her belly, cocooned by Zac's essence inside her.

So this is how it feels to be a Cynn Cruor mate.

She watched Zac put a shoulder holster on before checking and securing two guns in the slots. He then took another holster and secured it around his right thigh before taking another gun from the secret armoury and a short sword that gleamed in the dark. Faith knew the line that looked like the crest of a wave etched on the blade was silver.

Faith, can you handle a gun? Zac looked at her.

"Zac, I—"

Use the telepathic link. They will hear you. We took a risk speaking when we called the Faesten but it had to be done. We need to use our link now.

Faith swallowed. *I don't know if I can do this.*

Zac cupped her face in his hands. *It's only going to be for a while. Five minutes tops.*

The door to the bedroom crashed. Zac's hand covered her mouth to stifle the scream. Faith's eyes widened when Zac's own eyes changed colour to blood orange.

We have to go. He turned the knob and a secret door slid silently open. Zac bade Faith to precede him as he secured and hid the remaining weapons. With one look at the bathroom door, he followed Faith, securing the escape hatch behind them.

****

Kamaria walked into the room, her werewolves sniffing the bed. Her gold eyes locked on the evidence of the Cynn Cruor's intimate moments, her nose acquiring the mixed scent. She smiled and looked around. The sliding doors leading to the patio and beach remained secure. Both Scatha and her minions had been watching the place to see if the Cynn and his mate would leave that way, but they didn't. She moved around, walking into the bathroom. There was a lingering smell of the two closer to the closets. Her eyebrows met in the middle of her forehead. A secret door, perhaps? Kamaria was about to open the closet when she heard shots fired. Her face cleared, knowing she was about to claim a minor victory that would lead to a major coup.

The sooner she captured the fire binder the better.

****

The screech changed halfway to a gurgle before the Scatha fell to the ground, a silver bullet in his neck. Zac whizzed and beheaded him, the ashes mixing with the sand. Three more Scatha rushed at him from different directions. The sand under Zac's feet was no match for the swiftness that he shot and slashed at the transfuges. God! What he wouldn't do to have his wakazashi and tanto together. It didn't matter. One of the Cynn Cruors' strength was adaptability, whether it was the terrain or the weapon. Variable situations, different logistics, the same deadly results. A Cynn Cruor warrior only had one constant in their lives.

Their women.

Then he heard Faith scream.

He spun around, roaring. "No!"

A werewolf had Faith in a stranglehold, its furry arm locked across Faith's throat.

Ice veined through Zac and his heart plummeted. He was ready to sprint to her side when Faith catapulted herself in the air over the werewolf. She grabbed hold of its neck, twisted, and broke it as she landed behind the body, which looked as though it

Midnight's Fate

deflated before it reached the ground. In what Zac had never seen before, her eyes glowed with fire as did her hands, and she tore the werewolf's head from its body. Another werewolf pounced at her, followed by several of the mangy creatures loping towards them.

"Fuck!" Zac quickly dispatched three with bullets in the head, his aim accurate despite the targets being so close to Faith's own head. Before he could fell another one, someone shot at the heads of the remaining three from above, their blood and brain material splattering Faith. He looked up and saw Finn zeroing on several moving targets as he rappelled down from the EC 155 with the rest of the Cynn Cruor following. The Ancients leaped and dove to the beach eschewing the ropes for flying, transforming in mid-air. Two more EC 155 transport eurocopters dislodged more Cynn Cruor immortals.

"About bloody time," he muttered as he sprinted. "Faith!"

She mutely looked at him, shock making her more ashen in the moonlight. Zac swiped the rest of the blood from her face. "Faith, I know you don't like killing. I'll ask the chopper to take you back to the Faesten if you want." Despite the blood smears on her face and suit, Zac still found her devastatingly beautiful.

"No." She swallowed, her chest heaving with effort, her glowing eyes pinning him with an irritated gaze. "I will fight beside you. If you stop me, I'll kick your arse."

A slow grin made its way onto Zac's lips. He wanted to crow with pride. Faith Hannah was going to be a formidable opponent in battle, and he wouldn't have it any other way.

"McBain! Six o'clock!" Graeme shouted as he

landed ten yards to Zac's left, falling over two Scatha.

Faith looked over Zac's shoulder, her eyes widening before Zac spun around to face the enemy. In less than a second the rest of the Cynn Cruor stood beside Zac and Faith.

"Holy shit," Faith breathed.

"How many down?" the Eald asked.

"Nine including the two Temple landed on, Sire," Zac replied, then he turned to Graeme with a mocking grin. "Ouch."

Graeme snorted, brushing of the sand off his suit.

"Temple, I thought you said forty." Zac's brow rose as he turned to watch the Scatha-Were line facing them.

"She's called some of the packs," the Deoré spoke softly, answering Zac. Quiet rage laced her tone. "She wants an all-out war."

Chapter Thirty-One

A hundred yards in front of them, several werewolves and Scatha stood in line behind Kamaria and Dac Valerian. The lycan shifters' eyes glowed yellow in the night, their tales swishing behind them, their muzzles pulled back in snarls. Some of them had thrown their heads back in as though silently baying at the half moon. The Scatha's eyes glowed green, their jowls yapping in glee, their claws scratching by their sides. The waves began to lap at the feet of all those on the beach. The breeze rustled the leaves of the trees and tropical foliage that made an incongruous backdrop for a deadly confrontation.

"I swear these Scathas' evil stinks so much not even an acid bath will get rid of it." Graeme shook his head in disgust, eliciting several chuckles from the group.

"Odds are two to one at the moment." Finn slung his sniper rifle over his shoulder before crossing his arms over his huge chest. "I can see other werewolves lurking by the side lines. Looks like they're watching what the outcome will be." He nudged his chin at the direction of the trees where pairs of eyes looked like suspended fireflies.

"We've been through worse," Roarke said, looking down at the chamber of his own assault weapon to check on the safety as the rest did the same. "But I'm not going to underestimate them. Our experience fighting werewolves is nil at best."

"Remember what I told you of the were blood in the Kinaré, Hamilton." The Eald spared him a glance. "You will know when and when not to strike." He looked around. "Assault weapons at the ready?"

There was a barrage of clicks, all weapons' safety locks disengaged.

"Aye," the Cynn chorused.

Zac turned to Faith, giving her one of his guns. "You need this, Faith. Don't say no."

Faith took the gun with a nod and smiled at the relief in Zac's eyes. He faced their enemies with Faith beside him.

"Formation." The Ancient Eald ordered.

The Cynn Cruors dispersed across the beach. The Ancients stood in the centre. Roarke, Finn, and Graeme flanked them. Andrés and Bianca, Zac and Faith stayed together and were two paces behind the Cynn's first line of defence. Cynn Cruor mates fought side by side. Their assault weapons held in their hands. Zac felt the bloodlust roll though him, hiking his impatience as he waited for the other side to attack. This was just like old times when battles raged between the Cruors. For over a century, the battles fought were more like pocket skirmishes, sporadic encounters between the two races. Valerian had always hid behind human leaders who vied for world domination, using them like a puppet master, letting them take the fall while he continued to build his own empire on the backs of the evil that was the foundation of his every deed. Zac was going to enjoy killing as many Scatha as he could. Too bad he had to kill werewolves too. The Cynn's fight wasn't with them, but they sealed their fate by aligning themselves with the Scatha Cruor.

The journey to La Nahuaterique wasn't what Zac expected. He had been hell bent on finding an antidote for the special silver. Instead, he'd stumbled on a cure he never even thought was possible, a secret he'd never divulge, and a woman he never imagined he'd be blessed with. He found a solution to the Cynn Cruor's problem and obtained a jewel who held the key to his heart. After this battle, he would take Faith to visit the place he had once called home. He would bring her to where Colm was buried. He'd had on occasion been able to visit Colm during his sojourns and he was the one who was beside his old friend when he breathed his last. He would return with Faith to where Colm was buried and tell his friend that he had finally found someone who made his life more meaningful. He'd also take Faith to the place where he was born and in doing so, perhaps he'd be able to finally let his past rest and let fate take them both where it chose.

We will not be able to speak to each other after this, Cynn Cruor, the Eald said. *You all know what to do and while your mates fight beside you, keep them protected.*

Kamaria is mine, the Deoré growled.

As it should be, the Eald stated.

No one dared contradict her.

It wasn't necessary to respond to the Cynn Cruor progenitor. They all knew how this would go down.

Suddenly the Scatha and the werewolves surged forward. The Cynn Cruor picked their targets one by one, their bullets and flechettes slicing through the foreheads and throats of both Scatha and werewolf alike. Screams or rage and gurgles of death filled the night air. No matter if either enemy flew, the Cynn Cruors didn't miss. Bullet casings landed on the sand by their feet as they shot at each diabolical wave after diabolical wave. They thought they had hit everyone when a new wave of werewolves took over the line and the remaining Scatha flew over the Cynn Cruors. As one the Ancients soared to the sky and came down with an ash fall as most of those who tried to break through the Cynn formation were decapitated in mid-air. They sprinted towards the line of werewolves and Scatha, slashing everyone that made a mistake of fighting them, both of them hell bent on finding their nemeses.

"Protect the Eald," Roarke shouted.

The Cynn Cruor and their mates advanced, pinning werewolf and Scatha with silver as they came until the ammunition was spent from their assault weapons. Roarke, Finn, and Graeme threw their spent weapons and whipped out their handguns as they advanced. Zac continued firing both his guns until he too was empty. He whipped the sword he secured earlier on his back and started hacking. Faith remained beside him. If she had to move away, it wasn't too far. They worked in tandem for most of the time. Just as she was about to run out of bullets, Bianca shouted at her and hurled a dagger at her which, Faith deftly caught.

Faith didn't realize that she could be in her element while fighting. All her life she feared death, feared killing others because of her good deed gone wrong. She now understood why Zac killed, had an inkling of why it had to be done so that more good was kept in the world and less evil allowed to flourish. As she shot and hacked through bodies that were far from human, she started to feel the bloodlust that raged through Zac, could feel the euphoria of how something that was used to do wrong had to be done to make things right. Zac's memories of how the Cynn Cruors lost so many of their own to defend the human race only spurred her to protect Zac and his brethren.

This was her life now. This was her fate.

And she wouldn't have it any other way.

****

Kamaria threw werewolf after werewolf at Alaghom Na-Om's path. Her niece kept throwing the werewolves off with a swipe of her arms. Yelps and whimpers of pain surrounded them. Kamaria didn't care. Until the plan she reluctantly agreed to with Dac fell into place the fire binder was her trajectory. She saw the woman parry both Scatha and werewolf alike, water splashing against their legs as they came at each other by the shore. Greed surged through Kamaria. She wondered whether instead of using the fire binder as a bargaining chip, she'd kill her instead and take the essence of her fire blood into her. The thought of the Cynn Cruor immortal's blood inside the woman almost made Kamaria wretch, but she would do anything to absorb whatever power anyone had to cement her position among the lycans.

She looked around. Where was Dac? She growled when she saw Dac and the rest of his transfuge leave the fray, her wolf eyes narrowing to slits when the Cynn Cruor leader chased the Scatha leader. Alaghom was left wide open. Kamaria's muzzle rippled as she smiled. She saw the fire binder grapple with two werewolves, but her mate was not far behind. All of the Cynn Cruor immortals had their hands full, staving off the lycans that suddenly swarmed the area. Kamaria licked her nose, tasting and smelling victory in the air. In less than a second, she veered towards Alaghom's direction. Her niece had her back to her. Kamaria jumped, extended her arm above her head.

Once she landed, she would have Alaghom Na-om's head in her hands.

****

The Eald sped through the forest, his magick pulsing through his hands as he hacked his way through. He reached the first Scatha and decapitated him, running through the ash that blew against his face. He did the same to the second. He heard Dac laugh and his blood boiled. He blasted his way through the Scatha Cruors, hurling them against tree trunks.

Then Dac spun around and hurled himself at the Eald, plunging a knife into his side. The Eald roared, the agony spreading like wildfire.

Silver.

Dac plunged his dagger again, his grin maniacal in the dark.

Dizziness nearly caused the Eald to black out.

Were they wrong? Did he and Zac misdiagnose the effect of the special silver?

Dac cackled as he moved away. The Eald rolled on the ground, pain searing through him as he tried to get up. His lungs constricted as he tried to suck in air, his blood falling to the ground.

There.

The Eald felt it. The silver was being pushed away, the pain dulling to a throb. The tightness in his chest slowly eased.

His magick and power surged. He clenched his jaw as he felt the magick inside him demanding release.

Wait.

Dac knelt beside him and whispered in his ear, "Tonight you die, Ieldran."

"I don't think so," the Eald said softly before he twisted and hit Dac's chest with his palm. The magick surged through him, pulsing with such force that it hurtled Dac several feet away. The Eald stood slowly, watching Dac's face pale with incredulity.

"Tonight, *you* die."

Then the Ancient Eald heard the Deoré and Faith scream.

****

Zac saw the werewolves converge on the Deoré as the Eald chased after Valerian and the rest of the Scatha. Werewolves were everywhere. This wasn't the fight he wanted. He had no quarrel with the shifters. What the hell was this going to do to the Cruor wars? A three way war was not good at all, and Zac was afraid the damage was irreparable.

Suddenly Zac saw something fly in the air, heading straight towards the Deoré. He immediately launched himself towards the Deoré, parrying the blow aimed at the Deoré's head. Pain exploded on his chest and across his neck. He felt his blood erupt from his throat, his life force slowly ebbing away.

With one last thought he spoke to the woman he loved.

I love you, Faith.

****

Faith fell as something sliced across the front of her neck. She had deflected each and every werewolf attempt to swipe at her throat. Her arms and thighs burned every time the claws ripped through her suit, but her wounds healed immediately. But this time the pain was unbearable. Dread closed in on her. She couldn't breathe, the air locking inside her lungs as though she forgot to exhale. She looked at the carnage around her, searching for her mate. Her eyes moved towards the Deoré, who screamed as she pulled the she-wolf's head from her body. Faith's eyes fell to the ground at the Deoré's feet.

"Zac," she screamed.

All fighting stopped.

Faith sprinted towards Zac. "Oh God, no!"

Zac's blood was everywhere. His eyes moved to look at her.

Faith.

"You are not going to die! I won't allow it!" Faith felt her own life seeping out. She placed her hand over the gaping wound on Zac's throat, but the blood pushed between her fingers.

You will be with me, Faith. Always. Zac's breathing was becoming more difficult. Every inhale brought more blood soaking the sand.

"I want to be with you, Zac McBain. I want to die with you," she screamed and sobbed at the same time tears pouring down her face in torrents, falling on Zac. "You can't bloody go ahead of me. Don't leave me."

Faith felt the pulse beating underneath her finger giving in.

This wasn't happening. Fate couldn't be so cruel as to take away the very reason she had forgiven herself, the very reason why her heart started learning to come to terms with her curse. She corrected herself.

Her gift.

Zac's pulse slowed down.

Flashes of Zac smiling, laughing, and that look that made her melt every time they came together swirled around her. She wanted them back. Not just as memories, but as expressions she would see when she woke up in the morning, as they walked, as they laughed, as they fought side by side, as they made love. She wanted to see him crease his furrow in concentration, see the muscle ticking on his jaw, his eyes narrowing when she watched him talk with the Cynn Cruor about how to defeat the Scatha Cruor.

She demanded them back from the immortal lying between life and death.

Heal him.

Zac's pulse was now far in between.

It was that voice again, the same voice that came to her, stayed with her whenever she used the fire blood.

I can't. I'm weakening. I will be gone soon as well.

Why are you giving up at the time of your greatest moment? If love bound you to each other, so will it bind the wounds that momentarily claim you. If you want Fate to stand by you, to see how much Zac means to you, heal him with everything you have.

Faith could no longer feel Zac's pulse.

With a guttural scream Faith didn't think would come out of her, her heart broke. Her blood roared in her ears like an oncoming tide about to drown them both. Cries of disbelief surrounded them from the Cynn Cruors, but Faith only saw the walls of flame that rose in a towering wall around them. Fire flowed out from her like lava, bloodied orange, and glowing with heat. Her skin thinned and still she screamed, tears falling in torrents as her anguish fuelled the healing fire inside her. Her fingers sought Zac's pulse, desperately seeking even the faintest of movements, afraid that she had wasted time. She would never be able forgive herself if Zac was truly lost to her because of her hesitation, because she wasn't confident enough to heal the very person she should have healed above anyone else.

Something moved underneath her finger. A faint

pulse.

Faith quickly latched on to the movement and blasted it with her fire blood. The heat seeped through her fingers and into Zac's throat, coursing through his veins and adding to the blood that Faith had given him earlier. Her forehead pulled together as the blood entered Zac's heart to help steady its beat. She saw his heart move, expanding before it began to pulse. Zac jerked underneath her, gasping for air.

The fire inside her blazed.

She buried her other hand in the sand, clawing at the cooler grains underneath, eventually finding purchase.

Zac heaved a huge breath, then choked. The air passing through his windpipe sounded like air being blown through a reed.

"Stay with me Zac," Faith said through clenched teeth, eyes closed in concentration, setting aside her anguish to heal the man she loved. Soon the blood started to fuse the severed nerves, Zac's carotid artery, before treating his skin. Next, she moved her hand over his chest, where the rest of Kamaria's claws had ripped through him and allowed the fire blood to do its work.

Then she was done. As the wall of flames slowly dissipated, Faith looked at the face of the warrior she had given her heart to. She touched Zac's face and flinched at its icy coldness.

"I've done all I can, Zac," she wept softly. "Please don't die. Come back to me...please come back to me."

She didn't care who saw her. It didn't matter because no one would bother her.

No one would bother them both.

Faith stretched out beside Zac, placing her head on his chest.

"I love you," she said softly as her eyes closed and

tears continued to slide down the side of her face.

She was beside Zac amidst the carnage, sleeping beside the immortal she loved.

Lying on the sand that the intense heat had transformed into a beach of glass.

Chapter Thirty-Two

The tide brought sea foam to the beach, the sound of the waves sighs of relief that it had reached the shore. Faith walked the lonely stretch of sand, her gait slow and deliberate. She turned her head away and brushed the tendrils of her hair that stubbornly stayed across her face. Her bare feet indented the wet sand, her dress flattening against her torso. Sighing, she took the elastic band from her wrist and secured her hair in a ponytail. As she reached the beach house, she turned to face the horizon. She lifted her head to look at the sky. Grey clouds were beginning to roll across the heavens and it wouldn't be a sunny day for long.

This time she knew it wasn't the Ancient Eald's doing.

She stopped and looked down at the sand. The glass that she had made had been broken into pieces and thrown to the sea as far away as it could so that no one would be the wiser and question how there could be such a huge tract of glass on the beach.

Kamaria was dead. Dac had escaped again.

But all of that didn't matter. And as though she had conjured him, arms belonging to the warrior she belonged to heart, body, and soul encircled her from behind.

"I missed you," Zac whispered in her ear. Faith sighed and gave him access to her neck, which Zac licked and nipped.

"I only took a walk," she replied. "You, McBain, still need to rest. It's been just a week. The scar—"

"Will remain and I will wear it with pride because you brought me back. A battle scar of death that's a badge of life. Not everyone can lay claim to that. And why do I have to rest, when I have a fire binder at my beck and call?"

Faith turned around and gave him an affectionate swat on the arm. "I can only do so much, immortal." Her eyes watered, tracing the scar on his neck with butterfly strokes. "I thought I wouldn't be able to bring you back. I had never done that before. Oh, dear God, Zac, when I couldn't find a pulse...don't fucking do that to me again. If you die ahead of me I will kill you."

She placed her arms around his neck. Except for the scar that lined the base of his throat, Zac was in perfect health. He had difficulty talking the first few hours after the battle, but Faith kept at it, placing licks of flame in increments against his voice box. After the battle, the Cynn Cruor immediately placed a mat on the soft sand closer to the house so that Faith could temper the heat by holding on to the earth. Tiny balls of glass were scattered around them, as though a young boy had thrown his marbles helter skelter in the sand and forgot to put them inside its container. Zac's dark blond hair was slightly longer and wavy that it occasionally fell over his forehead. His hunter green eyes twinkled. Faith nuzzled her cheek against the thick shadow covering his jaw.

"Hmm...I liked the way your face felt between my thighs." She sighed.

Zac had agreed to rest to aid the healing process, but that didn't stop him from insisting that he also needed to make love to her, reminding her that sex was the Cynn Cruor's healing balm.

Zac laughed softly. "I'm happy to oblige again. I like it that I have your pussy on my face before you rock and ride my cock." He molded her body to his so that she could feel his desire for her.

For a long moment, the breeze wafted through their tropical retreat and the water lapped at their feet, their footprints appearing and disappearing with the tide, as Zac's passion filled kiss filled her beyond the brim.

Faith laid her head on his chest, her heart continuing to race after the hottest kiss her immortal ever gave her. "Do we really have to go? Do we really have to return to Manchester?"

"You know we do." Zac placed his chin on top of her head as he enclosed her in his embrace. "The Ancients bade us to stay as much as we would like to. Andrés and Bianca have said the same."

"It was magnanimous of them to take in Xavier and Felipe. Xavier has been following Hector around trying to learn as much as he can from your brethren."

"The brothers have never been in better hands than they are with Trujillo," Zac replied. "Not everyone gets that chance. And you, my love, you also have unfinished business in London. I need to come up with a new type of serum, and I won't be able to do that here when the rest of my equipment is in Manchester. The sooner we are able to find a more stable way of injecting the silver from the *Specus Argentum* to the Cynn Cruor, the better our chances of surviving any injury. Roarke, Finn, and Graeme are expecting us in a week's time yet, but I know Dux was anxious for me to return. It's not only because they want to return to their mates. I think it has something to do with Colin."

"Did he tell you what it was?" she asked with concern.

Zac shook his head. "No, but I have to admit that Colin was quite subdued, aloof even. When we left the cave to return to Trujillo he just kept to himself and Craig inside the eurocopter. Dux and the rest didn't bother him, but I know that they were also wondering what had happened to Butler. He's never like that. He always cracks a joke even in the midst of battle. Call it a coping mechanism but this time, it was different. I never got a chance to ask Craig what was wrong before they left. Whatever it is, I have no doubt it is something to do with the Scatha. The war isn't over yet."

"The only saving grace we have is that many of the werewolves have decided to leave in peace," she said.

"That's something I'm relieved about too," Zac agreed. "I didn't see what the Deoré did."

"Neither did I." Faith closed her eyes as she relieved the moment she thought Zac would never wake. "Bianca said that everyone had been stupefied at what I had done, turning the sand into glass. That display of power made the werewolves surrender. It wasn't only that. With Kamaria gone, the werewolves and their alphas wanted to disappear, but the Deoré howled for them to stay. When many realized that the Deoré was the Lycan Shaman's daughter and heir, many bowed before her, lowering their heads to the ground in reverence and fear. Apparently, the Deoré's father had been legendary. The shifters didn't know what was going to happen to them now that the heir had returned."

"If anything, the Deoré is fair. She has been a great source of counsel for the Ancient Eald," Zac said.

"Yes, she was." Faith nodded.

****

Alaghom Na-om looked at the remaining werewolves. Her eyes zeroed in on the Alphas.

"I did not come here to fight with you," she started. *"I am a shifter just like you. I have no quarrel with you. But I am also the Cynn Cruor Eald's mate. My fight is with the Scatha. Hurts have been perpetrated by Kamaria's lies and her desire to lord it over all of the packs. That is not what I want to do. What I want is for us to live in peace."*

The werewolves looked at each other as they changed back to their human forms.

"How?" One Alpha moved forward. *"Kamaria promised us—"*

"What did she promise? More power? More freedom?" She challenged. *"And for how long will she give this to you? Several years? A lycan's lifetime? Will that power be given to your heirs once you die?"*

Everyone was silent. Roarke, Finn, Graeme, and even the Ancient Eald surrounded Zac and Faith. Andrés and Bianca flanked the Deoré as did the rest of the Trujillo Cynn warriors, mortal and immortal alike.

Her voice carried over the sound of the tide.

"Kamaria is gone. Her promises don't hold water with me. I make my own promise and I will keep it. From hereon, we will all live in peace. I am the daughter of the Lycan Shaman who wanted nothing more than to live in harmony with humans. The Cynn Cruors have always protected the human race and we will continue to do so. I will continue to do so. If you keep to yourselves and live in harmony with the humans, I will help you not give in to the quickening on the night of the full moon. You have my vow."

"That's not possible!" a shifter from the crowd said.

"I am living proof." The statement was delivered so quietly, but the effect was enormous. Growls and whimpers rolled like on coming thunder and the

shifters' shoulders slumped, unable to deny the power she wielded over them. A powerful mantle she reluctantly placed on her shoulders to keep the peace. "The quickening will be upon you very soon. The Cynn Cruor will shelter you. But if you decide to side with the Scatha..."

Alaghom scanned the crowd of shifters, her eyes suddenly glowing even though she retained her human form.

"I will personally hunt you down."

The shifters knelt on both knees and bowed before her. Alaghom could feel the dormant force inside her come to life.

"It is done, Father," she said softly. "Rest in peace."

****

"Not all of the packs decided to stay?" Zac posed it more as a statement.

"Unfortunately no. Not only do we have the Scatha to contend with now. We have break away shifters as well."

"I was afraid of that." He sighed. "We need to get back more than ever."

Faith looked up at his visage.

He looked at her, his hand sensuously going up and down her back before squeezing her pert derriere. His eyes crinkled in amusement. "What?"

"I love you. I'm so happy you came back." Faith clung to him, feeling his hard abs against her stomach. She just wanted to crawl inside his skin and stay there.

"I never left, Faith." Zac kissed her on the mouth, a sweet lingering kiss that made her sigh with need. "Kamaria's claws didn't completely sever my head, but I thought I was dead. I could feel my life leaving my body." He placed his forehead against hers. "You brought me back to life in more ways than one."

She kissed his neck, smiling against his throat when she felt the rumbling growl, and Zac pushed his arousal against her belly. "For once I'm glad that I'm a fire binder. It really is a gift. I understand now what my grandmother taught me all those years ago." She cupped his jaw, her eyes pleading at Zac's green depths. "Please don't put me through that wringer again. I don't think I'll able to go through that another time. Promise me."

"You and me both." The sides of his mouth ghosted to a smile. "I promise."

Faith's laughter lit her face, then her smile turned seductive. "However, there is something I wouldn't mind going through over and over again."

Zac chuckled, his voice lowering to a sexy drawl. "By the time we're done with this beach house, Trujillo will have to install another bed."

As before, there was nothing slow about the way they undressed each other. The flame they now both carried in their blood heated their passion to blazing levels as Zac devoured her mouth with his, and Faith sucked, teased, and mated her tongue with his. She cried out in delight when Zac sheathed himself into her to the hilt, kissing and swallowing his groan when her pussy fluttered around his cock. No foreplay, nothing pre-empting their insatiable hunger to come together. Just the touch of Zac's tip against her opening was enough for Faith to flow with liquid heat. Tasting would come later, at a much leisurely pace. For the moment, the fusion of their bodies surrounded by the opalescent glow and the giving and taking of blood against the beating muscle inside them was what mattered.

Zac slowly withdrew and entered her again, each time harder, deeper, then faster. Faith felt her release tightening inside her, as Zac lengthened and thickened. She held on to his hips as he rocked her higher, causing her body to arch and offer her breasts to him. Higher they both went, their moans reverberating around the room until Faith screamed and Zac buried his fangs against her breast, drinking from her as they both drowned in their flood tide.

And as they floated back to reality cloaked in the knowledge that they now completely belonged to each other, it didn't matter where they were in the world.

Anywhere they went, together they were home.

Epilogue

Dac watched the waves part as Kamaria's yacht sliced over the waters. For the first time since the werewolf fished him out of his capsule after the siege in the Isle of Man, he finally had the luxury of drinking the dead she-wolf's bottle of Hennesy Ellipse cognac. Her liquor collection was his now, so was her yacht skippered by a new captain after the previous one tried to kill Dac in grief for the loss of Kamaria. It didn't take long for Dac to subdue them. Many of those who decided to side with the Scatha had similar if not the same proclivity towards human trafficking and drug smuggling.

Kamaria. Dac allowed himself a small amount of regret. A beautiful piece of ass now fertilizer for tropical plants. He should have done her a long time ago.

He moved his neck slowly. Any other time, the pain would keep him smiling, but not today. His eyes narrowed. He had shot the Eald with the silver that was meant to kill him instantly. He recalled the moments that his dagger corroded with silver had plunged into the Eald and scowled when the Cynn Cruor leader had packed a punch of magick, hurtling him against the nearest tree. Yet he had been there on the beach, stronger than ever. Even the Cynn immortal who had taken the bullet for Roarke Hamilton had lived. Impossible!

Or could it?

He had to read the human's diary again. He berated himself. Not only did he feel that he was getting weak, but he didn't like the vile taste of feeling incompetent. He would need to speak to the werewolves who agreed to side with the Scatha to find out what they could unearth. Right now, he needed to consolidate his hold on the Scatha Cruor.

But won't wonders ever cease. The Ancient Eald was about to kill him when the Deoré and the fire binder screamed, taking the Cynn Cruor leader away. A Scatha Cruor who witnessed everything, left his hiding place to take Dac back to the yacht. Fury replaced his shock at seeing who it was that when he stood up, he backhanded the Scatha, who whirled at the impact before falling to the ground. The fallen Scatha looked at Dac with glowing green eyes before his rage disappeared. Whether Dac's suspicions were correct, it didn't matter. What he needed to do was watch the Scatha carefully. The immortal never gave him any reason to doubt, but at the back his mind, Dac knew something was different.

The Scatha he was thinking of appeared and sat opposite him on the plush appointed deck.

"Does the shifter know where we're going?"

The Scatha nodded, resting one foot on the edge of the low coffee table. "He's much a greenhorn, but he'll get us to England soon."

Dac looked at the amber liquid in his glass, the alcohol rising in a thin film above the cognac. "And the Scatha?"

"They will be waiting when we dock."

"You better be right."

"Why shouldn't I be? No one has taken your place as head of the Scatha Cruor, Dac. They're too afraid of you. You've done this before. Disappear and then appear when someone was too cocky to take your place."

"I'm not so sure this time," Dac said, almost to

himself.

"Don't give in to self-doubt, General. It doesn't become you."

Dac's eyes flashed. His companion nonchalantly arched a brow. Dac raised his glass to his mouth, drained its contents, and stormed off. He couldn't find any trace of deception, yet he couldn't stop his unease. He would find out what this Scatha was hiding one way or another.

Herod watched Dac leave before looking out to sea. His heart beat loudly in his ears, something he didn't like unless it was because he had just sliced his blade across the shoulders of a Cynn Cruor. All that changed in the blink of an eye. Why was he feeling this way? This sudden change of heart? What did he care about what Dac's plans were? Why did he care about what happened to the Cynn Cruor when all throughout his immortal life he had decapitated so many?

Herod's eyes glazed over, remembering that one night when he'd met with the enemy. He had forgotten about that night until he caught a glimpse of the reason for that clandestine meeting.

He had to tread carefully now. No, he had no intention of becoming the head of the Scatha Cruor. He just wanted to make sure of one thing.

Dac could never know about his son.

His son who was a Cynn Cruor.

Discover other titles by
Isobelle Cate

Cynn Cruors Bloodline Series:
Rapture at Midnight
Forever at Midnight
Midnight's Atonement
Midnight's Fate

The Mana Series:
Lakam
Amihan (coming soon)

Connect with Isobelle Cate Online:
Isobelle Cate's Facebook Profile and Page:
https://www.facebook.com/AuthorIsobelleCate?ref=hl

Follow Isobelle Cate on Twitter:
https://twitter.com/Isobelle_Cate

Find Isobelle Cate's Books on Goodreads
https://www.goodreads.com/author/show/7191925.Isobelle_Cate

Email: isobllecate@gmail.com